Praise for After Kafra:

'A quiet triumph,'

- *RTE Entertainment Ten*

'Compassion and a feel for the underlayer of Irish rural life,'

– *The Irish Times*

'Martin Malone writes eloquently in his novel *After Kafra* about the psychological impact of witnessing war and slaughter on ordinary soldiers. Malone has an original take on the Lebanon - he sets the bulk of his story at home after a particularly bloody tour,'

Henry McDonald, *The Observer*

'A powerful, truthful and harrowing novel about the harsh realities of peace-keeping and its human price,'

– *The Independent*

By the same author

Us (2000)
The Broken Cedar (2003)
The Mango War and other stories
The Silence of the Glass House (2008)
The Only Glow of the Day (2010)
Valley of the Peacock Angel (2013)
The Lebanon Diaries (2009)
Deadly Confederacies and other stories (2014)
Dark Rose Days (2016)
This Cruel Station and other stories (2017)

AFTER KAFKA

Martin Malone

451
Editions

After Kafra
Second edition, 2018
Published by 451 Editions
Dublin
www.451editions.com

The first edition of *After Kafra* was published by
Poolbeg Press, Dublin, 2001: www.poolbeg.com

ISBN: 978-1-9999075-0-1

Cover and interior design: www.Cyberscribe.ie
Cover image: Tany Dimotrova https://themeforest.net/user/tanydi

For Colin and Barry

About the author

Martin Malone is an Irish novelist, dramatist and short story writer. His first novel, *Us,* won the John B Keane/*Sunday Independent* Literature Award and two years later his novel *The Broken Cedar,* published by Simon and Schuster, was shortlisted for the International IMPAC Literary Award. He is a former military policeman who served six tours as a peacekeeper in the Lebanon and Iraq; *The Lebanon Diaries* is a memoir of this time, and much of this experience is themed in his work. His novel *Valley of the Peacock Angel* explores war atrocities in Kurdistan in 1988; this title, *After Kafra,* now in its second edition, looks at PTSD experienced by a former peacekeeper. His short stories have been broadly published and anthologised, his stories and dramas have been broadcast on RTE and BBC and he was shortlisted for the BBC World Service Short Story Competition. He is based in Kildare.

AFTER KAFRA

Chapter 1

Harry Kyle dreams about thorns of Christ growing briary on the roadside, of air sweetened by orange and lemon groves, of banana plantations, fruit bagged in garish blue plastic, protection against heavy winter rains, yellow sandstorms, the sea's withering breezes, and an added bitter coldness that falls with the darkening of day. Of mush terracotta soil, drying under the wild caress of a Mount Hermon wind. Of a pale sun in grey-white cloud, hundreds of seabirds raising a cacophony, feeding on the remains of a harvest reaped by gelignite fishermen.

His dream eye sees grey Israeli patrol vessels bobbing on a shoreline not theirs, passing the gaping eye socket of a Moorish keep, its sun-scorched walls soaking in the smoky aroma of mint leaves burned by loved ones of loved ones who can love no more, in a Muslim cemetery that reaches as far as tall iron gates set like black teeth between marble columns. The cry of the gannet, the shush to shore of stormy waves, the first time of seeing another's blood on his hand, and how it hurt, without actually causing him physical pain.

By the time he parks the Chevrolet jeep and unloads his pistol, returning the Browning to stores along with Sam's Sten gun, night has drawn in and the evening air is cold. He and Sam say nothing.

In that silence he wakes with a wide-eyed jolt and a constricting sensation in his throat. His sweat rich, thick and warm on his forehead, his temple veins throbbing. His dream ending as it had begun, with soap staining his hands a bright red.

Harry Kyle stares at the darkness until the darkness stares back. A stiff wind blows, sweeping across the Curragh Plains, blowing flecks of rain against the new PVC windows. June's naked buttocks lean into his and for moments he snatches comfort in her heat, before easing from bed.

In the kitchen he makes tea and brings the steaming mug into the living-room, and sits on a fireside chair, a breath of cold ash catching in his lungs. He sees the darkness and the amber streetlights of the Curragh Camp through the quarter of window revealed by the blind. The wind plays down the throat of the chimney and sometimes it falls silent. Its silence is a silence of the ages, of wisdom garnered from the four comers of the world. In its silence Harry Kyle feels truly alone.

June's trying to figure out what the hell has got into him, why he has a mourning-bell for a face, and why, sometimes, when disturbed by the kids, he yells at them, and at her, and what happened to his relaxed, easy-going manner. He asks himself, too. Continually.

He is home from a place he couldn't wait to leave behind. And now, by night and, when not otherwise preoccupied, by day, he finds himself in his combat boots, reliving, and thinking, and when not thinking... seeing.

He is weeks back from the Middle East, the tan starting to fade in the late autumn coldness. He'd put on a little weight that June said suited him. He hadn't been training, he said. He was twenty-eight and liked to pump iron, see the muscles flexing in his forearms, feel the perspiration trickle down his spine. But now, only lately, the inclination to train had deserted him.

He can never wash his hands enough. June appreciates that, the new ultra-hygienic Harry. You could eat your dinner off his hands, if you didn't mind the smell of Dettol.

He finishes his tea and rubs his hands together. He was raised on a small farm in a comer of Kildare. Land and livestock he'd come to hate as much as his parents – parents who refused him a loan when he was badly stuck, saying that their money was tied up in investments for three years. The words came lame from his mother's mouth – too lame to be true. It hurt him, too – the way they shut out his kids.

He is home, but not home.

His mind is elsewhere, his grey eyes on Lebanese soil, his nostrils taking in the rich red earth, baked by the hot khamsin winds and freshened by the early autumn rains and sea breezes that chase and drive cracks in the hot winds, making crevices for the rains to steal through.

It is Saturday. He wakens in his prefab accommodation and lies on for a few minutes. A brown army blanket tacked across the window blocks daylight, except for a tear in the middle revealing a single bright eye.

Reaching a hand from under the green mosquito netting he thumbs a switch on his Sharp radio and listens to the BBC World Service News. The air smells of last night's mosquito coil lying as ash under its small aluminium plinth. In spite of the deterrent, one buzzed by his ear in the middle of the night and fattened by his blood had paused long enough for him to snap it dead with his hands, its burst carcass staining the netting.

The Ghanaians guarding the barracks keep wood fires going in braziers they fashion from barrels and stand around these at nights with their FN rifles slung over their shoulders, chatting with the Lebanese army sentries who show up on parade most mornings and leave the soldiering on the streets to the Amal militia.

The Military Police detachment operates from a long building with an eaveless veranda. On ground level the sandbag parapet soaks up rainwater that streams down the valleys of the corrugated tin roof. Some of the bags have burst, spilling sand, and others are beginning to unstitch. Replacing them will pass the time and afterwards he'll type up that Final Traffic Accident Report and get it off to HQ.

Sam the Fijian is on the Duty Desk this morning, taking weapons in from some French UN soldiers who intend visiting the ruins of Tyre.

Harry reads last night's journal, checks the ablution area for cleanliness and the dry toilet for emptiness. He is the oncoming Duty Desk and, if there aren't enough buckets to flush away the waste, the toilet clogs. Sometimes the off-going Desk doesn't bother to replenish the buckets and people just dump their loads and walk away. Then if you want to crap you have to use an Arab toilet and squat over a hole and it isn't easy to read a newspaper in that position.

Knocking on the kitchen door he enters. You always knock beforehand. This is done to let the rats and mice know you're coming in. He checks the cupboard above the sink. If there is a rat or a mouse pinned he'll only have coffee for breakfast. By right he should leave the traps until after breakfast but that affects his appetite too. He can't sit at the oilcloth-covered table and eat, not with the image of a dead rat next door, its black eyes glassy, its ringed tail hanging limp, its piss and shit staining the newspaper laid on the shelves. He raps on the long press and, eating a breath, swings the double doors open. Blankety-blank. The trap set, its rasher missing, its blue sewing-thread frayed.

Sam says a Ghanaian has eaten the rasher. Probably the rat, too. He doesn't like Ghanaians. It's a racist thing with him. He doesn't like blacks. He is serious when he says this and he a dusky colour himself. A true Fijian without the light colouring the Indians had brought to the islands. Harry is sure he means he doesn't like Africans but doesn't go down the road of asking him. The whole colour issue can raise its ugly head and refuse to lie down. But he derives great craic from the things Sam says to the lads, things no white man who wanted to own wrinkles would dream of saying. That's how the day starts. Checking rat traps, eating breakfast, listening to Sam locking the French weapons away. Bitching about the Ghanaians singing jungle songs by the braziers last night, eating the donkey they'd skinned that evening. Going on to say that he's checked with Ops, and the AO is quiet.

Harry sighs, eases the cabinet's drop-leaf down and screws off the brandy top, filling a small glass. Something to hold and stir, to catch his stare, rather than to drink. The wind moans and dies. Traffic begins to fill the roads, headbeams on.

The radio set crackles with activity. Ops telling the various battalions to go into shelter. Some place in NEPBATT is after being hit. He picks up the gist of it as he enters the duty room. Sam is already in flak jacket and helmet, carrying his Sten gun, the Investigation Box sitting at his feet, saying he's called the others out of their beds to man the desk and as backup in case they need them.

Sam isn't too sure what has happened, but something serious has and Tyre MP have to respond ASAP.

Harry gets up, sips at his brandy, and tugs on the blind, revealing the full window picture; beyond the road the Curragh Plains flare into a broad expanse of lush green carpet, patterned with furze bushes. Grey skies, pylon wires holding chorus lines of birds, racehorses nudged to gallops by jockeys with collars zipped against the cold, a spill of chips on a wet footpath, and treetops of distant woods. He isn't in Lebanon... but telling himself that and showing his eyes the proof doesn't keep the bad dreams away.

They drive quickly along the coastal road, passing sand quarries, a half-built hotel – someone's second thought – and twisted railroad tracks that once carried the Orient Express, before wheeling a left turn up Burma Road, hearing gunfire in the distance and the sound of a tank loosening its chamber.

Harry bites his lip, fingers sleep-crust from his eyes, and returns to the armchair.

They don't speak much in the jeep. He drives steadily, not rushing. All he can think about is Ops sending the Battalions into shelter and the MPs out in a soft-top jeep to investigate an incident of which they know nothing. The unknown mission.

It mightn't have been so bad if he had had time to steel himself.

Reaching a checkpoint they are flagged down a narrow, rutted road by Nepalese soldiers. Harry knows the village but its name escapes him. Sam says Kafra. He is right. He parks in front of the UN post and is met by an officer who brings them to the scene. Scene. A soldier's broken body lies on rubble ground by a whitewashed wall, his severed right hand beside a railing guarding an aged olive tree, bullets spilled from his rifle's magazine, the weapon's buttstock shattered. And cats darting in and out of the small square, feeding on flesh. An old man carrying a black bag shooing them away, picking up pieces. There is more. Sam touches his ribs to show him.

A woman's foot wrenched from her body sits upright and close to Harry – blue legging, shiny bone like chicken-bone and sinew – blown off her feet. Her foot forgotten about in the rush to get her to hospital. The officer mentioned that, hadn't he? Eighteen years old. The old man breathes her name but it passes by Harry. The old man's eyes meet his. Harry thinks how they have no depth. The bag opens.

Harry Kyle eases to his hunkers, pinches the girl's foot and lowers it into the bag and then watches Sam go through the same procedure with the soldier's hand.

For moments Harry stands there, feeling a numbness in the pit of his belly. Gathering his thoughts, his belly ice-cold, he goes about his work.

He takes photographs and measurements for the sketch.

Names of witnesses for the statements that will follow. On the way to Tyre they stop in NEPBATT HQ and snap photographs of the body for the Final Report. It isn't his first time seeing a dead body. But the others were of old men and it seemed sad but natural that they should die.

This is wrong. Bodies torn, the souls wrenched from them.

The Nepalese soldier, a week left to go home, home to a wife and four-year-old son, who would have only a scant memory of his dad. The young woman...

He'd always known that someday this would happen. His eyes would be called upon to see such a sight. He hadn't believed he'd handle it so badly. Hadn't thought for one moment he'd wake up in a cold sweat, that the sight of bloodied limbs would haunt his nights and his waking hours. Seeing them in the ordinary things he did.

Imagining June's foot in a blue legging, seeing the kids missing a hand; horrific thoughts sailing across his mind and sometimes making a return jockey. And cats crying in his nightmares in a demented craving for the taste of human flesh.

The weapons weeks logged in, the blood on his hands, and the washing, the constant washing, because his hands can never be clean enough. And he tells himself he washes not because the girl's foot was dirty and covered with the dust of her day, but because he is fearful of being tainted by the evil done to her, while now and then he acknowledges it is the sight and the feel of her foot he wishes to scrub from his memory.

He hears the door opening, but doesn't look up. Its hinges need oiling.

"Harry?" June says.

His "Yeah" is low.

"What's wrong?"

He sighs, "Nothing."

"It can't be nothing."

Tell June? He hasn't told anyone. He and Sam went back to Tyre, rang Ops with their findings and while he typed up a report Sam sieved kava into a basin and later they drank it, and beer, loads of cheap Lebanese beer. Getting sick and Harry knowing that his vomiting had nothing to do with mixing his drinks.

He tells her. Inching the words out – June waiting for the bits to fall with an eagerness in her blue eyes, as though with his words she can piece him back together and make all the nightmares go away. June believes in building bridges with words.

June's fingers stay on her lips. He has finished and he waits for her to say something. Anything. He can tell by her she doesn't know what to say. Then he catches the smell of that day. It breezes into his nostrils as June goes outside to the kids. A smell of death, of war, perhaps of Hell. Yes, Hell. And he has a little comer of it in his mind all to himself. In the shade, where the sun doesn't shine.

Chapter 2

June makes coffee and sits by the kitchen table with her legs crossed. She's wearing those faded blue jeans he likes and that loose red blouse. The kids are playing out the back, in the garden. Winter sunlight is pale and the mid-morning November air has turned cold for the first time this month.

"Will you go and see someone?" she says. Her slender fingers rake her short brown hair and then she adds, because of his silence, "Will you?"

"No."

"How long is this going to last?"

"Is what going to last?"

"This shite – shouting at me and the kids, the silent moods – you're like, oh, I don't know. I just don't."

"Say it."

June puts her forefinger to her lips as though to stay her words. Both their coffees are growing cold.

Tony starts crying. He's three. Always crying. June blames his teeth, says they're cutting his gums – all you have to do is look at him and his red cheeks – patience is needed. Her voice goes small and hard when she says "Patience".

June goes out. Harry feels the blast of cold air on his face. He sighs and follows her.

"He slipped in dog-shit, Harry – Jesus, didn't I tell you to pick it up this morning?"

"I forgot."

The smell is gross. June lifts Tony on to the table while Harry eases off his wellies.

The heels thick with shit. He calls Derek in. Derek is five and has his mother's soft blue eyes and his dad's dark hair.

"Yeah, Dad?"

"Stay in here until I clean the yard."

"I want to play — "

"Get in, I said."

"Dad — "

"In!"

Outside he scrapes the dirt up with a shovel and buries it under a holly bush that grows against the boundary wall. Barney, the black and white terrier, grey face and grey arse, hides in the back of his plastic kennel — knows he did something wrong but hasn't got an idea what it is.

He washes the wellies under the outside tap and leaves them to dry on the sill. Derek is out gathering leaves, moping about and sometimes kicking at a burst ball. The air is tinged with the smell of kerosene. The oil-burner roars. Its heat shimmers above the conical top of its aluminium chimney, in the way he had seen the heat do on the runway at Beirut airport — wavy air.

See someone? Who? A shrink? That's not what she said but it is what she meant. She doesn't know the army — the way it works — for fuck's sake, he's a sergeant, he wants promotion, wants a job — go and tell them he suffers nightmares and what'll happen, eh? In the clutches of a shrink and then in front of a board and before he knows it he will be signing on in civvy street. Have all the nightmares you want and good luck in the cup and fuck you.

The chimney! Derek. Jesus! Climbing on to the kennel, making for the roof of the burner shed. The fumes. May as well be sticking his head under a car's exhaust pipe. He lifts him down. June raps the window. Says he always plays up there with his men.

"The fumes," he says, pointing.

June makes a face.

"He could burn himself against the chimney."

"He didn't when you were away."

She closes the window to drown out whatever else he has to say. He goes into the shed and slips on his Dunlops and makes for the Curragh Plains. June calling after him, to remind him that he's to baby-sit at three. He doesn't answer.

He crosses the road opposite Coogan's Shop, Barney going on ahead, chasing crows instead of sheep, then rolls in the grass as he waits for Harry to catch up. The plains are soft from the overnight rain, beaded with sheep dirt and hoof imprints left by racehorses coming and going from the all-weather gallops. The last of the summer gold clings to the furze that lies on the plains in green swathes, except for the occasional patches burned black by vandals. It is the same every year, around this time, the kids burning the gorse in the days leading up to Halloween. When Harry is almost near him, Barney the terrier heads off again. By now the Wicklow mountains and their skies of canvas blue are behind them. There's the sound of a train in the distance – cutting across the Sunday emptiness.

There's a place he likes to make for on his walks. A ring fort partially hidden by furze, affording a view of the Hill of Allen and the bite the quarry company had stolen from it, this legendary fortress of Na Fianna. He had taken the boys there once but it had been a biting cold day and the woods frightened them, the swaying of the trees and their creaks when the wind played them like a musical instrument.

"I don't like it here," Derek had said. "It's creepy."

Harry carried Tony and felt his small fingers tighten on his collar jacket, his head pressing into his neck. He turned around and let them play awhile in the gravel car park while he sat in the Nissan Micra reading the Sunday Tribune and its piece about army deafness claims. Last spring, a sting of winter in it, he was a week from travelling to Lebanon and about five months away from the carnage at Kafra.

At the ring fort he stands on a grassy hummock, Barney losing himself in the furze in pursuit of the rabbits they had stolen upon. He never catches any – just does it for the excitement of the chase. Harry sighs and lights up a cigarette, pocketing his silver Zippo as he draws hard and exhales. The strain in his throat is less than what it was – the fresh air and long walk unravelling what he felt were knotted veins – but he still feels primed to cry. Cry, Jesus, cry. Over what?

He has two lovely boys, a wife whom he loves and who loves him he thinks, a house, a car, no pressing money worries. Good health. So – why are the tears lurking like clouds in his eyes, waiting to spill?

Harry gives the eye of his cigarette a sad look. A drink. He craves a drink. June had shot him with hard eyes this morning when she saw his brandy glass on the coffee table in the sitting-room. He had brought a lot of booze home with him – bottles of whiskey, liqueurs, arak and brandy – duty-free presents he had intended to give away but had now decided to hoard for Christmas. Why give those people who hadn't answered his letters a gift from overseas? Why should he think enough of them to do that, when they didn't bother their arses to scratch him a few lines?

"Who are you getting at?" June asked, the surprise at his tone visible on her lean, pretty features.

Who was he getting at? No one in particular, just friends he considered friends but who now, he believed, didn't really give a tuppenny fuck for him. None wrote back. None. Did that say something about him? Say it with flowers, the old TV ad went – say it by saying nothing, by leaving the page blank?

"Nothing – no one. I'm just keeping the booze – do what you like with the rosary beads and the other stuff."

"It's not me who should be giving these things to – "

"I'm not doing it."

"They'll be around to see you."

"All with hanging hands."

June sucked in a breath. Her cheeks tinged red, "What is wrong with you?"

That was before he told her. Before she knew. He may as well have not told her because her knowledge of what he is living through has not improved her tolerance. Instead, and he might be mistaken, but doubts it, she has if anything become more exasperated with him.

He takes in a breath. Scattered around his feet are broken mushrooms, trod upon by sheep, lying about like Last Supper bread the apostles abandoned when told of the betrayal. In the distance a train emerges from a tall and dense hedgerow, pulling few carriages, heading towards Dublin, losing itself behind the fox covert.

Harry takes in the time on the G-Shock watch he bought from Santosa in Tibnin. A one-armed shopkeeper of Lebanese descent from the Philippines. He settled in the mountains, in the Irish Batt area, because it was his wife's place and she wanted to die there and be buried in the grounds of the Crusader castle on the hill with her poet mother and professor father. "It is the way," he said, with a shrug of his narrow shoulders.

It's time to head back. Barney leads the way. For an instant Harry feels and tastes the richly sweet Arab coffee Santosa used to make him. An old man scratching a living in a war-tom land, while in the back room, on a mattress on the floor, lay his wife, the heat of life bleeding from her. Always complaining of the cold – and the sun at its summer strongest. Why think of Santosa? Is it because his lean face, the cracks of a hard life in it, remind him of his father? He had found the resemblance uncanny. So much a near ghost of a near ghost.

He sees grey-blanketed horses trotting along the gallops, dotting the air behind them with flecks of earth. Sees an army Land-Rover patrolling the perimeter wire of the Ammunition Depot, cutting in along a track by a World War II pillbox.

He walks quickly, flicking his cigarette ahead of him, stubbing it with the ball of his foot. June's getting her hair done in 'Shapes and Shades' in Newbridge. They're going out tonight. It's a surprise, she told him. Destination's a surprise.

Tomorrow he's back at work. Reporting into barracks at nine. Back to the grist of the mill. A quick month is the month's leave after a Lebanon tour. Not long enough, Harry feels, to leave the Lebanon behind you. Entirely.

Barney waits for him at the edge of the road. They cross together. There isn't much traffic on this road on Sundays – weekdays are another matter. He takes in the new windows June had picked out and had installed in his absence. All he had to do was pay for them when his Leb money came through, she said.

She talks of new windows and meals out and clothes for the boys – normal things – while he thinks of abnormal things that happen in a faraway country – where shelling and gunfire occur frequently enough to be called normal events. Where everyone, cats included, does his or her best not to go hungry.

"I was watching you," June says, when he enters the kitchen.

The boys are looking at a cartoon on TV. 'Zombie Island,' Derek says.

"Watching me?"

"God, that long face of yours would depress anyone."

He says nothing.

"You'd think all were dead on you or something."

"I've something on my mind – I've already told you."

She nods, "Maybe you'll shake it off when you go back to work."

Maybe, just maybe, June is right. Work might help. He says he feels as though his mind is full of hot coals. She says he needs help – he can't keep waking up in a cold sweat and shouting in his sleep. Disturbing the house – what will the neighbours think?

"They say nothing about the rocking bed." Sarcasm – there isn't any rocking bed.

"Don't make light of –"

He says, "I'll be fine. You're right, once I start back working."

The itch for a drink rises from deep in his belly. He says he's going for one, just one. He won't be long. Back well before it's time for them to go out. Completely forgets why June wanted him back early from his walk – to go get her hair done.

Chapter 3

"I'm sorry," he says, when he returns and realises why she's cool towards him. No hair care – fucking dope he is to forget, to come between a woman and her hair stylist.

"They only open for a couple of hours on Sundays."

"I said sorry."

"They're closed now," she says, taking in the kitchen clock. "Leeds were playing – you know I follow Leeds. I just..."

"My hair's a mess."

"It isn't."

"I said it is – it badly needs a cut."

"You and your fucking hair! Will you give me a break? How short do you want it? It's too short as it is."

June takes in the two boys sitting on the rug in front of the TV. He knows what she's going to say before she says it.

"I don't like that language being used in front of the kids."

"Don't annoy me, then." Jesus, he used to have such a clean tongue. Once he went six months without saying fuck – now it's a resident word on his tongue.

"Annoy you? I'm the one who should be annoyed. You're not pulling your weight around here."

"You're always saying that you got along fine without me for six months – everything I fucking do you come along and do after me – what's the point in me making beds and you redoing them, washing the floor after I've just washed it?"

"You only half-do things."

A silence falls between them.

He whispers "Like you, is that it?" His look is an edge of double meaning.

He shakes his head – what the fuck is wrong with me? Why am I losing the rag? Fuck it!

Anger swarms through her like a smouldering fire suddenly blazing to life.

"You better get out of here, Harry, before I say something I'll regret. I'm not going to argue with you in front of the kids – no matter how much you might like that."

She breaks for the phone. He watches her digit the numbers and feels a pinch of guilt. He has a big mouth with a runaway tongue. Harry goes to her and puts his hand on her shoulder and says, "Look, I'm sorry."

She shrugs his hand away. He lets it fall like a leaf, slow and easy. June had a certain reserve towards him before he left for overseas – and that distancing went on when he was away, and it's still here, alive and throbbing, as real as his nightmares. After cancelling the babysitter for the evening she faces him, her hand on the cradled phone. "Leave me alone, Harry – don't say anything – just leave me alone."

He stands outside the front gates. Wrought ironwork June's dad put up a week before he died. A man with lug ears – a legacy from his rugby-playing days, days when he made the Irish team panel and missed out by one place on an Australian tour.

Scratching his cauliflower ear, taking in the test swing of the gates. Harry thought he didn't look well, something in his pallor, his eyes full of the weight of bad news he had not yet broken to anyone. The gates squeak as Harry passes through. Derek Senior – things aren't being done in his absence; gates left without oil, gutters growing grass, cracks left in the paving slabs, blocked shores and the gable end peppered with the dried mud imprints of footballs kicked there by Derek.

Things Harry hadn't got around to doing yet, in spite of June's reminders.

He breaks for Frank's Pub a mile down the road. A pub with a mock facade of Tudoresque panelling that faces the road and the Curragh Camp. An icy wind blows from the west, catching him full in the face. He steps on to the Curragh verge before cars drive by him. He was hit a few years ago while walking on the side of the road, spun like a spinning top, fortunate his kitbag had taken most of an impact that had left him unconscious with a pair of broken ribs. The doctor said he was lucky. Lucky? He said he'd hate to see his unlucky cases.

He takes his pint to a corner table by an open fire and sits down. Gets a craving for a Hamlet cigar and returns to the counter. Breaks the Cellophane on the thin stick and lights up – uses a match because the wick in the Zippo is spent. There are few customers and the barman is a surly character with a small nose who grunts a response when Harry says there is frost in the air.

Harry sips at his beer, takes the cream off with a single quaff and wipes his lips. Pounding head, knot in his stomach, tight throat – nerves dancing a jig. Looks at his hands – his left is missing two knuckles, smashed on a soccer pitch when an opposing player stood on them. A light film of dark hair on the backs of his hands, fingernails clean, a cut on his thumb beginning to heal – hands.

He is missing a hand. The soldier. An olive-skinned hand with dirty fingernails and a wart on his thumb, the angry red pulp of the severance showing. A slab of meat with five fingers – his right hand carries a long lifeline – a pure lie.

Stop thinking. Think of something else. Anything else. Forget Lebanon and its stink of death. Forget about it. Home, he's at home, drinking a pint. Not out there. There is 4,000 miles away. That's a fair distance. You wouldn't walk it in a day. No, sir. You would not. Amazing how the mind can take you to a place – in instants you can revisit your childhood, a holiday, a moment in your life, switch from one scene to the next, spanning decades. But what happened in Kafra is taking over, staying in his mind, lurking – a predator memory chasing others away. Stop thinking.

He hurries his pint and then leaves. Pauses a short way from the door and draws in a deep breath. He shouldn't be alone – he should be with June – having that meal or doing whatever it was she had planned as a surprise. Her hair done. They had lots to talk about. He had missed out on so much with the kids. Six months is a fair chunk out of their lives. They'd gotten bigger in his absence. They were six months older than the mindset he had them in. Older, not babies. Tony potty-trained, out of Pampers. Derek pronouncing his words clearer. June organised – doing the things he used to do and doing them well, from gardening to basic car maintenance. He could be dead and they wouldn't miss him. Could be missing a hand and they wouldn't miss it.

Stop.

He walks on. Thinks of June. Twenty-six years old and beautiful – classy figure. Likes to paint river and forest scenes and write poetry. When she was six she lost her mother from cervical cancer, an only child raised by a father who never remarried, who devoted his life to bringing up his daughter. More of a brother than a father, more of a friend than either. Harry said she was lucky. She said she knew. Waited for him to say something about his parents and when it wasn't forthcoming, asked him up to dance. That first date – eight years ago. Christ. Time. Goes too fast or too slow – only in certain cases does it not move at all – in nightmares, for instance.

He walks on. The road is long and dark, a country road losing its status, becoming something of a secondary road as more people use it to avoid the jams in Kildare. Passing through the Curragh Camp, Brownstown, and taking a left at the fork to drive past the Japanese Gardens and on to

Monasterevin where the traffic would have thinned enough to allow smoother progress. He uses the route whenever he visits his brother Al in Castlebar. A younger brother who works in a restaurant managed by his lover whom he met in Canada some years ago, when he lived and studied there.

A trained cordon bleu chef. Al calls Ivan his companion. It's been a while since he saw Al. He'd written to Harry a couple of times during his Lebanon stint. He hoped that things weren't half as bad as he had read in the papers and seen on the TV.

Three times worse, Al. The Israelis called their offensive against the Hizbollah *Grapes of Wrath*. Harry caught the blast from its tail end. Right up until the last hour no one knew if his outgoing chalk, to replace the troops in Lebanon, would take place. Already, the rotation chalks scheduled to relieve the current battalion had been delayed by a week.

Harry watched the news on TV, constantly, seeing places he would come to know well; Tyre and Beirut in Lebanon, Nahariya and Metulla in Israel. Rockets fired from the backs of jeeps hidden in dense orange groves, civilian cars blasted by Israeli jets, even an ambulance en route to Najib Hospital was taken out, engulfed in black smoke.

June asked what he had asked himself, "What in the name of Jesus do you want to go out there for?"

Why? For the experience – he was twenty-eight – a soldier for six years, and you listen to fellas talking in the barracks about their tours and it gets so that you want to see the place for yourself. The idea grows on you. There's the money aspect, too – the thoughts of new windows to keep out the Curragh draughts had softened June's objections but, still, occasionally, she told him she wouldn't mind if he cried off and stayed at home. He sensed she meant none of it. He had traded peace of mind for what – new windows? New fucking windows. Imagine.

He is almost home. They bought the house five years ago, moving from a flat in Kildare. A dingy hole of a place above a dry-cleaner's, where the walls were blackened and mice scudded across the attic at night. He worked part-time in the pub across the road, squirrelling money away towards a deposit for a house. There was a place they looked at in town but the house in Brownstown was larger, cheaper and nearer to his barracks in the Curragh Camp and Derek Senior who lived down a leafy laneway in a small cottage. All that extra work hadn't earned them enough to make up the shortfall and it was Derek who gave them the money, almost all his savings, giving him and June the sort of start most couples only dream of.

He felt a little envious of June, having someone who would give till it hurt. His own parents were going to have a damn good try at bringing their money to the grave with them. Three years— he hasn't spoken a word to either in three years. They live on the same small farm in Sunnyhill, on the Kilcullen road, that the Kyles have lived in for three centuries. A fine redbrick house with a long chimney stack, a range of stables that once lodged a Derby winner and which had, the last he knew, housed beagles belonging to the local hunt. Not a word in three years to either — June was shocked by the extent of his bitterness. He never spoke of what had happened to cause such a marked alienation of people who had, after all, brought him into the world and reared him. And he realised that his inability to air his feelings was a failing, perhaps his greatest flaw. During an intimate moment June pondered aloud if he could shut her and the kids out to the same brutal extent. He responded by telling her not to be stupid.

Locked out. Barney barking until he is told to quieten. A sliver of moon in a cloudless sky. Stars bright but not as bright as those that burn over Lebanon. Hall light on. The glass side panel adjoining the door reveals June's bare feet on the lower stairs, painted toe nails reminding him that she had planned on taking him out tonight. Why? Had she something to tell him — bad news she wouldn't break in front of the kids? Why is he so fucking paranoid?

The door opens. She can't bring herself to look at him. Up the stairs – her blue nightdress ending above her knees. He, left to close the door and take in the scent of her moisturiser, his "sorry" a weak whisper that doesn't make the landing, falling well short of the bedroom door that closes with a soft but resounding click.

Chapter 4

He wakens early with a sore neck and stiff lower back. Remembers. Massages his neck. Hasn't dreamt. Harry rolls up the sleeping bag and fluffs the settee's cushions. Draws the curtains and raises the blind. The early morning light is almost an inky blue, the frost glitters on the road, not a hard frost, just a foretaste of what lies farther down winter's road. A rash of stars in the heavens.

In the kitchen Barney gives him a baleful look, arches his spine and then moves to the back door. After Harry lets him out he fills the kettle, listens to its early sizzling, his mouth dry and his stomach sick at the thoughts of returning to work.

In all, between overseas training, the months spent abroad and on UN leave, he's been out of barracks for nine months. Feels like much longer, but not long enough.

The burner kicks in and the pipes and radiators start to creak. Seven am.

If he were overseas he would be washed, dressed and breakfasted by now. Standing on parade, waiting for the CSM to take the inspection. Answering "Present" to the airing of his name.

"Traffic Section—Halverson, Alifoh, Bamberger, Sadimaki."

"Investigation Section – Opare, Konasau, Valimaki, Leszek, Kyle."

If not in camp he was either on a day off or on

detachment; he had spent a month in Metulla, living in a house in Dudovan Street, another month in Nahariya – Israeli towns – three weeks in Beirut and two months in Tyre. He was seldom on parade but near the end of his tour, after his spell in Tyre, he had got a run of them.

He sips at his tea, and butters the bread that has sprung up lightly toasted. Hears the door opening. June – she moves like a ghost – so quiet – you never hear the fall of her feet.

"Good morning," he says, quietly.

She says nothing. A truculent set to her chin, like her anger has dug in. June touches the radiator, yawns, rubs the sides of her eyes as she looks through the window at the creeping light. Massaging her thoughts to life. She's wearing a white woollen dressing gown, not belted at the waist but hanging open. Sees her breasts and the shaded vee of her fanny through the light blue nightie. June yawns and sighs and turning to the laminated counter, says, "Is the tea long made?"

"I've the kettle on to make a fresh brew." Conciliatory tone.

"Will you bring Derek to school? Tony might sleep on and I want to get the washing going." Belts up her gown.

"Yeah, right, no problem."

"I need the car at dinner time."

"I'll drop it down."

There's a brittle peace between them. He senses that she so much wants to rail against him it pains her to stifle her words. But she does so because she doesn't want to shatter the boys' peaceful home-life. Perhaps senses that if she were to drop the reins the arguments would be endless. On top of that she is struggling to come to terms with the changes in him. Her thoughts are like storm-driven clouds. They show on her face.

"About last night he begins.

"Not now, Harry."

"Later on... "

He nods. Moving to her he puts a hand on her shoulder. She says, "What's happening to you – why are you like this?" He says nothing, just removes his hand. Hadn't he told her? Why won't she listen?

"You're so moody, so bloody contrary, so unreachable." "Unreachable – I don't turn my arse to you in bed, do I? I don't draw away under your touch, not that you touch me anyway. The night we had when I came home – is that it? My fill?"

"You're a bastard."

"Language – the kids."

"I wouldn't mind if you were any good at it."

Abruptly, he turns from her. He had put it down to being tired. Landing at three in the morning in Dublin, the customs check, the long winding drive to Cathal Brugha barracks, collecting his luggage, almost five when he finally reached June, who was waiting in the crowd for him, their car idling on the barrack square. Keeping the heat.

That meeting – the warmth, the love – so apparent, and then at home in bed, the rise of her leg and the land of her onto his thigh brought no response from him. She couldn't understand his reticence, his not wanting to take her in a hurry. He wasn't like a man who had done without sex for over six months. In the end it happened but it was less than satisfactory for both of them. A duty performed. What should he have told her that night? That his hands felt dirty, that he smelt the blood on them, that he could never get them clean enough, no matter how many times he scrubbed them?

Said that tears flood to his eyes without warning, that the last thing he felt like doing was making love. The last thing he wanted to happen was to feel the flesh of another human being pressed against his. But it hurts too – the fact that she does not want him. Derek comes down. Bright-eyed, curious, looking about the kitchen as though he could see the atmosphere.

"Are you fighting with Daddy?"

Harry and June look at each other, glances as sharp as hail flailing against a window.

"You're always fighting," Derek adds.

"Were talking ... " Harry says.

"Talking fighting."

June sticks his waffles under the grill, making unnecessary noise. Harry takes in his eldest son. So small and vulnerable, impressionable. Pyjamas worn-looking and short at the cuffs and ankles. He had new pyjamas but he prefers the old ones. Like the past, Harry thinks, comfy – compared to now.

"Will someone turn on the TV?" Derek says.

"Yeah... I will," Harry says.

"Something useful for a change," June mutters.

Teletubbies. No – thank God it's only Tony who likes those. *Power Rangers*? Derek says, "Yes." Changes his mind and goes for *Ninja Turtles*.

Harry shaves in the bathroom, clears a patch in the mirror's mist and scrapes his face. Takes in his eyes. Grey blue – cloud and sky – not the washed blue of June's. A port-wine birthmark on the angle of his chin that ensures he shaves cautiously – a rushed shave, the slightest of nicks and the blood would flow for an age. He has slightly hooded eyes and a straight nose that dips near the end. More rugged than good-looking – not in the least bit handsome but neither is he ugly. His teeth, his smile, features he didn't of late reveal much of, were probably his best. The mist covers the mirror and he no longer sees himself. He had wanted to examine his looks because he wanted to see himself as others would – wanted to see if he could hide the truth in his eyes, hide Harry Kyle's marbles, the ones running wild in his head. If you looked deep within you might actually see him drowning.

Derek is quiet in the car. Hates school he says. Hates fucking school. They're a mile down the road. The way ahead icy in places and the frost like sheets thrown over the gorse. "You shouldn't be cursing."

"Can't help it, Daddy – will we go to Dublin, shopping, just the two of us?"

"Not today."

"Hate school."

"Hate work."

"You fire guns – I would love school if I could fire a gun."

"Guns are bad."

"Guns are good – don't they kill monsters?"

"Yeah."

"So then... "

Kids. June wants him to have a vasectomy. She'd been at him last Christmas, kept telling him to think about it, but then she stopped asking and he took that to mean she had grown unsure about his having the operation. Last week she mentioned it again in a roundabout way. Said she didn't want to have any more kids. She couldn't hack the notion of going through all that pain again. Twice was enough. He said nothing.

"Are you listening to me? I don't want my body being ripped apart again."

He said nothing just to annoy her. And his silence did annoy her because she knew he felt the same as she did – he thought two kids were enough and also knew that the doctor had advised her not to risk having any more.

Two kids enough? In what way enough? Affordable? Two was affordable.

If you want to spoil them a little then two is the limit. How long would it be enough? June might change her mind in three years' time and so might he. What then? Fly in the face of medical advice? On the other hand June had gone close to death's door while having Tony. Silly then to think they really had a choice. Stupid and mean of him not to understand June's reluctance to make love. She isn't on the pill. Could never take it – the side-effects had an adverse effect on her health – disturbed her biological balance. And there are times he wants her and times he doesn't – times he bums with desire and times he is repulsed by the idea of touching her, touching flesh, any flesh. Best to heed the warnings – besides, were you doing souls a favour by bringing them into this world? With all the bad things that could happen to them – the Kafras, the airplane crashes, the whole damn variety of diseases, to have them face the whole gamut – tears, pain, loss, love, laughter, joy – for fucking what? Wouldn't they, these souls, be better off not knowing fucking any of it? Christ, he'd win, if there were one, the Mister Negative Award.

He parks on the triangular island opposite the church and the school. Ten to nine on the black-faced clock under the green mosque-style dome.

"Come on, son."

"I'm not going."

Harry looks over his shoulder. Derek's eyebrows are furrowed, showing his displeasure. He wears a navy uniform with a crest of St Brigid's cross above his heart. A navy tie with an elastic neck sits slightly askew under his collar button. Harry smiles. He stays with Derek in his line outside the classroom. When the bell sounds Derek says, "Daddy, bring me into the classroom, okay – and don't tell Miss Moore I was cursing or there'll be trouble in the house when I get home."

"Sure, just for this morning, son, okay? And I won't say a word about you cursing."

"Yeah, okay."

Late, he was late for work. Almost. In the car he rings up his work number on his mobile and calls in sick, on a day's Uncertified Sick Leave. USL. Not the done thing after having a month off – but fuck it. He'll be okay tomorrow. Ready.

Takes a coffee in a new cafe and reads the complimentary newspaper. Small place, full of the smell of frying and grilling and chatting women. Steamed-up windows. A grey morning, not cold, a good morning for a brisk walk.

Outside, he calls June on his mobile. A silence when he says he'll be home in an hour.

"What do you mean you'll be home?"

"I took the day off."

"Jesus, Harry – you don't need the day off what have you to do? Where are you? Is Derek in school?"

"Of course he's in school."

"Where are you?"

"In town – Kildare."

"Catching Mass?"

He doesn't detect sarcasm – hope, perhaps? June is half religious, while he believes he has seen enough evidence to suggest that there is no God. Because no God, all powerful, would allow so much pain in the world. As far as he's concerned that is the bottom line.

"Yeah sure, and confession – look, I'm on the mobile, expensive, so I better go – see you in an hour."

He parks outside the ruins of Black Friar abbey. The National Stud and Japanese Gardens branch off the ruins. Not the usual volume of tourist traffic this morning – he remembers that the gardens close for the winter and so too the restaurant and horse museum. The place is quiet. Ghostly quiet.

He walks a pathway through old, slanted headstones, bypassing the ruin's thick walls, making for a bench facing the lake. A cigarette between his lips, third of the morning. Coughs. Sits, crosses his legs and takes in the clear lake waters, the quiet ripple on the surface and thinks how he feels a little better this morning. He had slept last night and hadn't been to Lebanon. Didn't feel the urge to have a drink.

Closes his eyes and breathes in through his nose and out through his mouth. He smells the scent of the pine trees behind him. His tongue finds a sliver of scone between his teeth but can't shift it. He doesn't use his finger – people at their ears, mouths and noses get on his nerves. He smiles – it wouldn't do for him to get on his own nerves, would it?

He is warm in his green husky jacket, so warm he feels a little sleepy. Better now, feels composed, a little confident – amazing what a good night's sleep can do. The way a cigarette soothes the mind. The morning air – so quiet and peaceful – a balm for the mind. *Then he smells oranges, fresh oranges and imagines a trailer-load emerging from the groves. A smell of oranges.* Good Christ! Opens his eyes, takes a deep breath. Home. Ireland, Kil-fucking-dare – not South-fucking-Lebanon – can a smell be a ghost?

Harry gets to his feet, brushes the cigarette ash from the end of his jacket, checks for burns. One burn is enough – on the upper sleeve, done by someone else's cigarette.

Oranges. Breaks for his car, walking hard, so hard that if someone were to see him he would think Harry was fleeing the scene of a robbery or hastening to some important conference. If someone were to see his hard walk merge into a jog he would think Harry was in a hurry to leave something behind, very far behind.

Chapter 5

June ignores him when he arrives home. He senses her anger, disappointment and bewilderment – there is nothing he can say or do to make things okay – she is angry because she can no longer reach him, disappointed because she thought she understood him better and bewildered because Harry never missed a day's work on a whim. Letting her down, letting himself down. She can't see the wind that has forced him to dip his flag.

Tony plays with his Action Corp figures on the kitchen rug in front of a mute fire. He has the hands chewed off them and some of their black weapons have bite marks. Teething hard. Strawberry cheeks. His favourite soldier is a character with a black eye-patch. He carries the figure everywhere as though it were a talisman of sorts.

"Some of us can't take sick leave," June says on her way to the line with a basket of washing, biting on a clothes peg to cork her sarcasm.

He puts coffee into the percolator and unfolds the Daily Star. Tony wheels a jeep back and forth and rolls it across the floor. It swerves and runs under the armchair and collides with the skirting-board. Smiles, claps his hands. Looks at Harry before going to gather his toy. In bits – a miniature version of an American Willies jeep – just enough essential parts – World War II vehicles still in use with the Israelis, albeit with slight modifications. Tony hands him piece by piece to put together as if daddies were there for that sort of thing. Picking up the pieces.

Tony's words aren't distinct – but then neither were Derek's when he was at that age, and look at how much he has come on. It runs in the family on his side – poor oral communicators. It's like there's an in-built fear that their words might betray them.

"You needn't think you're going to sit there all day – under my feet," June says.

"No, no – just going to have some coffee – the shed needs sorting out. Change the bedding in Barney's kennel."

He sometimes senses resentment in June's tone that she is the one who has to stay at home. She is good with computers and has a good manner towards people. She often says she misses that daily contact with adults, that there's a marked isolation to contend with for the stay-at-home mother. At the same time she realises that it simply isn't worth her while working – by the time a childminder is paid there's little left over. She talks about going back to work when Tony starts school, perhaps something part-time before then. In a shop, but not back to the one she worked in for five years. She says some of the people she worked with and her employers pretend not to see her if she comes across them, say during shopping in Dunnes. It's as though by leaving she had in some way slighted them. The conditions were bad in that electrical shop on the main street. A cold, draughty building, more suitable for use as a warehouse than a shop – small wonder that it wasn't making a profit. She had never had a falling out with them. It's something she can't understand. He tells her it will be the same when he leaves the army – people just get on with their lives – you're no longer part of theirs. It is the way with things.

"Why didn't you go to work?" June says, sipping her coffee. She's sitting in at the table.

The windowlight enhances the copper in her brown hair. Her face is long but her eyes are large and round and so very penetrating.

He shrugs, "I don't know — this day is like — like taking a deep breath before you dive into a pool."

"Are you going to see the doctor?"

"No."

"You — "

"No."

"Will you listen to me? Just listen"

He nods. Favours her with his right ear. Listens.

"If this thing that happened to you is going over and over in your mind you need to do something about it — you're as mopey as hell to live with — the kids can't relax around you — you shout, you're curt, distant, cold..."

"Jesus... "

She rakes her temples with her fingers, "It's like I've gotten a new man in my life. You're drinking too much — for God's sake, Harry, just do something about it."

"You left out sex."

Her eyes fall to her coffee. Tony pushes his jeep again and this time it turns over.

He is annoyed because one of his soldiers won't fit into the vehicle. Throws the figure across the floor.

"Tony!" June says.

He ignores her and carries on playing with his other men.

"I said you left out — "

"I know what I left out. I said it's like living with someone else... I don't know you, Harry. You're not the fella who went abroad, who I dropped at the gates of the barracks. You're not him at all — you're only a remote resemblance — the last Harry you could talk to and know he wouldn't overreact — Harry, you're a powder keg."

"That depends on what's said or done to light my fuse, June."

A dawn morning, the last days of April, light streaking the skies. The car heater blowing out warm air. A searching cold wind chilled him to the bone. A smell of turf smoke from the boiler-house chimney. The last kiss, her tears warm against his face. Drying instantly when they drew apart. She said she'd miss him and that he was to take care. Keep the head down. He couldn't say anything because of the strain in his throat. By the time he could say something all he could see of June was her silhouette in the car and the bright red rear lights turning a comer. He rang her that night from Lebanon. Easier to talk and say the things he missed out on saying, easier because the pain of parting was over.

A different man? Yes, but there was something different about June, too. He couldn't quite put his finger on it. Something had changed. It wasn't just her lack of interest in having sex with him. Though that was saying something – perhaps more than either of them realised. After all they had made love before he went abroad, if not regularly. In spite oftheir fears about her becoming pregnant. What then? A lover? No. Surely not? The temper rises in him at the notion. Don't be stupid. Stupid. June wouldn't... simply wouldn't. "I've a thousand condoms in my suitcase," he says. Feeble humour – he shrugs, "I suppose I should have that op'." June's fingers knit each other, "It's down to you – do you want it done?"

He sighs. Coffee? No. Cigarette? Yes, but not in front of Tony. "I do. Of course, I do."

"Then?"

"I was thinking about getting a penile enlargement done first."

"I don't like that sort of talk in front of the kids."

"Tony doesn't understand."

"I don't like it."

"I was messing, that's all."

"Are you really going to have it done? Perhaps you should wait a little longer."

He nods but not convincingly enough to judge by June's dismissive shake of her head.

They've been through the mill on this before – what if

they separated and he wanted to have kids with someone else? He said he never even thought of such a thing happening. How could she? June had smiled, "One of us has a brain."

"What if you meet someone, June?" he asks now.

"What?"

"I suppose it'd be off my conscience that you didn't use my flute to commit hara kiri."

"You can be so disgusting do you know that?"

"I know that. Sure I know that."

June gets to her feet. Barney's barking. Postman must be on his rounds.

He says, "I'll ring today and make the appointment – with your fella in Clane. He's a super-snipper, I hear."

She says, "It's your decision."

She's a little distant, like her brain is chewing on new thoughts he'd given her.

"Will it hurt much, I wonder?" he says.

"Not enough – never enough."

A woman with a clipped Northern Ireland accent scribbles him in her appointment book for Wednesday week.

"That'll cost two hundred pounds, sir. Will you be having a local or general anaestheic?"

"Local."

June says he must be mad, go for the general. He is still on the phone as she whispers but he says with added emphasis, "I'm sure – yeah, local."

He wraps the call up and says, "I don't like the notion of being put asleep – it's scarier than the notion of being... you know?"

"Awake to what's going on?"

"Yes."

"I suppose – given the way you jump about the bed in your sleep these nights – it's the best choice, the safest one for you."

"I hope you come back as a cow in your next life – again."

Silence. A long-drawn-out pause broken by Barney's barking and Tony's tired little whimper caused by the discomfort in his mouth.

He checks the hall for letters while June sees to Tony.

Bills – ESB and Multi Channel, a letter from Al, invitingthem to the launch of Ivan's book of poetry. Notes the day and date – Saturday week. He'll have to check the duty roster tomorrow. See how he feels after the op. He couldn't drive with swollen balls. Not to Castlebar, could he? Too far. But by then the swelling could be down. June won't travel. She likes Al but finds Ivan overbearing. He never stops talking – it's because his mouth is loaded with hot air from his barrel chest, she says. June's tongue would slice apples.

"Baby-sitter... " she says.

"Yeah, I know."

"You go."

"Is there no way we could get – "

"For a day but not for a weekend – besides, this little rascal," she tickles Tony's chin, "is cutting some big teeth."

"We could bring them the kids?"

"Not on your life three hours cooped up in a car with two kids and you having your tantrums."

"Tantrums?"

"You know what I mean... living in your own world... war zone."

"Thanks – tantrum. Tan – fucking – trum."

"Get a life, Harry, you're losing the rag over nothing. Yes... tan – fucking – trum is right. " June sighs.

He sleeps on the sofa. Becoming a habit. Wakes early. The stillness of night. Creeping towards dawn. A brandy. Last finger measure. Make it last. A day at work ahead of him – the operation, what else? He sits in the dark, glass cupped in his right hand, a cigarette in the other, its red eye glowing. He rarely smokes in the sitting room because June hates the smell, says it will destroy her good furniture. On another night the smoke alarm in the hallway had gone off.

June took strips off him, lighting on him with language that would straighten a bishop's crozier. So, he'll restrict himself to a single fag and his brandy — then climb into the sleeping bag and search for some sleep. Tired... so fucking tired. Sleep. Jesus... just one night's good sleep... not a lot to ask from a guy who made blind men see, is it? Not being over-demanding, is it? It's not another prayer on your altar for a Lotto win. Do You know what I mean — it's not a fucking lot to ask.

He dreams of a quiet night in Lebanon, back in Naqoura — awake with only a sheet covering him. Stifling. A floor fan creaking as it circles. Smell of mosquito spray, smell of feet, of sweat, of beer. Loud snores from a comer bunk. Barty. Another boozy night. Drunk in action, in Pablo's Bar, admiring the new barmaid, Hetta. Tits squeezed into a green tank top, revealing much except the nipples. Harry is almost sure that Barty wanks in his sleep but never wants to find out for definite. Awake, alert — stop the snoring, unplug the fan and there would still be the shush to shore of the waves, the buzzing of mosquitos. Always a noise. Always a scene in his head. Takes in the glow in the dark crucifix hanging from a nail in the Formica wall. Strikes up the Our Father but the words are silent on his lips. Mental prayer — stops short of finishing. Climbs from his bunk, the mosquito net falling into place behind him and eases his feet into flip-flops. Pops the fridge open, and lifts a beer, Lebanese Al Maza — pulls the ring outside. He is wearing his striped boxers. Only. Picks a spot under a frangipani tree and sits on the dry red earth to sip his beer. Ice cold. Closes his eyes. Cold. It isn't just the beer that's cold. It is the night. Opens his eyes and sees the rocks on the beach and the thick foam beating against them — the barrack's pale perimeter lights make the rocks resemble snowdrifts. Cheeping insects, a sudden burst into barking by one of the Norwegian drug dogs. Quiet then... a white cat on the prowl along a tin roof. Harry is perspiring heavily. Polishes off his beer, thinks of a Chris de Burgh song as he leaks against the wire fence, 'Ship to Shore'. Thinks 'Piss to Shore' as he hears the scraping noise. Something being dragged. Curious, he moves from the fence and the tree. Looks up and down the small rectangular parade square, pans along the Quartermaster's Store, the Duty room and cells, the offices. Still the noise. Behind him. Close. So close he gets the smell of blood. He turns, hands spread in front of him in a defensive position. The girl is very pretty. Short and slim. Young. Naked. Coming closer, dragging her leg — she has no foot. She is looking through him. Her eyes so brown — colour of washed chestnuts. But his eyes don't fasten on her eyes. It is her wounded leg, its tattered blue legging, and he hears, somewhere very close, a cat's low miaow.

Wakes with a jolt. A sensation of falling. Did he cry out? He prays not. Looks out the window at the Curragh darkness. Hears the wind on the rise. Closes his eyes — so tired, so very, very fucking tired.

Chapter 6

Work. Army work is different from other kinds of work. Al says it isn't work but play. What do you actually do? Fire your weapons, run a little and be there for your duty and so on. Suffer a little tedium. Now, in a kitchen, you work in a kitchen. You slave. No time for tedium, Harry. Army tedium — Jesus — yeah, loads of tedium. Waiting about. Thinking nothing is going to ever happen and when it happens it's over so quickly you're left to wonder what life is all about. How the fuck can ten minutes give him so much trouble? A single war scene from all the war scenes in Lebanon? Then this one is his. Isn't it? His. Soaked in by his eyes and filtered into his brain. Indelible images. Branded on his soul. A tough guy melting.

June says that she needs the car to go shopping. She'll drop Derek into school. He says he doesn't mind the walk to work, it's not far, will give him time to group his thoughts, rein them in. Map in his day. Whatever. He'll cut across the plains as it's shorter. June appears to be apprehensive. Her eyes are holding him at arm's length.

Something's on her mind, other than him, other than the cracks in him she sees and the ones he has told her about.

A mild morning for November — a pale moon the night appears to have left behind and a jet's fading contrails. A short winter? He hates the Curragh winter, how the winds meet on the plains and the grasslands fill up with rain puddles and mucky patches where racehorses make to and from the gallops – how frozen puddles trap sprigs of yellow flower, last of the furze gold, and how hailstones, like mother-of-pearl, necklace lone shrubs. Winter's a prison.

The grass squelches under his Wellingtons. Sheep shy away from him – there's the stench of a decaying carcass from the furze that he hurries to escape. A stench of a dead sheep or a dog killed by the ire from a farmer's shotgun, or meat sweetened with poison. He enters a copse of spindly pine and emerges onto a footpath that leads right to the Camp, up the narrow, winding hill to his unit.

His unit is stationed in three large houses, redbricked buildings showing their age. The first, at the comer on a bad bend in the road, houses the Miltary Police Company's provost sections, the second the Investigation Section and the third the Administration Wing, where the CO has his office. A corrugated tin fence hems the bones of old trees long cut down and burnt.

Swoops in a breath of air as he takes the steps leading into the Duty Room. A whiff of kerosene – the turf fire's done away, the unplastered brick walls holding a yellow emulsion, new windows. Improvements. Good. No more nights on patrol dragging in binloads of turf for the Orderly Sergeant and then being told by him or her that time flies. Tea break over. The turf smoking towards a red heat and the bastard standing with a smug grin on his face, saying "I'd love to let ye stay, boys, but orders are orders. You know yourselves." Favourite words of Maxie March, fucker. And who should be the first one to greet him? The old bollix himself.

"Ah Jaesus, you're back."

He's sitting in an easy chair, hogging the radiator the way he hogged the open fire. A face full with big red nose, round green eyes and receding chin. Old Sweat. They say that years ago he earned a medal for bravery by jumping into the Liffey to save a woman. There are those who say he threw her in and then remembered she was carrying his money.

"I'm back, yeah. Back. Sort of obvious."

"You're needed – there's a lot of lads after taking the oul redundancy."

"Who?"

"Willie Keane, Todd Walsh, Piper Kelly, and who else, let me see, Sean Malone, Eric Samuels."

"Eric's gone?"

"Yes, gone – thanks be to fuck. A waster, that lad. Owes half the camp money."

Maxie sniffles and rises from his chair. Tunic buttons undone, belt flapping from the black stays on its sides. His hair is oiled and slicked. A cowboy book spread on the desk. *Riders on the Range* – dog-eared comers. Maxie's tobacco-stained finger trails down the Duty Roster.

"You're in the Investigation Section."

Harry nods. Okay, he can live with that. Shirt and tie – look like an office worker instead of a soldier policeman. Maxie shakes his head, "I hear you'd a bad trip."

"A bad trip?"

"With Qana and all."

"I wasn't in Qana."

Maxie says, "All those kids – all those civvies killed in a UN camp. The Israelis don't give a fuck, do they? Not a fuck do they give."

The doorbell rings. Harry sneaks a look out. Mrs K. She'll talk the arse off Maxie about stray dogs and cats and God bless the days when the MPs would go out with a shotgun and get rid of them. Blow the arse off them, big time.

A bad trip? Probably Barty and his big gob, telling the lads how Kyle was crying out in his sleep like a banshee. Bastard.

Barty Dobbs is married living in. His marriage lasted two weeks. One summer's morning he arrived in barracks and found that he had no tunic in his locker. Pedalled home like crazy. Front and back door locked – lazy bitch in bed. Pegged a pebble against the bedroom window. Her pretty face pressed to the glass. Colour drained. Breath-misted window. "What, Barty?" she said, raising the sash window.

"My tunic, Emma. Come on I'm late – the fuckers will charge me for absence."

Flight of a tunic. Barty stared at the sergeant's stripes on the sleeves. His lean, hard face like well-weathered stone looked up at the window. Then he kicked in the door and pounded upstairs – screams and a wrestling match and Barty's thick lips and the sergeant's missing teeth and the whole thing a joke on the lips of the unit.

Barty laughing at himself though bloodshot eyes – on the piss for a week. Now, he's off the drink, off the cigs, and going with a girl (Barty's thirty-eight but all his women are girls to him) and thinking of moving in with her. He's slow to trust anyone. Then Harry couldn't blame him for being like that – like wrong turns in life, a person can only take so many wrong tunics.

Harry leaves Maxie to deal with Mrs K, searching out his locker in the large room off the hallway. He had left a new shirt and tie, a Dunnes Stores special still Cellophaned, iron-free, in his locker before leaving for Lebanon. Harry likes to be organised – besides June would have given it away to one of those charity agencies – something like the way she used to put flowers he bought for her on her dad's grave. It made him feel as though she valued nothing that was his. Shirt's crinkled – iron-free, me hole – so he runs an iron over it in the Common Room. Then he heads for the Investigation Section Offices, passing a half-hearted stab at a memorial to their fallen comrades – a weeping willow in the middle of a ploughed garden. Hexagonal paving slabs point to the tree, like a road going nowhere. A red railing plundered from only God knows where – some whorehouse's closing-down sale – leans for support against earth-filled steel cannonball holders.

Climbing the stairs. Familiar creaks at the fall of his feet. Curlicues of pipe-tobacco smoke make a sky of the landing, the odour is of old socks smouldering on a fire.

"Har... " husky voice.

Karl Dunne. The Company Sergeant, suffering from MS – doesn't usually try the stairs. This must be a good day. In the office Harry takes his hand. Loose grip from the other. Feels the wart on the back of his hand. Thinks of that other wart.

"Good to see you," Karl says. Bites on the stem of his pipe. It gives a soft plop when it leaves his lips. He keeps looking at the pipe, eyes avoiding Harry's. Harry recognises the mist in his eyes. It's caused by a strain in the soul.

"And you. Good to see you, Karl."

"Enjoy the trip?"

"Parts of it."

"Only parts?"

"Yeah, parts, Karl. Nothing's perfect, eh?"

Karl riffles some pages, tells him what cases are in progress – mostly Mickey Mouse stuff – break-ins, vandalism, just one serious case involving an alleged sexual assault.

The woman in question is a private. Tough-talking. Takes mickies off a conveyor belt but didn't want this particular fella poking her and got highly insulted when he insisted that she wanted it.

"It's your case."

"Mine?"

"Yeah, the file's there – just wrap it up by taking a few statements – write up the final."

They talk some more, then Harry senses that Karl is winding down. Batteries low. The others in the section – Pete McKee and Sarah O'Toole are on a day's leave. Dougie's gone to Cork to interview some captain and Fleece Moore is in Bosnia, putting in his last tour abroad before quitting the army on pension.

In the small kitchen downstairs Harry makes tea and brings up two mugs. Karl says "thanks" when his is left on his desk. Harry knows that he doesn't really want tea.

"I'd love to... " Karl begins, falls away, egg-blue eyes distant.

"Love to what?"

In the background on a Sony radio Pat Kenny is talking to a woman whose son committed suicide in prison. Breaks for the news.

"Be able to go overseas again."

Harry slugs on his tea. Karl isn't the sort to open up. Everyone knows what he has without his having to tell anyone. How is that? Medical confidentiality, my arse. Secrets leak. There isn't a secret that exists that isn't pushed from someone's mouth – a secret's like a baby – it has to come out sometime. Anyway everyone knows about Karl's medical condition without anyone knowing the originator of the leak – typical, Harry supposes. He's married but not married. His wife, can't remember her name, did a runner a few years ago. Soldiers' marriages go to the wall for reasons as widespread as cloud on a grey day.

"I'm fucked, Harry."

Harry sighs, "How long?"

"Three, four months, that's all."

"Jesus."

"I've lost weight and get the shakes really bad. This is a good day. Eye of the storm... "

Why tell him? They're not exactly friends. Harry had always thought him aloof and somewhat distant. He was about thirty-six with good political pull, so it was said. The reason why he had attained the rank of CS so young, ahead of people senior to him? Others less kind said he had achieved so much because of the favours his mother bestowed on the old CO, Flapper Canty. They call him, "Mammy Stripes" behind his back. Of course, behind his back – stabbing someone in the chest doesn't quite hold the same appeal. Harry had thought it was old-fashioned begrudgery and perhaps most of it was, but knowing Cathy Dunne's form – she'd ride the hump off a camel – he allowed for a small vestige of truth.

"Sorry to hear that." What else could he say? Have a happy death? Hope you die *intact*?

Karl nods, drums his fingers on the table, nudges a file away as if it is a dessert he just hasn't the appetite to touch. He sighs, "I better go home."

Harry thinks it strange how Karl's lips move after he has finished speaking. Silently repeating his words. It's only peculiar to him because he hasn't seen the tremor of Karl's lips for six months. A lad can forget a lot in six months. That notion gives him a small comfort.

Harry watches the other's slow progress, his unsteadiness, the way he has to feel the wall with his hands. Slow shuffle towards the stairs – Harry moves out to the landing, talks about the sex case as they descend – poised to break Karl's fall – a fall he feels sure is imminent. It doesn't happen.

"How are you getting home?"

"Maxie will organise that."

"I could have rung him. You could have."

"You know Maxie – to get him to do something you need to see him face to face, otherwise, it's 'fuck him – let him wait', that's how he is. The most disobliging fucker God ever put on earth." His forefinger shoots up, "And besides – I like to walk – walking is fighting the fucking thing. Walking is a little fight back. I'll walk as long as I am able."

Alone in his office Harry finishes the dregs of his tea. Karl's getting a lift home in the patrol car. He lives on the Green Road, a shoot of road past the golf club, beyond Donnelly's Hollow, through trees that reach out and touch each other, canopying the road, in a bungalow with a facade of Wicklow stone. A house he and June had considered buying a long time ago but couldn't raise enough money.

Lights up a cigarette, opens the file on the sex case, and shakes his head, closes it. He'll get a start in the afternoon – right now, he wouldn't mind a brandy. His throat itches, every bit of him itches for the juice that makes his eyes go light on the world, and his heart forget the pain he feels for others. Detached – it's his own fault for not remaining detached – you've got to keep yourself detached from what others are suffering, because if you don't you can't help them, you can't help yourself. You end up being good for nothing – if not, then good for very fucking little.

Chapter 7

To break the silence between them June asks, "How was work?"

He is sitting with Tony on his lap watching a cartoon on TV. Derek is out the back kicking a ball about.

"Fine. Old Maxie March is still there."

"Pervert."

"He's not a pervert."

June hands him tea. Tony asks for a biscuit. When Daddy gets attention, then son must get attention. Kids are gas.

"He put his hand on my arse at the Christmas dinner dance one year."

"That doesn't make him a pervert."

"It does in my book."

"It shouldn't. Jeezus, you're a hard woman. "

"If he put his hand on your arse how would you – ?"

He goes to reply but June goes on, "See, you'd say he was a pervert."

"No – queer."

All the same."

"No, it's not. Al isn't a pervert. Ivan's not a pervert."

June sighs, "I think you're just being awkward."

"I'm not. I just don't like you getting a dig at people in a roundabout way."

His tea is milky white and too sugary. Not the way he likes it. He puts Tony down and empties the mug into the sink, washes away the tea cloud.

"That's the last time I make you tea."

"I like my tea strong... you must have got used to making it weak for someone else when I was away."

He smiles but June's face freezes for an instant, the span of time it takes her to realise that he is only kidding.

"Dad – he preferred his like that."

He has nothing to say – feels as though he glimpsed something behind a mask that slipped, a brief show of an unrecognisable truth. Tony's wiping his hands free of crumbs and Barney's licking them off the lino.

"Did you get your leave?"

"Leave?"

"For Ivan's book– "

"Yeah – no, I'm off that weekend – I didn't have to apply for leave."

He tells her about the fellas who have left the unit, about Dobbs shooting his mouth off. The weakness that came over Karl so quickly that it looked like he had suffered a power cut. She parts her lips to say something but then joins them.

"What?" he says.

"Nothing."

"You were going to say something."

"You're sure... sure about having this vasectomy?"

"Yeah. Two kids are enough to have in this lousy hole of a world."

"Charming viewpoint – are you ever going to cheer up?"

"No. Yeah, sometime, hopefully – please God or whoever."

The back door opens, "Da, Da... will you play soccer with me?" Derek says.

"Sure."

It's almost dark. Black clouds rove the skies – a smell of rain on the wind. Derek asks why is he always looking at the skies. "Come on and play. Come on, will you?" Looking at the skies.

Night duty — closing the gates over. Crackle from the Motorola set in the Duty Room. The air warm, the aroma of freshly watered flowers replaced by the belching diesel fumes from the French guard patrolling the large military base. They go by every hour, leaving their quarters at the French Wadi Gate, passing UNIFIL Hospital, Italair, Camp Tara, the Customs House, MP Coy, Pollog, French Eng Coy and the Transport yards and Admin offices. Young soldiers with white shoulder scarves signifying their unit. Blue berets sitting on their skulls as though made to measure. While on foot their scabbard-encased bayonets clap against their thighs.

He sits behind his desk; the club is closed, Monday night. No one is drinking or if he is it is in his billet. Sam is in the Quartermaster's stores, sharing the last supplies of kava with his pals. He has never mentioned Tyre or the scene of the shelling. Not since they arrived in HQ a week ago. In the evenings Harry hears the Fijians singing hymns in Fiji House which was built on a rise across from the MP camp. Afterwards the constant pounding of the kava roots into powder is like the lonely beat of a lost soul on Heaven's closed doors. Rubs his eyes. Looks at his nails. The TV is silent. An old western on Lebanese TV not worth troubling his ears. Silence. There is a prisoner of sorts in one of the cells adjoining the Duty Room. A middle-aged Palestinian called Khodi who has spent nineteen years in an Israeli gaol for carrying out an armed raid in Jericho, after crossing the Jordanian border. A small man, broken and bent, who is allowed to come and go as he pleases within the UN confines. Short fuzzy hair going grey, his skin so dark he could pass for being a Ghanaian. Living in No Man's Land — kicked out by the Israelis, not wanted by the Lebanese and Jordanian authorities. He receives monthly visits from the Red Cross and the occasional call in from Robert Sexton, the journalist, who keeps his story alive in his newspaper column — the written word is Khodi's life-support machine. Keeps him from being forgotten. Now and then Harry sees Khodi staring at the setting sun — going down behind the ruins of a Moorish keep, losing itself beyond the horizon — he talks of Palestine and his hatred of anything to do with Israel, a name that makes his lips curl as though the spittle in his mouth has turned sour.

He is in his room with his arak, had said goodnight an hour ago. Flip-flops falling softly on the red concrete floor. Harry could see in his eyes a certain inner suffering, caused by things he has witnessed or perhaps inflicted. A real sorrow.

His own sorrow is what? A pain? Or is it more angst? A variation of Khodi's — except where the little Palestinian has hatred he has bewilderment. Sheer and utter, and fucking incredible bewilderment.

Teth Lifoh, his relief, reports in early. A large Ghanaian sergeant always smiling, always. Talks of Liberia and the fighting there and Harry sees pain in him also, but Lifoh has left the bones of his nightmares behind. It's finished, he says. Over cans of Guinness Lifoh drops his guard and speaks of a firing squad, putting it across in the third person, like it had been someone else involved. Another man's finger on the trigger. Another man's bullet that pierced flesh, minced innards and shattered bones.

Then, drink talk is drink talk and who really gets to know the true score in a man's mind?

Lifoh, smiling through the storms, is someone Harry admires.

In the club, the walls festooned with plaques and unit pennants that travel the years, preserving the names of all the MPs who have passed this way, Harry taps boiling water from a Burco and brews coffee. A ceiling fan clicks annoyingly on its slow turn. The club is empty. Cold. The kerosene heaters turned off. A spread of newspapers on the low tables. Old news. Sam breezes through. Looks about and whispers. "Kava — Harry?"

Nods. Early shift in the morning, but fuck it — Lifoh will get him up. Has the muscle to lift him and his bed and drop them in the Duty Room.

There's four in the dimly lit stores. Sitting on mats around a large wooden bowl containing the milky-looking kava, each clapping hands before accepting the proffered coconut shell and scooping a portion of the liquid and polishing it off. Harry knows them all. Shakes hands. They wear parkas and tracksuits against the night chill, only exposing their feet to the air by wearing flip' flops.

No guitar tonight, no singing — the kava is almost gone and another shipment isn't due in for a week at least. They're drinking some Sam had squirrelled away. Sam has a thick moustache, is tall and gangly with owlish eyes and tattoos of crucifixes on his wrist. The other wrist Harry can't see because it's deep in his parka pocket.

It is another Sam who produces the photographs. The quieter than quiet Sam. The one who doesn't fish for shark and play pool. A tall man with an incipient paunch and a wedding ring dug into his finger, that you just knew he had never taken off and never would. Passing the pictures around — talking in monotone cadences.

Talking about the refugees sitting around the camp, waiting for the Israeli shelling to stop so they could return to their homes. Not knowing that more than 105 of them would never see their homes again.

The shells rained in. He was running after the first had landed, had grabbed a kid and was running. The little fella was crying for his mother. Then, the shells fell, and when he looked down he saw that the boy had no head.

His eyes mist, his voice chokes. He falls silent.

The photographs. A woman burned black, sitting in situ. A kid lying like he was asleep — an orange bodybag unzipped beside him. Awful sights Harry's eyes didn't delay on. Harry knows that the man hoarding the photographs has serious problems. He is passing them around — look, everyone — this is what my mind sees — see, my mind isn't lying — look at the photographs. Look.

"What's that you're drinking, Daddy?"

"Medicine." Baby whiskey.

"What's wrong with you?"

"I've a cough... getting the flu... come on so, are you ready? Pass the ball."

Later, when the kids are in bed and the kitchen is cleaned, June says Derek is looking for some of Daddy's medicine. He has a cough. A forced one.

"You're tippling away, aren't you, on the sly?"

"It was only a drop. Half a – "

"Playing with Derek – some example to give him. Isn't it?"

"I'm full of bad examples – going away to Lebanon was one – but you wanted new windows, didn't you?"

"Don't lay that at my door – you wanted to go."

"I had to go to shut you up."

"How can you sit there and lie?"

Silence. Lie? He had lied. Of course he wanted to go to Lebanon. It was his idea. And he had suggested getting in the windows to soften June's protestations, not that any were forthcoming. She, as he did, suspected that they needed the separation. A lot of bickering going on over small things, nonsensical things, things that only two people who have known each other for a long time could fight over. Rows such as they were having bled love from the body of a marriage. But now, now when he thinks about it, things were better between them before he left.

There wasn't this current strain between them, this gulf. So distant, and yet they are both trying, trying so hard to make things normal between them. A vasectomy? Surely they had a future together when that was being done? Hadn't they?

No guarantees. He should know that – no guarantees in life. Except one – but you think of that if you want to walk on the dark side of life and end up buried before you are dead.

There's no doubt she has changed. In his absence she has become more independent – stronger – resentful of him as he tries to slot back into the run of things. It's as though she believes he is trying to usurp her. If he were dead she could do without him quite nicely, thank you very much.

The kids are in bed; their stories told and prayers said. The kitchen has lost its heartbeat or so it seems in the after-silence left by the boys.

"Why do you say things to annoy me, Harry?"

"I don't know."

"A new hobby?"

"Can we drop it? I don't want a row."

"Neither do I – tell me something though – where do you see us in five years, even three, a year even?"

He shrugs.

"You don't know – I don't know... no one knows," June says.

"What exactly are you saying?"

"We mightn't be together."

He lets her words sink in. They're still sinking moments later. What she's really saying is that she isn't going to put up with his moods forever. But he's also quick to sense that she's saying something else – but her path is too oblique for him to read, yet.

"Am I living under a threat?"

"I won't stay married to a drunk."

"I'm not a drunk."

"No... perhaps not yet, but you're getting there. Jeezus – I remember the time you wouldn't touch the stuff and that isn't so long ago."

Does he have to engrave the fucking thing on his forehead? Does he have to spell out Kafra for her over and fucking over? He can't sleep and therefore he drinks. He thinks of things – thoughts he can't turn away from – sights and faces – a film he can't turn off. Drink blurs the images, dulls a cat's miaowing, but he can never drink enough to totally blur the images. No matter how he tries.

"Do you know what I have?" he says.

"What?"

"A haunting – I'm being haunted – by people's faces and a cat's cry, a cat I seldom see, but always hear."

A pinch of weariness and some intolerance steal across her features. June's voice is tired but blunt. "Get help. I can't help you. Please, Harry, go get help." Help. The army only keeps its madmen on when they remain silent. Is he mad, heading there? If and when he shakes off the nightmare thing he'll be a dipso – swings and fucking roundabouts. Swings and fucking roundabouts.

Chapter 8

As half-expected, Karl doesn't show this morning. Rings after nine to say he won't be in. The others in the office have statements to record from people and after tea depart for the different units in camp. Pete and Sarah have a thing going. It's easy to see, the way they look at each other – the way he and June used to look at each other – with a certain hunger.

Harry waters the cacti plants in the main office, and files some reports in a cabinet with handles missing on its top and bottom drawers. Sex case. Karl had dosed him with a nuisance investigation, one given to him cold, that would probably result in a court-martial or a civil trial. Why wait until he came home – why pass the ball to him? A headache. Drinks his tea. Camomile, milkless, must bring in some honey to sweeten it a little, as recommended by the package's instructions. A nice fucking soldier indeed with his taste for honey and herbal tea.

He sits at his desk and opens the file to read the case notes. Karl has a neat handwriting style, easy on the eyes, concise.

> "Pte Enright reported to her Company Commander, Comdt Peadar Heffernan, at 09:10hrs on 10 Oct 96. She alleged that on the night of 09 Oct 96 she had been sexually assaulted by Sgt Dougie Smart of A Coy, 4 Reg Tac Coy. Pte Lucy Enright reported to this office on 12 Oct 96 and a statement was recorded from her, to the effect... "

Read the statement later – carry on with the notes. Gardaí informed? Yeah, okay. Normal procedure. Smart is currently serving in Lebanon. Staying a year out there and had been home on leave during the incident. No statement taken from him. Witnesses? One. Possibly. Not to the actual assault, but someone who can place Smart in Enright's billet with Enright. Again, no statement was recorded.

This guy Williams is currently overseas, too. Doctor's report – where is it? Shit. None. Did Enright go to hospital?

Harry sighs – this happened six weeks ago – ample time to have all the small points taken care of – for fuck's sake. It's the small points that get bastards like Smart, if he is the culprit (open mind, keep it) off the hook.

He reads Enright's statement. Once, twice, yeah, on two occasions she'd been with the sergeant before. With? Did she mean she'd slept with him? A couple of times? Just once? At all?

He came into her billet that night. It was about eight or nine, maybe in between. She was on heavy – having her period – why didn't she say it or perhaps she had but Karl or whatever female MP was with him during the interview had preferred to write on. Yeah, Sarah – it would be her. She likes to dress up the truth a little. Make shit palatable to the eye.

Lucy had been out all day on the rifle ranges and was feeling tired and dirty. In other words she wasn't in the mood for taking shit from anyone. Smart had been drinking. Not too much. He wasn't unsteady on his feet or anything. She told him to get out. When he showed no signs of moving she told him, "to get the fuck out". He stayed and closed the door behind him. Said he had something for her. An 18 carat gold puzzle-ring – a number of thin rings banded together – something to do with love and fidelity and the rings not staying intact if the wearer was untrue. A Middle East variation of the Claddagh ring. She said she didn't want it. He got thick, extremely thick and went for her. Throwing the ring at her. Calling her names.

Names — what fucking names? Bozo, Mary, what? — why didn't they ask what name he called her? Names? How the fuck did Karl get promoted? Yeah, remember — Mammy Stripes.

Smart took out his penis. He shouted at her to suck him. She told him to get out. This gets better and better. She told him to get out? Screamed more likely. He wouldn't budge. Then he grabbed her by the throat and walked with her to the bed. She couldn't speak his grip was so tight. She was on her toes. It hurt... he hurt her a lot. He threw her on to the bed, ripped off her top, fondled her breasts, touched her between the legs and freaked when he found out that she was on. Started throwing things about. Then Williams knocked on the door. She didn't see Williams but she recognised his voice. He said he couldn't wait any longer, that he had to bring the car back to his old man. Smart called her a stupid cunt and left.

A stupid cunt. Karl's pen must have got brave.

What next? See Williams... see Smart. But they're in Lebanon. So shouldn't the file be forwarded to the Battalion MPs? Makes sense. The Gardaí are interested in the case. Bound to be more than interested given the spate of women gone missing in the Leinster area. So, Enright must have also made a formal complaint to the guards. Hasn't dropped her complaint — sometimes they do, when they get scared of the hassle — so it looks like she's determined to have justice done. Fair do's to her.

Photographs taken by the MPs on the night. A couple of throat shots — visible red marks. Green eyes full of tears. Pretty oval face. Brown hair. Long — obviously rolled in a bun when on military employment. He had grabbed her by the hair, too. She looked like someone who had gotten the scare of her life.

Yeah — need to see her, too. Before he saw Smart and Williams. Get in touch with the guards and speak with Pat Roberts, the investigating officer.

The phone rings just as he makes to pick it up. The

Command Sports Officer reminding him about the trial match in the afternoon. Harry says he'll be there. It's ages since he last kicked a ball. He must get back in training with Kildare. Though the last thing he and June need is his absence on Sundays – home games are bad enough but away games eat the arse out of Sunday time. "Family time," June says. Roberts isn't in. Won't be until tomorrow. Best time to catch her is about nine. Harry looks at the phone, smacks his lips. There's some hooch that was recovered after a break into a mess some months ago. Vodka, whiskey and Malibu. He stares at the property cabinet. No... no fucking way. No fucking way.

Enright's army vest is in there, too. In a brown-paper bag – her blood on it – where Smart had cleaned his hands after touching her. It should be with Garda Forensic. Blood. His stomach feels sick. So fucking sick. Looks through the window. He doesn't see the leaves falling from the trees or the blues of the Wicklow hills – what he sees is *a mosque and its dome and the shocked faces of Nepalese soldiers as they wave them down a rutted road into the village. Sam easing the jeep to a stop when an ambulance inches into view. It rolls past. In no hurry* – Not now! Don't dwell on it.

Do something – speak to... He rings June. Hurrying his forefinger along the digits. Dial tone.

"Hello?" she says.

"It's me."

"What's wrong?"

"Nothing – nothing – I'm playing soccer after lunch, so... "

"And?"

"My gear?"

"I don't know, Harry. I haven't seen it. Did you check your locker?"

"No."

"Some investigator you are."

"You always have the kind word."

"Harry — get a life and don't be so serious."

"I don't know what I fucking rang you for."

"Neither do I."

June hangs up. Fuck it. If he's not saying the wrong thing, he's picking up something wrong. What the fuck is wrong with me? Snap out of it. Focus on something else. Sighs. Focus on all he likes for as long as he likes — for Kafra breezes across his mind like the wind walks the Curragh Plains — it doesn't let you know when it's coming or indeed, going. Landing on a spot, a time, a place in Lebanon, not necessarily in the proper time date sequence — images pre- and post-Kafra, and of the village itself.

Like now.

Passing King Hiram's tomb on the road from Qana, Harry pulls over. Sam had been tapping his shoulder for him to stop the jeep. His cheeks bulging with the breath he trapped in order to cork his vomit. Harry cuts the engine. The immediate silence seems to lean in on the soft top. Sam gets out and spews. It's dark. The retching plays on Harry's nerves. Lebanese stars bum brightly and the moon is full.

It's an hour after Kafra, half an hour since they had been to Camp Trishul, the Nepalese Battalion's HQ, in the Regimental Aid Post, taking file photos of the dead soldier, seeing what slivers of metal can do to a human body.

They had to take the long route home, avoiding the coastal road to Tyre because the Israelis were shelling the area. Harry is sweating and shaking. Jumpy. Perspiring heavily — his vomit leaking through his pores?

The wooded nowhere they're at is a bleak shadowy place; cypresses shivering in the cold breeze and insects cheeping in the undergrowth. Down the road Hiram's tomb resembles a black hunk of stone, blacker than the night. The tomb of the king who had supplied Solomon with the materials for building the Temple.

"You okay, Sam?"

"Yes, okay... fine."

"Fine?"

Nods, "You?"

"Okay... looking forward to a beer."

Sam opens the back door and removes his flak jacket. A helmet hits the ground. The noise from its impact appears to momentarily startle the night into silence. Picking it up he puts it on the back seat, then drinks water from a bottle and hurls the empty into the darkness — spits out a rinse.

"Let's go," he says.

"Yeah, okay."

They crawl into Hassan Burro barracks an hour later and wait for the Lebanese soldier to raise the boom. There's a group of soldiers huddling around a glowing brazier. All of them smoking cigarettes. Laughing. Harry parks the jeep in a large veranda, the walls of which hold murals, aged and weather-tarnished, that were villa scenes in the Ben Hur movie.

Home. He had never thought for one moment that he would call this rat-infested kip 'home.' Perhaps he meant "refuge'?

The gear is in the bottom drawer of his locker. Clean socks, multi-Studded football boots with the muck from his last game hard as old Christmas cake on the soles.

Harry changes into a tracksuit he had brought home from Lebanon. Blue with the UN emblem done large and in navy on the back and small above the breast — olive branches holding the world in the join of their stems.

He is the first to arrive at the pavilion and sits on the steps outside the long corrugated hut to lace up his boots. Other players start arriving. Some he knows; others he doesn't. One boots a white Mitre ball onto the pitch and Harry goes to warm up.

The grass feels soft, cushiony. This is when he enjoys

playing football best, when it isn't late into the season and you're playing with old knocks carried over from previous matches and your toes are sore, and the weather's lousy. Today is a cold day, cold but not biting cold and no wind to make a fool of your passes. He almost made the grade as a full-back in the League of Ireland, but he hadn't the burst of speed you need to make it at that level – reading the game and marking tight saved him from being embarrassed by flying wingers – though soccer's like life; sometimes your failings are cruelly found out, and his were, enough times for coaches to dismantle his teenage dreams of earning his living from the game – so now he plays in a league that doesn't require a demanding fitness level, with guys like himself, and younger players still young enough to cradle a dream, and older guys who play on for too long and invest in gammy knees and weak ankle joints. But the pleasure of playing soccer is abating – each year the team changes faces and he feels less comfortable when he climbs into the bus. There's a new manager this season, Billy Bryan, a proper dope – the sort who'll drop a good player just to let him know who's the boss. Harry's not going to bother playing this year. Maybe next season. Maybe.

He reflects later, back in his office, on what had made him lash out at his opponent. A short, stocky guy who'd been niggling at him all through the first half and for most of the second. A player with limited ability – a kicker, not so dirty a player that he would get himself sent off, too cute for that – he just got in little digs, made them appear accidental – aggravating things more so than hurtful. And Harry had fallen for it, retaliating and getting sent off for his trouble. The first time it had ever happened to him. He was a cool player, never dirty, hard but fair. Never got involved in fisticuffs, would never let another player have the satisfaction of knowing he had got to him.

Until today. These days a lot of things were getting the better of him.

He packs his gear into a plastic shopping bag and

makes for home. Its begins to drizzle as he passes the bus stop outside the Orchard Park estate. The shelter's Perspex sheets have been vandalised, and lie in pieces on the road, path and grass. He would love to catch the fuckers red-handed. For what? He asks himself. So he can drive a fist into one of them – just to make him feel good in himself for a few seconds – is that why?

Divert his anger and frustration and tilt at the wrong windmills.

Jesus – Kafra's running deep – he's a fucking soldier – it's a war scene. For fuck's sake, cop yourself on. Come on. Quite the booze, get stuck into the job, forget Kafra. Forget. It's like telling himself he should piss through his ear.

He doesn't want to go home. Doesn't want to walk into another row, be the cause of one. Right now, as the roof of his house shows above a knoll, he bets June is wishing he isn't coming home for the exact same reasons, or close to them. What he thinks is confirmed by the absence of their car.

Chapter 9

He picks yellow leaves from Barney's aluminium water bowl and rubs the dog's ear. The oil-burner bellows a little as he turns the key in the back door. Eases off his shoes before entering the kitchen. The house is warm and a briquette fire is set and waiting for a match. Crisp crumbs on the fireside rug and dried tea-drops next to the armchair and some crayons lying on a *Tom and Jerry* colouring book – so unlike June, who likes a clean and orderly house.

He showers and changes into fresh clothes. Just one small drink and he'll get the dinner on. Just one and he'll help Derek with his homework without getting annoyed.

Just one and he'll tell Tony a bedtime story without making a compliment of it.

The temper rises in him. Is this why she's cleared off? Because she'd taken the booze he brought back from Lebanon and had either chucked it out or given it away and didn't want a scene when he came home and found out? Not a piss drop of booze in the house – 12-year-old Chivas Regal – shit – how could she?

"Easy," she says, when the boys are in bed.

She had said nothing when he produced a bottle of wine, Ed's Red, during dinner. Looked at him the way bad guys look at good guys on TV – with sheer contempt.

"I don't want you drinking in front of me or the lads. You know why. You're not stupid – as it is rows start too easily between us."

"It's nice to have a drink at the end of the day."

"But it's not just the end of the day with you, is it?"

"I'm not gone wild on it. The way you went on anyone would — "

"You soon will be if you don't check yourself."

She doesn't touch the wine. He tells her it's smooth and fruity. She says he's not smooth but is definitely fruity. Harry feels as though a certain darkness has entered his soul, a darkness weighted so much that he finds himself wondering about June, about how long more they will be together.

He doesn't want to lose her.

"I got the wine for you, for us. If you don't want any drink in the house — that's fine, really. Fine by me."

June spreads her hands on the table. She's wearing a tight blue T-shirt that shows off her breasts. Her lips are full and he suddenly wants to touch them, run the tip of his small finger along her cheek. Wants to take her here, in the kitchen, on the sofa, she sitting on his lap. Naked, the TV on, the lights dimmed, the fire throwing shadows on her lithe frame. He wants to cup her breasts in his hands and take them to his lips, feel her wetness with his hand, the thrust of his cock into her. Wants her. "Don't," she says, when he moves to her.

Don't? Before he has even touched her. It's as though she has read his mind and found the contents off-putting.

"When I can't, you're not happy — when I want to, you turn me down."

"Not here — look at the state of the place. I need a bath."

"I like you dirty."

"No."

He feels his erection dying. Freshens his glass with wine, tinkles her unused glass with his full. "Cheers."

Tony gets his story. Derek extracts a promise from him to play soccer tomorrow. He tells June he's still going ahead with the op. He says it quietly, in bed. Her back is to him, the lights on. The house is quiet. June's breathing soft and light, not betraying the troubles in her mind. He lies on his back. Wants to reach out and touch her shoulder but thinks twice about it, as he would about putting his hand on anything icy.

"June?"

"What?

"Nothing."

He braves his hand.

"Don't knock the sleep off me."

Comes out cruder than he intends, "I'd like to knock the arse off you."

"Jesus... "

She climbs from bed, hitting the lamp switch, "Don't start a fucking row, right. I don't want to have sex. Okay?"

"I'm not a fucking monk – monks would get a ride quicker."

"That's all it would be to you, wouldn't it, a ride?"

He sighs. Why didn't he keep his hand off her shoulder when he knew he should have? There's nothing he can do or say to retrieve the situation. He loves her. But he can't bring himself to breathe the words. He suspects that she doesn't love him. Suspected it before he left for Lebanon and suspects it now.

In Lebanon it showed in the trickle of short letters she wrote – she was too tired to write, she said – don't forget I've two kids and a dog to look after while you're sunning your arse out there, looking at all those Israeli beauts. He felt like writing back and telling her he was into picking up body parts, too. But she wouldn't object to his doing that, would she?

That's acceptable because he wouldn't be enjoying himself. "I'm out of here," he says, taking his pillow.

"Run, go on."

"Fuck off, June, will you?"

"Don't you dare speak to me like that."

"Listen – just leave me alone."

He goes downstairs, enters the kitchen and brews tea.

Strangely, he feels light and dark in himself, as though some humour has spilled into his basin of gloom.

Absolut Vodka – come on Devil, where are you? My soul for a bottle of Finlandia or Absolut Vodka – come on! "I'm going to count to three – if it's not in front of my eyes by that time the sale is off – I'll keep my soul. And you can go fuck yourself." He makes do with tea. The devil must still be in Kafra. Anger and frustration push at the seams of his sanity. He sits by the fire and stares into the dying embers. Wishing he was dead, wishing his life would pass as quickly as a fart in the wind.

Someone has got away with murder. For it is murder, as far as he's concerned, to aim a tank's cannon and fire into a village where civilians have congregated to buy early morning pitta bread. Musa, the old man, the village Mucktar, who holds the black bag, brings him and Sam down a lane way into his tiny cafe. His wife clucks and cries, cries and clucks, while they sip at her strong coffee and shake their heads. Harry runs his finger along the Arab graffiti polished into the table. Swallowing bile. The old man's English is poor but he doesn't have to speak to relay his thoughts – suffering is an international language. The girl's mother comes in – white scarf awry – loud in her lamentations, beating the air with her clenched fists. The black bag at Musa's sandalled feet – holding his vacant gaze – as though he didn't know how it got there.

Someone else, a middle-aged man, takes it, mutters and leaves. Musa sighs relief.

Harry nods at Sam. It's time to leave. They pass through the square on their way to the jeep. Old women are throwing buckets of sudsy water on the blood, washing it away, into the cracks in the concrete. Bits of tank shells swept away too, the larger fragments already gathered by Harry and Sam. In a few minutes the place will look, except for the blood-speckled whitewashed walls, as though nothing evil had ever happened. Sam carries the evidence bag that contains the soldier's wallet, the broken magazine with its 7.62mm rounds, his dog tags, while Harry carries the man's bloodstained flak jacket, his helmet and his FN Rifle. In the distance there's the thud of tank fire — the bang of a warplane breaking the sound barrier makes Harry's heart go fast with fright. He tries hard not to show that the sonic boom has given him a start. Says nothing. They put the bags in the back. Sam's hands can't stop trembling on the steering wheel. He says he can't drive and that he might take them down a wadi. Deep down into a wadi. He slips from the driver's seat and while Harry finds his fingers are just as shaky as Sam's he drives, because there's more work to be done, and he just wants to put space between himself and Kafra. Although he is sure that no distance will ever be far enough.

Why is he here? In Lebanon? Keeping the peace? Fuck that, picking up the pieces, standing by and watching women and children and old men being slaughtered, typing up a fancy reportso it can join all the others that rest in some top nob's fucking filing cabinet. Problem is the Yids are getting their arses kicked by the Hizbollah and they're lashing back with their planes and artillery. They'll stop shelling if the Hizbollah halt their guerrilla attacks on their civilian towns and refrain from killing their soldiers — a kind of high-grade kiddies' stand-off in a playground. And the UN, UNIFIL, United Nations Interim Force in Lebanon, dishes out food, medicines and some money to villagers, shows a tangible presence on the ground, bears witness to the human destruction and tells the world. Standing by, Harry thinks, just standing by. Watching the skies of Lebanon burning crimson.

He falls into an uneasy sleep in the armchair. Wakes with a familiar ache in his neck. Cold. Shivers dance along his spine. It's five by the large wall-clock's stubby blue fingers. Another day at the office, another day at the fucking coalface his marriage has become. All his fault? Mostly his fault?

He stirs himself and makes tea. Barney is pawing at the door to get in. He doesn't do that unless he's really feeling the cold.

"Good lad... sit down, sit... go on."

Dog's an eejit, so grateful to be indoors that he circles the kitchen, his nails loud on the lino.

"Barney – sit!"

He issues a sorrowful look and troops to a comer behind the table. Starts licking his paws. Sulking.

Harry takes a sleeping bag from the hotpress and breaks for the sitting-room – he might get two hours' rest if not sleep before it's time for the house to waken.

He sits and thinks. Can't rest. Well, rest the body, okay, but his mind is cruising in fifth gear, not dropping gears to round the bends.

A spill of Lebanon photographs by his side – the albums he bought are empty and waiting for their sleeves to be filled – of Tyre, the souk with its fish stalls, a cow's carcass hanging from a hook with a cloud of flies in attendance, the sluice channel choked with detritus, the smoky air, a man waving at him to stop taking pictures. Sam on his knees showing off the tuna he bought as a present for the Fijian Officers' Club in Naqoura, The MP Detachment and behind it the long rows of tanks abandoned by the Palestinians many years ago, rusting away, a tank graveyard.

The tour of the Phoenician ruins and the Byzantine cemetery known as the City of the Dead with guys from MP Coy whose names he has already forgotten – Baalbeck, outside Beirut, in the mountains and its spread of Roman ruins. A picture of himself alongside one of the Columns of Jupiter – an insignificant figure beside the girth and height of stone, the snow-covered Lebanon mountain range in the background. Photographs – in Israel, too – at Metulla of the Good Fence, a tourist spot where a Lebanese woman passed her sick child through a hole in the security fence and returned a week later to take him back fit and well. T-shirts carrying the slogan, "Better a close neighbour than a distant brother.'' In Netanya where Woody the Whore worked her face into a snap. A reach over her middle years, a tout for Israeli police and also for the MPs, who is considerate enough towards her own sex to give only blowjobs to men whom she saw wearing wedding rings.

A Nepalese corporal called what — Dexy? Yeah, nickname. Had terrible English — put the phone down if things got complicated for him. Either that or he would keep repeating over and over, "Hello, MP Detachment Netanya," till the caller got pissed off and hung up — something he preferred to happen — knew enough to know it was impolite to hang up on someone, and felt better if it was the caller who did the insulting. A fellow you could bollock for an hour but who would still be smiling at you when you finished, who on foot patrol would walk a step behind you. Never by your side, as though he was deferring to his better or something. Photographs of June and the boys, taken during an outing to the zoo a week before he left home, always on his bedside locker, are the first faces he sees in the morning and the last at night — if you don't include those he sees in his nightmares.

June puts her head around the door, glares at him.

"Miss your friends, do you?"

He gathers up the photos and puts them in their jackets. Follows June into the kitchen.

"Look — "

"No, you look, Harry — I've had enough of your shit, your moods, your — "

Their voices are low, like those in church. Thinking of the kids, wanting to keep the tension at a low flow.

"I'm sorry, June — it's a bad patch. We'll get over it."

"Will we?"

"I said I was — "

"You're always sorry over something."

"Have you nothing to be sorry over?"

She gives him a searching look. Says nothing.

"You seldom wrote to me — never rang, unless you're counting the time you wanted extra money sent home."

He can almost see the armour coming over her face. That's it. She has no more to say and what he has to say won't get through. It takes a lot for June to ignore him, to quit on talking things out — it proves just how pissed off with him she really is and there isn't love there for him — her eyes say more than she likes to reveal, let truths slip quicker than her tongue. How many times does he have to see it to believe?

Chapter 10

June suggests that she come with him to the private clinic in Clane.

"I will go in — I won't chicken out — you don't have to make sure of it." Smiles.

He hasn't had a drink in three days and has cut back on his cigarette intake, too. Then he was never a heavy smoker nor indeed a heavy drinker. But, yeah, June's right, he is heading that way. His incipient beer gut, his poor fitness levels are things he has come to dislike about himself. He caught June looking at him from the corner of her eye, as though she were reading from a menu that held nothing to her liking.

"You know you don't have to," she says.

They stop at red lights on a road being resurfaced. There's a pungent smell of hot tar and the noise of a steamroller following a truck. A man with warts on his cheek, the ridge of his jaw prominent from the toil, shovels tar grits from the truck-bed on to the road. Stitchings frayed and waving on his jacket's elbow patches.

Lights switch to green.

"I know," he says, taking off.

"I mean — "

"I know what you mean — you don't want me throwing this in your face -I won't. Besides, aren't we working on your doctor's advice?"

"Yes. Still."

"Still, nothing."

He drives beyond Clane hospital, knows he has missed the bungalow and turns around. He slows to a crawl as he keeps a watch on the houses he passes, earning toots of impatience from the drivers behind, and cops the small signpost signifying the clinic. Set amongst ash trees like an apology in a post-dinner speech. An east wind blows – savagely cold. The receptionist is called Clare. She doesn't tell you this. It says so on her name badge. She looks at him and smiles. Tells them to take a seat, pointing to orange polypropylene chairs by a floor-to-ceiling window. There are magazines spread across a Mexican pine coffee table and a day-old newspaper with a snot on it that turns his stomach. He turns the newspaper over so June doesn't see it – she'd hack up her guts.

He moves along the carpeted corridor and enters the surgery. The doctor is tall and lean, wears a dickie bow, no name-tag (does he think everyone knows him?). Long, intelligent face with sharp if not shrewd green eyes.

"I'm Doctor Callan."

Shake of hands, "Harry, Harry Kyle."

They go through the preliminary questions. The doctor's long legs crossed. Scratching at a questionnaire with a gold pen.

Age. Address – etc. Signing a waiver then in case he makes a cock'up, or a balls of it.

When Callan says that he smiles the way he must have smiled to thousands of others.

"I've done seventeen thousand of these – there's never been a problem, so relax."

Is he counting balls individually or in pairs?

He outlines the procedure in a clinical voice and after he finishes he says, "Okay, drop your trousers and climb up on the bed."

Perhaps he should have gone for the general anaesthetic? On the trolley bed he takes in the ceiling – there are fine cracks near the fluorescent tube – grows aware of the doctor and his syringe. Doesn't look — keep the image vague. Bad clouds in the offing. Closes his eyes a pinch. No more. Sighs relief. Waits for the numbness to spread. It's like having a tooth filled. Take a breath — under the knife, sort of. Laser treatment — no stitches. Right ball done. Jesus. Easy-peasy. A mild discomfort, that's all. He can handle mild discomfort.

Left ball! The fucking agony. The fucking agony — Jesus, thank God he snipped the other ball first or he was out of here. Fuck. The pain. What must castration be like? "Put this pad down your underpants — there'll be some slight bleeding, and your testicles will be swollen and discoloured for a few days. Nothing to worry about. If you're worried give me a ring, but you'll be fine. Now," he holds up two packages, "these contain test tubes... send the first to me in six weeks and the other six weeks after that... I'll write back and let you know the results. Meantime, continue to use whatever contraceptive method you and your wife — "

"Yeah, okay."

Abstinence.

June smiles when she sees him. Hand going to her mouth. She says she'll drive. He says he'll be okay, that driving will keep his mind occupied. In fact, he would love nothing better than to drive all day and all night.

"I hope this is worth it," he says.

"Worth it. How do you mean?"

"I mean there's very little point in having a vasectomy when you're not having sex to begin with — isn't that so?"

"Just drive, Harry."

He does that. Drives. The only words spoken in the car are radio voices. It is so for the half-hour journey it takes to reach home. It is so when Harry sits alone in the car waiting for the baby-sitter to appear beside him in June's place. She, Emma, says more to him in ten minutes that June would in a week. If he were a flower and water were June, he would be withered a long time.

Derek says Dad is walking funny. Harry says soccer is

out today, for him. June says there's fresh coffee in the pot. Asks if he paid the baby-sitter.

"Yeah, of course."

He notices that she has started to peel the wallpaper in the hall. It's only up a year.

Expensive, too, not a cheap sort of paper that looks grubby after a few months, like underwear worn for too long.

"I don't like it," she explains, as if that was explanation enough.

"We don't need this extra expense with Christmas coming up."

I'll be paying for it – you won't have to do a thing – so don't worry your little head about it. Okay?"

He stays his tongue. Last time he had done the peeling of the old wallpaper with a steamer and had taken away patches of plaster from the wall. June did her nut.

It took an age to get in a plasterer. Rarer than brain surgeons are plasterers, Derek Senior said. That would have been about a month before he died.

"I was – "

"No question of money though, is there? When it comes to you hightailing it to the west to see your brother."

She seldom calls Al by name. He's mostly his brother, rolling off her tongue like an accusation of sorts. He points out that she was asked to come with him.

A violent shake of her head. "I'll pass."

"The offer wasn't being repeated."

"Good."

Harry goes to say something but stays his tongue. Where is the sense in this verbal jousting? It only upsets each other and the kids. The dreadful thing is that they know it's bad for the kids to live in such an atmosphere. A war zone in their home and everyone suffering from the razor-sharp digs – he and June launching direct attacks at each other and the boys enduring the fallout; the stiff silences, the tense atmospheres, the intolerances, the petty spites, the lies. Kids know nothing about telling or living real lies. Adults do. The greatest secret of all to lose to your kids is the fact that Mummy and Daddy no longer love each other. On one hand the example they're being set shows them not to quit a relationship too easily, and yet is that such a good example? Isn't it better to untie the knot when people can't get along? After a period of them not getting on? Teach them that no one has to live with the vulgarities of a relationship breaking down? No one has to listen to his family being torn asunder by his wife and vice versa. But there is love in his marriage. He loves June. Loves her. And he might try to fool himself into thinking he doesn't, but it's a truth, a fact.

He does. You can't change how you feel for someone — he always wants to reach out to her through the clouds that are their arguments. But.

"I'm going to lie down," he says.

Silence from June until Derek tells her his daddy is speaking.

"A lie-down," June says.

"Yeah — don't feel too well."

Derek fusses. Small hand landing on Harry's forehead, look of concern in his round features. Harry had seen the hand coming, and buried the inclination to dodge it. "He's very hot, Mam. He needs some 7-Up."

Tony's taking an interest in the proceedings, drawing on his pacifier, moves closer and puts his hand on Harry's knee. The touch. He looks at Tony, at Derek, at June.

What had he done? Jesus, Mary and Joseph — pushed his kid's hand away. Why? He puts Tony on his lap and makes a fuss of him.

June says, "I saw that."

Derek goes back to playing with his action figures.

"Instinctive... I didn't know, I didn't think."

"The look of hurt on his face — how could you?"

Tony jumps a little on his lap, wants a horsy. The action

hurts his balls. How does he explain away the scare he got when Tony touched him? He had recoiled because the hand wasn't Tony's in his eyes; it belonged to someone else, someone whose face he didn't know when alive.

Easing Tony to the floor he moves to the sink where June is peeling potatoes.

"I... "

She looks at him hard, her lips like pink blades, eyes like cut stone, her voice low, barely above a whisper, "You can say and do what you like to me... but if I ever see you hurting one of the kids again – I'm warning you, Harry. Just fucking warning you. Don't. Right?"

What he intends saying is driven from his soul by her quiet ferocity. How many times does he actually have to tell her about the goings-on in his mind? When he first told her in the sitting-room she was unable to leave him behind quickly enough. All she said was that he should go and get help. He had gone for help – June – but she didn't want to know.

He says nothing, grabs his jacket from under the stairs, feels a twinge in his balls and plants his jacket back on the hook. Heads for bed instead of the pub.

Harry gets in under the covers and sleeps until the early hours of the morning. His eyes blink open and he turns on his back. Bed squeaks a couple of times. June's back is to him, clinging to the outer edge of the bed as though she had fallen asleep with a serious intent not to give him any of her heat. She never draws the blind against the night. He sees the amber streetlight across the road, on the Curragh side, a throw of stars in the skies, a full moon shadowed by drifting clouds. Hears the shifting of sheep alongside the road verge, a sure sign of bad weather. His eyes meet the first creaks of light in the skies and soon afterwards he gets up and showers.

Blue balls. But the soreness is leaving them. What did June see in him? A young man with hair starting to crow'speak, the sporting look going off his figure, a cigarette in one hand and a beer in the other. Someone whose nerves were almost shot, who couldn't bear the touch of his son's hand? Why doesn't she look deeper? Listen to the depth of his words and see the war going on inside him. She might see — she would see — if she could only look into his eyes without her own falling away.

Karl doesn't make the stairs this morning. He is drinking tea in the kitchen, still managing to look frail under a thick woollen sweater. The weight has dropped off him, and his movements have becomes a series of jerks, almost robotic.

The kitchen is tiny, cramped. Harry gets the smell of the other's Lagerfeld aftershave and sees a tiny speck of toothpaste at the comer of his lips.

"There was a dead mouse in one of the cups this morning," Karl says.

"Yeah, place is fucking riddled with them... whose cup is it?" Harry follows Karl's small finger to the initials done in black marker under the handle. "She'll freak."

"I threw it in the bin — the mouse — and boiled out her cup." "Don't tell her — Jesus — you know what she's like with mice and spiders."

"Pete... she's doing a line with him, you know?"

"Yeah, yeah, I figured that out."

"Yeah, well, figure out what happened to his face when you see him — he's upstairs — herself is on a day's USL — the CO is hopping off me over people ringing in sick."

"We're — "

"Don't give me what-we're-entitled-to shit — he's bitching like fuck — I got it in the ear this morning from him. He's coming up later on, after the GOC's conference."

"So what are you saying — is he getting a dig at you for being out sick so much?"

"Doubt it, but you, you be bright and not smart with

him – you know his form – if he feels threatened he holds parades and inspections."

Pete sits at his desk. He has scrape marks on his cheeks and above his eyebrow.

"Jesus, Pete – what were you at – trying to ride the cat?" "Fuck off. Jesus – "

"Jesus what? Half your face is tom off – we're worried about you, Pete."

"Worried, me hole. Nosy, more like it."

Silence. Harry moves to the radiator and turns on the radio. Looks through the window and spots the CO parking his car in his space under the elm tree. Barty Dobbs is bagging loose leaves while Maxie March is heaving another bag into a smoking barrel.

"His conference must have been cancelled."

"Who's... the CO is back?"

"Yeah... coming this way, too. You better take that face into the jacks."

"Fuck," Pete says.

The CO is a well-built man with cauliflower ears that are a legacy from his rugby-playing days. This posting is a stepping-stone for him to a higher rank. He is the APM, Assistant Provost Marshal, responsible firstly to the GOC and secondly to the PM in Dublin for all policing matters in the Command. Harry lowers the volume on the radio but he can't distinguish what's being discussed between Karl and the CO. Busies himself at a computer when he hears the fall of feet on the stairs.

"Good morning, Harry – by yourself – Pete is out?"

"Yes, sir."

The Colonel looks around. There are tiny red cracks in his cheeks. He has large round green eyes that protrude a little, not quite a bug-eyed look but not far off, either.

They shoot some talk about the weather, about the changes in the political climate in Lebanon, about an upcoming rugby international match, and then, quietly, as though he has worked towards the point, asks how things are progressing with the sexual assault case.

"It's in limbo, sir."

"Limbo?" As if drawn by an invisible pen a frown creases his forehead.

Harry opens the pocket wallet and surfaces the green file, "There hasn't been a lot done with the case – and it's old, the witness and the suspect are serving overseas... "

The CO holds up a hand, pull out a chair and sits opposite Harry.

"Karl isn't well," shapes a face, "can't be helped, things like that happen, can't be helped. The thing is I'm getting it in the neck from the GOC. He wants some serious action on this."

"The guards have a more active role than ourselves in the case, don't they?"

"Not any more. Private Enright withdrew her allegation, went into the station and withdrew her complaint. The guards don't want to know. But we do."

Harry rubs his lips. The CO has a dithering voice, the sort that reveals a mind in disarray or one which is thinking of many things at once.

"So."

"So, sir?"

The older man shows a smile he probably didn't want to show and says, "There's a review party travelling to Lebanon next week, basically a sightseeing tour for some old fogie who's retiring from the civil service – you're going."

Harry feels his blood turn cold.

"I know, I know – you're only back from the place, but this is only for eight days, and while the others are swanning you'll be working, getting those statements."

Harry's voice climbs the rock in his throat. "Sir, the battalion MPs... ?"

"No. You're the investigating officer – continuity of evidence and all that."

Harry sighs, rolls his pen across the desk where it stops against a sheaf of paper.

"Does this create a problem for you?"

It does. He feels sick. What does he tell June? The kids – causing another upheaval in their lives. Fuck it.

"No, no... sir. No problem."

What else can he say? Sir, I have a fucking problem. I have nightmares and daymares about that fucking place. I recoil when my son touches me. The missus and me are all but choking the living shit out of each other. I'm on and off the bottle, dying for sex, had a vasectomy – look sir, if you don't mind – things are a little fucked up in my life right now, you know? So, I'll skip this. Okay? Pass. Yeah.

"Good. Ring Personnel Section in Dublin and they'll give you the travel details."

Harry stands as the CO leaves the room. Pete appears moments later.

"I thought the oul fucker would never go."

"I'm going to the Leb."

"You're joking."

"I wish I fucking was."

Pete nods and runs a hand over his gelled red hair. Looks like he's about to tell Harry something but doesn't come across. Says he's going home to see if Sarah has calmed down any.

Harry says, "How did you face coming in here this morning, Pete? How will Sarah... "

"You're asking me that – that's funny, I was going to ask you the same thing."

"I don't get you."

"Don't you?"

"If you've something to say, spit it out."

"I've nothing to spit out."

Harry comes round the side of his desk.

Pete sighs, "Look, Harry, I'm talking a load of shit – of course it isn't easy for me to come in here, and Sarah's the same. What's the slagging going to be like, eh? Can you imagine Barty and Maxie – cutting the arse of us?"

"Yeah, well – it doesn't matter what they say – they've been in your position, only in worse circumstances."

"Thanks."

"Sort it out, Pete."

Harry thinks how Pete can't look him in the eye. He thinks this as he sees him get into his Volkswagen jeep, and thinks it a third time as he reaches for the phone to break the news of his trip to June.

Chapter 11

June's initial reaction is to fall into quietness. He imagines the news steals across her pretty features like a fog steals across the Curragh Plains.

Harry sighs hard into the phone, "June?"

"Are you the only one up there. Why you?"

"I'm investigating the case."

"Jesus Christ – anyone would think you were a detective instead of a soldier."

"It's a present from Karl – he kept the case especially for me. Blame him."

Silence.

"June, look, he took it on himself but he's in no state

Beep, beep, beep, beep – she's hung up. Hung up. For fuck's sake. He sits and lights up a cigarette, exhales and puts his palms to his forehead as though to stem a tide of headaches. All going wrong – every fucking wheel on his wagon is coming off.

He passes Karl's office on his way out of the building, catching a glimpse of him behind his desk, but says nothing. He knew this trip to the Leb was coming up but hadn't said anything, had left it to the CO to tell him. Bollocks. Lebanon. Fuck.

He draws up outside on the gravel, hands buried in his jacket pockets, searching for the keys to the Astra saloon, the section's civilian car, and remembers that it hasn't been released from the workshops yet. Spare keys, no car. Angles his watch above his head. A little after midday. A half-hour to lunch. Heads back into the house.

"You knew, didn't you?" he says to Karl.

The office has a musty smell. A wall calendar is a month behind. Elton John's 'Sacrifice' is coming from a dusty black radio on the windowsill.

He nods, "I told the CO that I wasn't the one who was going to tell you."

"No – but you knew this trip was coming up – there's no way you'd have let Smart and Williams out of the country otherwise."

Karl's eyes travel to the ornate antique fire.

"You lined me up nicely for this and I'm wondering why." "Who else... Pete, Sarah, get real. Me?"

Harry stabs a finger. "I don't need this right now, and if –"

"If what, Harry? If you didn't see yourself carrying my rank after I kick the bucket, you'd tell the army to go fuck itself?"

That's it, too. Isn't it? For him to advance up the promotion ladder Karl has to die or retire. His death will happen a long time before he would have been due to go on his ticket. So, Harry is up years.

"I haven't got you dead and buried – but sure I want promotion. Why not?"

Karl cleans his ear with a biro and flicks his gathering onto the floor. Jesus – a dirty bastard. Harry's stomach does a flip. He always had dirty habits – even the notion of simply washing Sarah's cup instead of throwing it out along with the mouse was an unhealthy act. Sometimes, even if Karl is dying, it's hard not to be annoyed and disgusted with him. The thing is, Sarah will tell you he's a gentleman. Looks, speaks and acts like one. But he's not a smarmy charmer – he's sincere, she says.

Harry slips into the Wesleyan Café across from the HQ and orders a ham roll without the mayonnaise. Mayonnaise squirts everywhere. When he returns to the office Karl is gone. He doesn't show in the afternoon – you can take a lot of liberties when you're dying. *Liberties*? Karl isn't at work because he's physically unable to attend. What sort of a fucking *liberty* is that?

Tries calling June again but the phone rings out to the answering machine. Then calls the Sergeant Major in Private Enright's unit and asks for her presence in the Investigation Section office tomorrow. "Say – 09:30 hrs, Major."

He reads over her original statement and then the case notes, scribbles some questions he wants to ask, hopes Sarah will be in to sit in on the interview, and decides to finish up early. Catches Pete on his way in and tells him he'll see him in the morning. Asks him to give Sarah a ring and let her know about the interview.

Going home, he hasn't a bob to go drinking – deliberately leaving himself penniless so that he wouldn't succumb to the longing – he wishes for death to claim him, but only if it would give him peace of mind and a light heart. Regrets he has no money.

Early December skies are a cold, clear blue. Unseasonally warm for a winter month.

The night before last a big wind had taken the last of the leaves and they lie about the roadside verge in a great rustling veil of red, gold, copper and deep brown. Plumes of smoke rise from a series of cottage chimneys and a white goat leans against a corrugated fence to reach an overhanging shrub that hangs teasingly low but not low enough. The fence belonged to an old guy who died a while ago. It encloses an obsolete gypsy wagon, some aluminium advertising signs, a rusted Morris Minor and a small caravan on a concrete base, grass growing from its skinny chimney pipe, grubby curtains sealed. As a kid June used to play with the old guy's daughter – she didn't show for the funeral. Kids and parents – look at his own set-up – fuck, he hasn't seen his own parents for such a long time. Imagine. Years. There'll come a time when he has no choice in whether he sees them or not. They're so fucking thick – he could die before the two of them but they don't see things that way. Sad, really. It wasn't so much a falling-out he had with them as a gradual loosening of ties. It hurt when they didn't bother with the boys – okay to send cards and ring, but they never dropped around to see their grandchildren. Blaming June for creating an atmosphere while in fact they carried an atmosphere with them as though it were baggage. They didn't like the noises kids made; screechy voices and the smell of shitty Pampers almost drove them crazy. As for crying – peace, they liked peace. The peace of the grave before their time as far as Harry is concerned. Still, he shouldn't be as thick as them; he should go visit. Mend a bridge – be better than what they are. Sometime, someday. Must visit. Must respond to his mother's occasional card and call – her thinly veiled hints that suggest his old man hasn't much rope left to fray has made him a little anxious. Last thing he needs is a saddle of guilt. To look down at a hump of earth with wreaths and bouquets and try to come to terms with something there's no coming to terms with. A time for talking gone like a wish in the wind.

Entering the kitchen June ignores him. He smells the lasagne in the oven, the cheesy fragrance he loves. Derek and Tony are playing with their toys on a red rug.

"June?"

Silence.

"Jesus – you used to like to talk. There's nothing we can't talk out – you used to say that."

"There's a time to give up hope."

"What do you mean?"

He rakes his fingers through Derek's hair and then Tony's. Waiting for an answer.

He lets it go when she doesn't respond and goes to have a shower, saying he'll skip dinner, to have a double portion for herself. She knows how to get on his wick.

Ignoring him makes him see red quicker than any

words she might use. Ignoring the dinner she prepared for him makes her see red, too. No cross words, he tells himself. None. For the boys' sakes. Don't disturb the night. If June loses her cool she forgets about the boys, about everything, just breathes fire. Regretting all when the heat has cooled in her. So – don't annoy her. Stay out of her way. Right?

He lets the shower run for a few moments and then gets in. Letting the water rinse over his face and hair, needles of hot water – so relaxing.

Eight days in Lebanon. He feels sick. Thoroughly sick at the idea of going and being there.

The earth in Tyre, the small garden patch behind the detachment is red and has a rich fragrant smell. When he thinks about it later – the red earth – he wonders if it gets its hue from blood spilled over the centuries.

The Ghanaian soldier skinning the donkey behind the soccer goals invites him over for supper – donkey and yam. The head of the donkey is beside his right knee. The cook has a huge scab on his elbow and the attention of the flies doesn't appear to bother him. Perspiration beads his wrinkled forehead. The donkey's eyes are open. Harry puts away his hoe, says he'll drop round with Sam, the Fijian. The cook doesn't like Sam but is too polite to turn away a guest imposed on him. Isaac the Cook is a sergeant, a distant relation of Lifoh's, who occasionally visits the MP Detachment in search of items to augment his supplies – from bulbs to porridge, to the blue barrel of wine the French MPs had left behind when they rotated to Naqoura – all presented to him by Harry, much to Sam's visible if otherwise silent annoyance.

Ordinary days in Lebanon – when the gunfire is close you remain in barracks; when you hear of a doctor being shot dead for carrying out an abortion you avoid going into town. You steer clear of storms. There are no UN personnel stationed in Tyre town proper. The MPs and a platoon of Ghanaians in Tyre Army barracks are the longest reach of UNIFIL, except for Beirut, where a pocket of UN personnel work from UNIFIL House, mostly civilian administrators.

An ordinary day — taking the jeep on a right turn, heading into town — labourers, skinny brown men with cigarettes, sit on the roundabout garden, waiting for work, for someone to pull up and hire them for a day or hopefully longer. Men with faces hardened from constant toil and a dejected acceptance of their lot in life. The long line of Friday morning traffic into Tyre, passing the new streetlights the sea a vivid blue, travelling the isthmus Alexander the Great built to join the mainland to the island in order to breach the city walls — crucifying the inhabitants of the city along the causeway when he was finally successful.

Parking a short distance from the souk he follows Sam through crammed streets — an aroma of beef turning on a spit, a man wearing a fez pushes a wooden trolley that sells handbag-shaped bread speckled with sesame, chickens being roasted outside a restaurant, men striking bargains and some not, an Arabic song cutting the air, 'Habibi'.

The hubble-bubble of life. Stops. Freezes when the high-pitched screams of Israeli warplanes sear the skies above their heads. Lasting mere milliseconds, but the silence and the fear in people's eyes, that awful lull as they wait for the shells to fall, the silence to break — that fright will live with them until replaced by the next scare.

Slowly, like figures moving on a TV screen after a freeze-frame, life resumes. Harry watches the sky — now empty — skies so blue. Lowers his gaze to the horizon where the blue of the sky merges with the blue of the sea. Shades of azure.

Sam sighs. Rubs his hands. He likes to come in here every Friday, to this poky and smoky pool room in the Maronite Christian Sector. Harry never plays, just watches the breaking of the balls and Sam's expert pots that demoralise the local talent. He drinks strong Arab coffee and eats fresh pitta bread and olives. Some people are never more alive than when they're doing something or being with someone they love. Heaven for Sam is a cue-stick, chalk, and a billards table. Or was — the same way

Heaven was a good book, a slim cigar and tasty coffee for Harry — but is now a place where blood doesn't seep into the ground and eyes never hold fear.

Chicken and chips for lunch and then to Basra's on the main street to hire some videos — Kung Fu for Sam and a mixture of others for the guys in the detachment. The little Nepalese, Khadar, likes blues. He treated himself to a feel of a Norwegian MP's tit as she slept off a hangover on the couch in Netanya — Harry emerged from his bedroom to her screams, seeing through bleary eyes her hands around Dexy's throat, his eyes popping. In his best pidgin English he croaked that the blue film had filled him with evil ideas. Half-throttling him was satisfaction enough for the large woman — she didn't want him reported. Dexy was lucky. No blues. Harry reckons he'll treasure that feel of breast for the rest of his days, if not the hands on his throat.

Derek knocks. He wants to use the bathroom.

"Come in," Harry says, through the shower glass.

"I can't. I have to do my poo. You have to come out."

"Just a minute, good lad."

For fuck's sake. Can he not steal a few minutes to himself?

Dries off with a towel carrying the UN logo and opens the door. Derek stands there smiling, "I was only joking, Daddy."

"You — "

"I wasn't." Laughs. He brushes by and eases the door shut.

June is in the bedroom pulling out a drawer.

"That lad's a header," he says.

She slips on a change of knickers. Pink.

"Have you seen enough?" she says.

"No." Grins.

Moving to the window he stares across at the Curragh Plains; blue-blanketed horses returning from the gallops in single file, following a rust-coloured terrier, the spread of green gorse interspersed with new realms of black scorched by Halloween vandals – a lick of ancient trail called the Race of the Black Pig losing itself over the brow of a steady climb.

"When are you going?"

"I don't know yet – have to ring Dublin."

"Eight days?"

"Yeah... yeah, eight."

"How do you feel about that – given your problems?"

He faces her, "I'm dreading the fucking thought of going there."

"Go sick, can't you?"

"What do you mean?"

"They wouldn't send you if you were sick."

He holds up his hand, "What are you talking about? Say I'm sick? What will I say to them – I have the flu – or I have a mental problem?"

"What do you think?"

He says nothing, just turns from her. June carries herself on a sigh down the stairs.

His name was Damar Thapa. He was twenty-four years old and had a wife and a four-year-old son. He had a week of his tour left. He is lying on the table in the RAP.

Black hair cropped and unevenly cut. Eyes closed. Thank God. Closed. He is naked; injuries showing, left leg missing from the knee down, blood and bone exposed. Hand, right hand, missing too. A hand that would have caressed his son, touched his wife, wiped sweat from his brow.

Harry snaps the camera. No dignity in death. None whatsofuckingever. The room is silent. Cold. The walls disturbed by the flashing Olympus – sheets of lightning.

"He died quick," Sam says, fingering the tip of his moustache. They are alone, the three of them. The smell of disinfectant is strong. The smell of death stronger.

"How quickly, Sam?"

"The tank round hit him — glanced off him, it did. My Jesus."

Blesses himself.

He thinks of the man lying there — his wife and son thousands of miles away, unaware that something terrible had befallen them. Bad news travels fast. The thing is, his son will only have a scant memory of Dad. That's it, isn't it? His wife. Christ — maybe he's taking his death worse than she will? Maybe. Who knows? The fact is that he was a soldier in Lebanon trying to make a few bob for his family — fuck coming out for the medal, to be a peacekeeper, fuck that oul shite. It's money with most soldiers, no matter their nationality — from the French who tot three days toward qualifying for their pension each time they fly by UN Heli, to the Norwegian teenager out for the year to save money for that log cabin on the fiord.

Finished with the camera he and Sam stare for moments at the dead man. Harry sees in the corpse his own vulnerability, sees where his road will end, where all roads end, and he's so scared, so fucking scared. There's the sound of an approaching heli — blades clipping the air — on its way to collect the body and bring it to Rambam hospital in Haifa, Israel, for a postmortem.

Strange that Damar should die by Israeli proxy and that they should be the ones to examine the body.

He houses the camera in its jacket and nods for Sam to leave. Outside they catch the hard savage blowing from the rotors as the medi-heli hovers above the landing pad. "The girl was eighteen years old," Sam shouts above the racket. "Basima."

Harry takes the car keys Sam proffers — thank God he doesn't have to put a face on that poor girl. Just needs her details for the record.

He eases from the Camp, over the speed ramps, acknowledges the clip of heels and the salute, "Ram Ram," from the Nepalese sentry and heads the long way home because of the gunfire from the wadi beyond Quasimodos Curve.

He turns from the window. June has left the room, her harsh closing of the door calling him back from Lebanon. Go sick? Perhaps, she's right. But while she may have the right answer she has no clue as to what it actually means for him – how hard it will be to surrender his army career, kill his chances of promotion – and the fear, the fear that no one could help him is real, too real. He could be told that there is no getting better. That post-traumatic stress disorder is something you just learn to live with – cope. Is that what he has – post-traumatic stress? Perhaps. He – tough Harry Kyle? No fucking way – all he needs is a little time to pull himself together – time for the faces to fade from memory and his hands to feel clean. A little fucking time.

Time to blot out that fucking roll into Kafra — down that fucking rutted road — not knowing at that time that the ambulance rocking towards them was carrying Basima to hospital in Tyre. Not knowing that when he walked into the square the stench of death would assail his nostrils, that Musa would carry a black bag and Sam would draw his attention to Basima's foot. Damar's hand... his body rushed to NEPBATT RAP — rushed. Why rush a dead body anywhere? The Nepalese officer said that, "Rush... we rush him but we are too late." Did it mean that Damar lived for a while? No, no — he had died instantly. Sure of it. For fuck's sake, his leg and hand were reefed from him — his leg. They never found his leg. There was nothing left of it to find. It was made smithereens of — handy little titbits for the fucking cats. Fate can be so fucking considerate.

In Nepal a woman and a child went about their daily routine — probably preparing their home for his arrival, arranging a homecoming party. He wonders at Damar's personal circumstances — was he happy, did he love his wife? Of course he loved his son. The plans he had, his bad habits, did he think he'd die in a foreign land? Far from his family — then, we all have to die on our own, it doesn't matter how many are dying around you. There's nothing and no one who can lift that last living responsibility from your shoulders. God wouldn't do it for his own Son. The best you can hope for is that you know as little as possible about it when it happens. That you can look down on yourself and say, "What the fuck happened?"

What the fuck happened?

Chapter 12

It's a minute after five in the morning. June sleeps. He has a pain in his gut. Like there's a sharp rock inside. It feels as though he's been awake for an age. He lies perfectly still on his back with his eyes open but distant.

Tyre. Pool table. He is on his second glass of black coffee when the planes return. The café shudders. He sees dust rising from trembling floorboards and shelves — hears the plastic cord-ends of wall lamps give small ticks against the mirrors underneath.

Back from bombing the Bekaa valley, he thinks, or Sidon, wherever the Hizbollah are holed up. He tells Sam they'll make a move — any more frights and his heart will drop through his arse.

The jeep has a flat. Sam grabs the spare. He has big hands, thick fingers. It doesn't take him long. there's a kid of about eight in sandals kicking a dead rat about.

"Imish!" Harry says.

"Fuck you, UN Mister!" Runs away.

Harry hopes he washes his feet. Soccer, with a rat as a ball — Jesus, what a place, what a dive. He puts the flat in the back as Sam lowers the jack and tightens the nuts. All the time Sam is talking about his last tour in Lebanon — that he was in Tyre back then. The Amal — they had boy soldiers patrolling the streets carrying rocket launchers, boys no older than his sons back home. This trip he hasn't seen any of them around. Then, they lived in the Roman Hippodrome under the spectator rostrums and the MPs used to bring their instructors, rough men with woolly beards, the rockets confiscated by the various battalions. They'd sit in the shade of the trees on ancient columns laid low and drink tea.

Once, the boy soldiers lifted the live rockets from the jeep and dusted them off. Sam says when he thinks about it, now, how one of those rockets could have gone off and killed the lot of them, he breaks out in a sweat. Harry says to him as they head towards the roundabout, "The worst thing you've ever seen out here — the worse thing that ever made you feel lousy inside, Sam, what, what is it?"

Sam sucks in air, a double breath. Looks way beyond the windscreen. Changes gear at the roundabout. Harry sees that tic in Sam's right eye. It comes whenever he struggles to find the right word.

"I knew a soldier from a different island in Fiji — he was hit in an APC and killed. Some of his soldiers, yeah, take a video of it all and it ends up for sale in the video shops in the AO. That's the worse thing for me — his kids could get to see the film someday — their father's blood down the side of the armoured car, body slumped forward. So, I learn one thing — one thing." His finger shoots up. "I learn that no one cares about you. No one really cares — you got to take of yourself and the family. That guy who died — he would never have dreamed, never, that his comrades would take a video of a dead man and make copies and sell them. We got them out of the shops — but maybe, maybe, there's some out there still, Maybe in Fiji, maybe."

Back at base a message comes over on the radio, saying that the AO was off limits — no UN traffic permitted — shelling expected. The Israelis always warn UNIFIL when they intend to shell its area, that way if any UN soldiers get killed or injured they can hold up their hands and say, "We warned you — why weren't they in shelter?"

The next day it happens. Kafra happens.

Stirs himself from bed and dresses in his tracksuit. He is hungry for June but she isn't for him. Is it the sex he wants or just the feel of being one with the woman he loves?

Does he think it will in some way ease his disturbed mind? Bring some inner peace, wash away the fucking nightmares? Or is he just being lustful, looking for his bit, because it would take his mind off things, show him a pleasure, an ecstasy? If it was just sex wouldn't a wank do the job just as well? Use himself instead of using June to obliterate memories he didn't want to own. Thinking of masturbation draws his thoughts to his vasectomy and the test tubes on the wardrobe's top shelf. June might give him a hand when it's time. Hah – imagine asking in her current form – just fucking imagine what her response would be. Thunder looks and dagger words.

Can he blame her? She makes him feel like young trees on an old mountain – immature for his age.

Beyond the kitchen window, seeds of snow dance in the morning wind. The skies are watery. Barney lies in a wicker basket that is too small for him – his aged head lies on the lino, an ear raised like radar.

Al and Ivan's this Saturday for the book launch. Poetry. Bore the shite out of a sewer. But Al's only coming back to himself after being hit by a car last year – two brothers run down by cars – you'd think they were cursed – he doesn't need disappointments, no matter how small. Four months in hospital, coming out with metal plates in his skull, leg and arms. Ivan nursing him in their flat above the restaurant until he was able to look after himself. If Al hadn't got Ivan he would have had no one – yeah, go down Saturday and be bored, least he can do for the guy who gave his brother something to live for. Save Al from having a small disappointment at his absence.

From the foot of the stairs he calls June before leaving for work. She doesn't answer so he squeezes the doorbell twice before heading off — she can't say he didn't give her a shout at reveille.

Spots a lone magpie emerging from the furze, scans for another — two for joy. No luck — what's fucking new? It's cold, bitterly cold. The plains are matted with a fine powdery snow that scrunches under his trekkers. His breath haws the air and already he feels his lips begin to crack and bleed. Sensitive lips — makes a mental note to buy a chapstick. Winter has landed, accompanied by a trumpet blast of foul weather.

Karl is in, warming his hands on the radiator. Rolls his eyes to the ceiling to say Pete and Sarah are upstairs, that the mood between them isn't great.

"You look pleased with yourself over something," Harry says.

Karl's eyes widen, "Do I?"

"Like a cat that's got the cream — or about to get it."

He moves from the heater, eyebrows coming together, and says, "You better sort out that pair — they won't listen to me — I don't want to hear them at each other's throats in here. They can do what they fucking like in their own time — in the door and up the stairs they went, bitching. I could have been the CO listening to them."

"Yeah, right, I'll have a word."

Sarah's in the interview room looking over the case notes while Pete is starting up the computers in the office.

"How's the... " Harry says to Pete.

The big man looks up, flecks of green in his brown irises. Shakes his head. Harry recognises the strain in him because he has seen it a lot lately, whenever his face meets a mirror.

Sarah calls from the next room, "Harry — is that you?"
"Coming... corporal."

He knows that pisses her off — the fact he's a rank above her and that he's letting her know her place. He's unsure as to why he would want to piss her off.

Closing the door behind him he says, "Yeah?"

Sarah's thin with a long face interrupted by glasses. Her large eyes are closely set and remind him of the colour of the camp's redbrick under the glare of an autumn sun.

"I shouldn't be sitting in on this interview."

"Why not?"

"I know Lucy."

"You know Lucy — Private Enright?"

A nod. She's wearing a black trouser suit. You wouldn't see as much black on a dozen widows. His eyes find her nails. Long and painted. None broken.

"How well do you know her?"

"She's a friend."

Harry deliberates for moments and then says, "I need you in here with me. You'll just have to be a professional about it."

"I — "

"No debate."

She shrugs. Her fair hair is tied in a bun. Harry thinks of how she must look when it falls loose. It would take from the sharpness of her features and make her almost pretty. Three small moles are a ladder on her chin.

He stops at the door, looks across the hallway into the main office and sees Pete at his desk. "Two things, Sarah," he says without looking at her.

"What?"

He eases the door over. Meets her eyes and holds them. Her shoulders climb a little.

"One from the CS who hasn't the balls to tell you himself and the other is from me."

"Jesus, Harry -"

"He says you and Pete have to do your arguing outside of army time."

Her chin lifts in a small show of defiance.

"I'll be telling Pete the same in a moment — so give us a second together."

"The other thing?"

"Don't drink out of your mug. Don't ask – you don't want to know."

Pete is pale, so pale that Sarah's claw-marks appear more livid than yesterday.

"Yeah, I know. What can I do?"

"I don't know, Pete – Jesus, you've no kids, you're not married – no real pressures, know what I mean, and you come in here with a face like you've been attacked by a tiger. What do you want... signposts nailed to your forehead?"

"I'm mad about her."

"Is she – about you?"

He doesn't answer.

"She's mad at you and not mad about you."

"Yeah – I won't, I won't – she wants to give her oul one a lend of our money, five-grand we've got saved in the building society. That's what it's over, because I hate the oul cow – we'd never get it back, you know? Not a fucking hope."

"None of my business, Pete, and I don't like giving advice, but don't go against a daughter and her old doll – you either accept that or you don't, but it's a fact. Search for compromise – but if I were you, it's those marks I'd be worrying about – fuck, they're bad."

His eyes fill.

Harry says, "If you've got leave, take it... till they heal up a little."

"Yeah. I can't listen to Dobbs or March – they're having a field day over this shit. Bastards."

Harry plucks his brown Filofax from his drawer. He's some article to be giving advice to people on how to manage their relationships. Jesus. His own has a crack as bad as the San Andreas Fault. But at least he's never come to work marked, carrying external wounds and you'd only know he was bleeding inside if you looked at his eyes for long enough.

Sarah comes in and says, "We're in business."

She doesn't look at Pete. He may as well be one of the dust-motes caught in the shaft of light in the landing.

Pte Enright is in combat uniform, slightly faded from overwashing. Her black boots are polished, the rims dirt-filled. She's of medium build with short gingerish hair and very fine eyebrows. He wonders what stops the sweat from flowing into her eyes.

"Private Enright, my name is Sergeant Kyle."

A brief meeting of hands while Sarah opens the door to the interview room.

"Sit down, relax," Harry says, taking his seat beside Sarah and placing his hands on the desk.

"Now, I've asked you here because there are some questions I want to put to you and I hope to record them in statement form."

The young soldier's round face fills with apprehension. She glances at Sarah.

"But I've already given a statement to CS... "

"I'm aware of that — I have it here." Harry taps the file.

"So — there isn't much more for me to say."

"I think there is and I think you should tell me everything. I'm going to Lebanon to see Smart and Williams — perhaps next week — I'd like to have all of your side of the story going in."

"You've got all my side of the story." Eyes hard on Sarah. Pleading.

Harry sighs. What kind of a witness will she make at a court' martial? Strong, weak, hostile, a reluctant complainant? "Why did you drop your complaint with the guards?"

"I... "

She wriggles on the chair, hand touching behind her ear as though she had the answer hidden there.

"Go on."

"I just did — I just —"

"Just did?"

"I mean I want the army to deal with it — I think it's enough."

"The army to deal with it?"

Nods.

"Court-martial deal with it — give them a bollocking — how deal with it?"

"Transfer... "

"Them or you?"

Silence.

Sarah coughs and says, "Is there anything Sergeant Kyle should know before he speaks with Smart and Williams?" Christ! There is something. Fuck it — there is. It's written all over her face. Harry massages his temples. Senses there is.

"No," she says.

"Tell me," Harry says.

"I have nothing to tell you."

"You've been with Smart before — how about Williams?" Silence.

"Eh, Williams. Come on. Tell me about Williams?"

"No... "

"You're sure?"

Small shows of the tip of her tongue are like peeps of the truth afraid to reveal its entirety.

"Lucy?" Sarah says, coaxingly, with a small encouraging smile.

"No — "

"No?" Harry says.

"We're friends."

"Was he in your room when — ?"

"No, he wasn't."

"What sort of friend is he — close, talk-close or talk and bed-close?"

"Talking!"

"Just talking — are you winding me up — talking?

Sarah shoots a hard look at Harry. Goes to say something but thinks better of it.

He feels like telling her to keep her nails sheathed.

"With all due respect, sergeant – a man and a woman can be friends without necessarily getting up to something."

Harry bluffs, "He was in your room before – on some other day – want to tell me about it?" Her eyes run from his.

Harry points, "He shouldn't have been in your billet because it's against regulations – isn't that so?"

"He came in."

"Did he knock?"

"Yes."

"Who let him in?"

"He came in himself."

"Did you tell him to come in?"

"Yes."

"Well, you asked him in, then, didn't you?"

Silence.

"Didn't you?"

"Yes. I suppose."

"There's no fucking supposing about it."

Harry looks at Sarah and grimaces, "Tell you what, Private Enright, you go down into the kitchen, make yourself some coffee, have a smoke, and think of everything that happened that evening. Okay? Everything. How's that, and we'll see you here in ten minutes." A scraping of chair legs against the lino as Private Enright gets to her feet and makes her exit with a wounded look in her eyes, like she's getting a verbal mauling she doesn't deserve.

"What's your game, Harry?" Sarah asks.

"I need to know the truth. She's lying through her knickers."

"You're sexist – just because you have a prick doesn't mean you have to be one – do you know that?"

"Sexist. Maybe I am. But I know when I'm being lied to most of the time, and I know that it's not so much she's lying as withholding information."

"Perhaps we're all guilty of that from time to time."

A dig there. A flash of her claw.

"Tell me what you're feeling guilty over – using your nails as blades?"

"You're an easy man to dislike."

"Yeah, probably. But then, know what, I wouldn't wipe my arse with your opinion – you just listen in and learn – and keep your discussions with me on a professional level and not personal."

"Like you did when you asked me to quell my rows with Pete?" Her lips go hard.

"I told you in a professional capacity – and, shit, Sarah, I'm sorry, just fucking sorry."

Sarah nods, some of the hard face leaving her. Harry signs for her to fetch the private.

"Well, what have you got to add?" Harry says.

The young soldier looks away, her bottom lip quivering. Shakes her head, "Nothing."

Afterwards, alone in the office, Harry writes up his case notes and paper-clips the soldier's new statement with her old. Nothing much to add – she's lying and also up to something, scheming. But maybe, maybe, he was just being mean, taking his home life into work, venting his frustration a little? Reading too much into things.

"Basically," Enright said, "basically that's what happened – like I told the CS."

"Basically, you're bullshitting me."

She glared – kept her lips tight.

"So much for fucking look and learn," Sarah says, in the kitchen, when Enright has gone.

"She gave us a little, didn't she, about Williams being in the room with her on a previous occasion – mightn't mean a lot – then again it might assume some significance later on."

"Yes, I suppose it might."

"I want to give her a bad fright – want to give him

one – in the meantime will you check with the guards and through our own files to see if we've anything on him – in particular anything to do with assault. Likewise with Williams."

"Sure – what do you think she's hiding, if she is hiding anything?"

"Don't know until I interview the others." A pause. "She hates her unit."

"Can you blame her? It's a kip."

"This might be a way out for her."

"I think you're wrong. Anyway – "

"Anyway, I'll do up the report and let the big brass decide, eh?"

He smiles afterwards. God, Lucy Enright. Aged 21. Told him nothing at the start and told him nothing at the end. Fuck all in the middle, too – a hard lady inside. Bad idea to give her a break – maybe she got on her mobile to someone and sought advice?

How do you investigate her complaint when she's only half-telling you the truth?

Then, it's not really Enright who wants this investigated – it's the army. Their baby.

Discipline and all.

"It went well, I heard," Karl says, putting his head in.

"Fuck off, you."

"Watch your tongue. Rank and that."

"I'm going to Lebanon to be made an eejit of because she's holding out on something. These guys can whistle Dixie and I won't be in a position to contradict them."

"No one's asking you to be a fucking lie detector – stop whingeing and get on with the job."

"Yeah, right. I'll take everything everyone says at face-fucking-value."

"You broke the news to June?"

"Yeah, I did – I don't want to talk about it."

"Sorry I asked."

Harry looks at the door space for long moments after Karl has gone. Something sly about that fella. Midday – fuck it. Fancy a pint in the mess, wash down the Wes' roll? Good idea, Brain. Let's go. Just for one.

Chapter 13

The mess remains open in spite of all the loose talk about the authorities closing it as part of the Camp's revitalisation programme. Harry sits on a barstool, orders a beer and lights up the last of his Lebanese import Lucky Strikes.

No matter how often they do the place up or how much money they pump into it, the mess doesn't look as plush as it should. On a busy night the air gets tainted with a commingled smell of piss and cigarette smoke. The jacks aren't great – leaking smells and the urinals spill over because the plughole can't drain away the piss quickly enough – but, quit being negative – the beer is cheap and the place is cosy if not plush. Maxie March and Barty Dobbs are huddled in deep conversation at the end of the counter, smoke greying the air between them. Now and then one of them peels away and throws darts at the board, cigarette clamped between lips. Each had nodded at Harry when he walked in – Barty said, "Shush, Shush, Special Branch" – but Harry gave a look to suggest he wasn't Pete and wouldn't tolerate his shite.

Maxie snuffles. Loses his big nose in a Kleenex, "You're going back to the Leb?"

"Yeah."

Barty says, "Jaesus – I hope the guy in the billet has ear- defenders – what, with you being the banshee at night – sure I came home from the Leb suffering from sleep deprivation." They laugh, Maxie nudging the other.

He's a hateful little fuck, that old sergeant – his moonface is pitted as though to show the poison within – he loves to wind up people and make the snowballs for others to throw. Stands clear then – hands spread wide in a show of innocence.

"Isn't it a pity your mouth can't suffer from the same sort of exhaustion?"

"Ah... "

"Fuck off – you pair are just the unit jesters, a pair of bitter wankers – now fuck off, and keep your titters and your remarks to yourselves."

They're taken aback at his attack and swap uncomfortable looks. Facing the barman, Dobbs raises his eyebrows. Harry sees the comer of his sneering smile.

"You think you've no skeletons in the closet, Dobbs, do you? I'll bury you with bones if you don't leave me alone," he looks over Barty's shoulder, "and you too, you oul flute – you're a shit-stirrer, March, nothing but."

The barman taps a glass with a spoon, "Gentlemen, quiet, please."

Harry takes his drink and moves to a table in front of the large TV screen. Catches Maxie's "Can't take a bit of slagging," but lets it pass without comment. Jesus – why are people getting on his wick so easily and why can't he keep his tongue in check? Where has his sense of humour gone? He's at war on all fronts. At home, in work, with himself. Perhaps that's why his nerves are stretched so thinly on the ground – too many battles on his plate. He used to be so cool when it came to keeping cool. What is it the ex CO said? Sangfroid, yeah, that. He had that at one time.

Sky One News is on – scenes of flooding in India and avalanches in Austria. He looks into his beer and then sips at it. He feels as though he's going to burst out crying at any moment. He squints in order to drive back the tears and sips some beer to try and ease the strain in his throat. The images of bloated bodies in swollen rivers and the tips of chimneys showing like headstones above snow sickens him – he has first-hand experience of what smells and sights the rescuers, the investigators, will encounter.

But it has to be done. Someone has to clean up the mess and someone has to find out why such a thing happened so that it can be stopped from happening again. This is what he can't understand – he can't understand how policemen cope with the sights they must see at the scene of traffic accidents, sights of bodies cut to ribbons in wreckages – hospital staff – how do they cope? Are they all like him – full of nightmares and cranky as fuck? How do they go about their tasks each day with the knowledge they might and more probably will encounter something that will eat through their eyes and into their hearts?

Is he a lesser person, a lesser man, a cardboard effigy of a soldier? How does the ordinary Joe Soap cope when he comes across something horrific – like pulling a body from a river, listening to kids screaming in a house fire and no one able to get near them? How do people manage? Survive the horror of it all?

Basima turned eighteen the week before she died. She had been walking through the square after buying some bread when the shell landed. She lay on the ground looking at her leg where her foot had been severed. Her blood staining a patch, covering small weeds, a cigarette end, splashed against the wall behind her in a crazy artist's crazy strike of brush. Spaniel eyes fixed on her foot by the railing that protects a gnarled olive tree older than the village itself. Seeing her ankle bone and sinew – or had her eyes begun to cloud by then? Pain? Did she feel pain or had the shock numbed her?

Musa, through the interpreter, a young man home on holiday from university in Beirut, says the Amal had attacked the Israeli compound from the orange groves behind the village and that is why the shells landed in the village, to punish the villagers for allowing their groves to be used as a base for the attack. Harry nods. Musa has a navy scarf in his hand. There are long black hairs fastened to it.

Basima's. Musa's words pass through the interpreter — and Harry comes to know Basima. Walking the Virgin Parade on Fridays — hoping for the eye of the boy she fancied. She liked to read poetry, and she wrote poems, too. A song. She read Lebanese poems written by authors long dead and her favourite book was a collection of short stories penned by a great-aunt of hers who used to live in the grounds of Tibnin castle. Musa said she could relate to and knew the people in the stories. Harry holds the thin volume in his hands, touching the first few dog-eared pages, leaving his mark atop Basima's. Page 10 holds a thumbprint, as though someone had spilled coffee and hadn't cleaned her hands entirely of the fine powder — the ridges, loops and whorls are clearly visible. Basima's? Arabic writing — right to left — he follows a few lines — having no comprehension of what is being said. Just doing it for the sake of doing it — travelling the eye — path of another — a pilgrimage of sorts. A show of respect in lieu of attending a funeral. In lieu of saying a prayer.

After the first shell landed, the UN soldiers emerged from their base, about five, hurrying to the scene. Another shell landed as the first soldier hit the square, catching him flush, taking off his leg and his hand and slamming into the wall, bursting into an explosion. Perhaps killing him outright if he was lucky — not knowing what hit you is not the same as dying instantly — and finishing off the girl.

A further round struck the mosque, shattering its double doors. The last shell broke the mast above the UN position, leaving the blue and white flag lying on the pantiled roof, the jagged midsection of the pole showing like a long fingernail.

A grey day with cloud banks drifting across hilltops and mists forming in the wadis. A crying mother, leaving her to Musa to deal with — feeling it deeply that as a soldier, a peacekeeper, he and the UN had somehow failed her.

He takes the binoculars from Sam and looks south at the compound on the hill, one of a series of encampments that straggle an unnatural frontier, a buffer zone designed to protect Israel's northern territory from guerrilla attacks. There, on other hilltops flies the UN flag, dodging the bullets and tank rounds, sometimes not, sometimes being caught in the crossfire, sometimes walking away unhurt.

The compound has a high earthen bank — its lower region is circled with barbed wire and littered with anti-personnel landmines. A grey Sherman tank, a relic from WW II, stands outside the compound, its barrel pointed north towards Tyre. There's a soldier in the turret — a clean-faced youth with black shaggy hair talking down to someone in the tank — slight swivel of barrel. BOOM! The tank gives a little backward shuffle and smoke pops from the mouth of the barrel — some other village or town, not Tyre because it's out of range, is getting a pasting. More souls lost?

Who gave the order to fire? Who aimed and who fired? Do they lie awake and think about the consequences of their actions? Are they alive to think? If they are, do they say it happened in the name of war, that they were merely obeying orders? Wash their hands of it all? Try to? Succeed?

He's a soldier, obeys orders too — what would he do if he were in a similar position? Of course — he would pull the trigger. Hurl the shell. But civilians — women and kids and old men? Cop on — who suffers most in wars? Only those who can't fight back, who get in the way, who are in the wrong place at the wrong time, only the innocent.

They're the ones who suffer. Really fucking suffer.

"If you go too deep in yourself you'll fall in and drown," Sarah says, waving her hand in front of him.

"Yeah." Blinks. "Miles away."

"I noticed — I've been beside you for about two minutes — you didn't see me."

"Sorry."

"Drinking during lunchtime, Harry. That's not your style."

"Private Enright put a thirst on me. And you, you're not a regular here?"

"God, no – not with those bar-fleas – Dobbs and March – cutting the arse off anything and everyone. Just giving Pete a bit of space – he's taking a bit of time off to heal the war wounds."

Harry nods, sits up straight and taps a cigarette from the pack. Strikes a match.

"I just came over to see you. I'm sorry about calling you a sexist and – "

"Ah, look, forget it – we all say things in the heat of the moment – I said worse."

"I lost the head with Pete – I shouldn't have done that to him. It happened so quickly, I swear to God I didn't think about it – it just – "

"Sarah, look – "

"No, I just want you to know that I've never done anything like that before nor will I ever do it again."

"That's good. It's good when we learn from our mistakes."

"It's just that Pete – well, he can be so self-righteous, just going on and on and on."

Harry says nothing. He's not going to agree with her because he hasn't seen or heard Pete carry on like that. That's not to say he isn't pushy. It's just saying that he doesn't know that side of Pete – lads keep things hidden from each other – they just do. It's the likes of March and Dobbs who pounce on and take malicious pleasure in the failings or misfortunes of others. Vultures who feed on other people's wounded feelings. Maybe he's being hard on them, maybe he is – they've got their own share of troubles – what he does know for certain is that they like to make other people's problems appear worse than their own. Just to feel better in themselves.

"But one thing, Sarah?"

"What?"

"What's going down? I sense something's up — Pete let something slip the other day in conversation and you as well — why do I have the feeling every fucker around here knows something I don't?"

Her cheeks tinge a cherry red, "There's nothing... "

"Really?"

Her eyes fall to the red eye of his cigarette, "Not really." She goes to speak but Dobbs and March are walking past, muttering about some of them having work to do.

"It's June."

"June?"

"Yeah... Jesus, I shouldn't be telling you this. Or maybe I should... "

"Go on."

"Harry — oh fuck it — you'll find out sooner or later...

"

"What — Sarah, will you fucking tell me?"

"She and Karl... she and Karl, they were seeing a lot of each other when you were away."

A slap of ice hits his belly. He draws on his cigarette. Heavily. Like it's his last draw. He looks at her. Moves his lips and shakes his head.

"I'm sorry."

Anger hardens his features. That's why he's in good form — cat that's licked the cream — setting him up to go to Lebanon so he can... Bastard! Who's to blame?

He for going away in the first place, June for betraying his trust, or Karl for knowing what Lebanon is like, the biting loneliness that can grab a guy's spirit and make him feel he's so low down he can never get any lower? Apportion blame. Quickly. Analyse like you do everything fucking else, why don't you?

Sarah rests her hand on his — he looks at it so hard that she grows uncomfortable. She whispers "Sorry" and leaves.

Jesus Christ! Why does it feel as though he's got two guys in his jocks playing tennis with his balls? Jesus, how fucked up do You want me to be? Fuck off and give us a break, will You? What are You saying to me? I'm thinking too much about war – here's something to take my mind off it? That's not helping, Jesus. Not helping at all. About the closest he has come to praying for a long, long time. He takes in his beer and polishes off the dregs. Puts his anger under a tight rein. He's going back to work, and when he speaks with Bollocky, today, tomorrow, whenever, he's going to chat like he had heard nothing. He's going to chat with him about his kids, his home, his lovely wife. He's going to chat so much that the fucker will know what he's driving at. He'll know it as clear as day. He'll know he knows, and leave him wondering as to what he's going to do about it. And when.

Chapter 14

The balance of his Leb money appears on his weekly pay slip. He runs his eye over the incidentals while Karl drums a pen on the edge of his desk in deep thought and then jots something down. Apart from the ticking of the clock, a computer's humming, the office is silent. Sarah is upstairs, ringing Dublin to determine his flight arrangements.

"I see that you had a word with them," Karl says.

"You know I had – hasn't Karl put in for leave?"

Karl looks up, "You mean Pete." A piercing, slight frown is a disturbed wave along his forehead.

"I'm slipping – now, why would I have your name on the tip of my tongue?"

Karl senses the subtle undertones in Harry's voice, sees the shark's coldness in his eyes. Harry sends out his words in carefully clipped packages – saying amongst other things that he hates leaving June and the kids, that while you're overseas you live with a nagging fear that something might happen to them. You worry about how she'll manage if the car doesn'tstart on a frosty morning and she's stuck to bring Derek into school. You worry about things you wouldn't worry about if you were at home, because these things are things you do – from picking up the dog-shit out back to making sure the smoke alarm gets its weekly testing – waiting out there for the post to arrive and not receiving any letters, and sure a call is quicker and easier than writing, but a letter, you can read a letter over and over whereas a phone call is instant news and you're there in the kiosk trying to pick up giveaway nuances in your wife's voice – is she all right? Really? Are the kids fine? What is she not telling you? You wonder, Karl, what she isn't telling you. You know?

Their eyes lock. Harry sees the growing realisation in the other's – like an Israeli dawn, the sun climbing high and quickly.

Harry says, "You think out there – Karl – you think what if she's being untrue, what if some fucker is screwing your missus when you're out there – and that's bad, bad if it happens at all, but worse, worse if, can you imagine, it's someone you know, who you might once have called a friend. Then you think – no, she's not like that – but when the letters dry up and the calls aren't answered, and if they are it's by the childminder, you get doubts – and you begin to wonder does anyone in this fucking world care for you – because guys have blown their brains out over things like this – but shit, Karl, you know this, don't you? You've been there – you thought the same things I did, you've been through it before with your ex – you know what I'm talking about, don't you?"

Karl nods, holds up his hands, "Em... call came for you about a soccer match – I told them you were off to the Leb and mightn't be here."

"Yeah, iit's very important I go the Leb, for some people."

"You're driving at something."

"You know fucking well what I'm driving at."

"I... "

The CO coughs, enters the office, throwing a smile over the tension. Like a fire blanket smothering a small blaze, "I'd like to read Private Enright's statement."

Harry nods, "It's in the file, sir – I'll get it for you now."

"I'll come with you."

Derek kicks a ball against the gable end. It's almost dark, the early winter afternoon closing in. A chill breeze blowing. Derek is wearing an Arsenal woollen hat, minus the tassel he pulled off the very instant it was bought, a Peter Storm black and yellow jacket and runners with winking red lights — a week old and already he has the toes scuffed.

"Give us a game, Da, will you?"

"Sure — I take the wall as goals and you take the gates." These little things you miss, Karl, you bastard, playing ball with your son — being available for him. You don't miss Lebanon and doing very little for very little money — certainly not enough to buy the time you lose with your kids — and you can do very little about people being blown to kingdom come except pick up the pieces.

Literally pick up the pieces.

Derek puts his arms around Harry and squeezes hard. He does this as they wrap up the game and leave the ball in the shed. Harry sweeps him into his arms — kid's so light. Five, almost six — will be after Christmas. Jesus, where do the years go?

Doesn't seem that long ago when he came into the world — must be the worst pain in the world to bury your child — a grief from which there is no recovering — never mind what they say about Time the Healer — load of bollocks that — absolute bollocks. Basima's mother knows the pain. Above all else it is, he senses, the one sorrow he would not carry in life. "When I grow up I'm going to play for Arsenal."

"Good lad."

"I'm going to play in goal I am."

"That's great — sure you're a great keeper."

"Will you come and see me playing?"

"You bet — I can't wait."

Eases the door shut behind them and lowers Derek to the floor — Tony smiles and says, "Hi, Da."

"Hiya, son."

Smiles. Smiling through the pain. Herself is at the electric cooker — hasn't looked his way. He'll say nothing to her until she says something to him. But she always finds it easier to ignore him than he does her, so in the end he talks, pushing a piece of paper towards her. "I'm flying out next Wednesday and will be back Thursday week – there's the dates and times."

She looks at it.

"I think it's very important that you know the exact time and date I will be home."

June takes him in with a sidelong glance.

He's been remarkably cool for a fellow feeling a lot of pain, a lot of anger. He turns on a player during a training session and here he is – not thumping Karl and not railing against June – how is that? His moods are totally contradictory. Like the sea.

He cups her elbow – she shakes it loose.

"I know," he says, almost but not quite a whisper.

"What?"

"I know – I just know."

June reddens, flusters, hands shovelling her hair. She's not wearing a bra and he sees the points of her nipples – wonders if his lips have touched and hands caressed them.

"Is it true – you've been seeing him?"

She nods. Rubs her neck as though the truth were a guillotine and has hurt there.

Suddenly he boils and the swell of anger inside almost comes bubbling over the surface – he wants to hit her, headbutt her, drag her fucking screaming from the house. Almost, but he doesn't. And is repulsed at these notions that race through his mind like a runaway train with a cargo of evil thoughts.

His parents were fucking useless parents, but now he wonders – never hit a woman, his father said, always said, as though he knew there were times in life a man might want to, or a bad woman might want him to, to suit her own purposes.

His eyes fill with hot tears. Tears that sting, tears you know come from the heart. He blinks and dabs the backs of his hands to his eyes. There's that lump in his throat again and that goddamn awful shake in his hands.

The boys are sitting quietly watching *Tom and Jerry* on TV – each telling the other to sh – ush. He whispers, "Later... we need to talk later."

"Yeah, yes, later."

He senses neither remorse nor relief in her tone, just diffidence. She probably knows as Harry knows that he won't be emerging from the sitting-room unless it's to kiss the kids goodnight and take a leak. Anger, frustration and wounded feelings find room for a little fear, too – fear of losing June, losing the right to oversee his kids growing up. He knows he won't leave the house, which is the reaction she might hope for – but he won't because he has done nothing wrong. Nothing. Still – it's just short of criminal to stay in a house with kids and have an atmosphere squeezed between walls and under the roof – have them listening to shitty rows and trying to understand the reasons for the long, cold and poxy silences between Mum and Dad.

It's late. The house is quiet and in darkness except for the landing light. The temptation to leave and move into billets is a live idea – but he can't walk out on Derek and Tony – or is he just using them as an excuse to stay? No, no excuse. He could, of course, be magnanimous – is that the word? – and forgive her – if she wants forgiveness. But that's the rub, the real spit and shine of his hurt – she doesn't want to be forgiven. A trust is broken, his feelings walked on, and he'd better face it, because truth has come barnstorming from her comer and hit him a haymaker. She doesn't love him.

What has he done to deserve this?

It's been coming – come on – think – you haven't been getting on for a couple of years – constantly bickering, her heart cooling towards you for no particular reason other than discontent with her lot and over-familiarity and you're amazed that something like this has happened! Wakey, fucking wakey.

Be calm. Remain calm. And yet, in all this, she says that she doesn't want him travelling abroad for eight days. A ray of hope? Does he want it to be? How will he feel this time next week, next year, when the truth has lived with him awhile?

He smokes a cigarette, drains half a sherry bottle because there's nothing else to drain, and pops a sleeping pill. Wonders if there's any other booze in the house. Once, he found a can of Guinness in the kitchen, hidden in the shoe- polish box – one of the kids must have hidden it there during that hiding food phase – like they hid chips and sweets in places and then forgot all about them. The fear of famine is branded on the Irish psyche, June used to say.

He drank half, didn't enjoy it – Sammy lapped up his and looked like he would have enjoyed the other half.

He wakes before eight with a muzzy head and draws himself from the sofa. His stomach is upset and a headache is beginning to throb. He enters the kitchen, reaches for the phone and calls in sick.

Harry leans with his back against the laminated counter and waits for the jug-kettle to boil. The kitchen has three walls done with green maple units and off-white lino patterned with squares bordered by inshore green. A large PVC window faces south and the small back garden. It's the darkest morning of the year. Night-time sleeping on. Barney stirs outside, causing the security sensor light to flicker on and off. In the pale light he sees the winter bones of a pair of apple-blossoms June planted when they moved here about four years ago – she wanted a hammock she said, when they'd be big enough – something to laze on in the summer sun. She never got the hammock, and the trees – one grew strong while the other was a weaker version – like partners in a marriage? June – with her it doesn't matter what he thinks, and hasn't for a long time. Harry makes his coffee strong and sits by the cold ashes of last night's fire – the oil-burner kicks in and he hears June's first stirrings, her feet landing on the floor.

When she's in the room, in that navy dressinggown that's as old as their marriage, she says nothing.

"Why?" he says.

She shrugs, her back to him.

"He's a worthless scumbag with dirty habits."

"He's dying."

"So, he gets sympathy rides because of that, does he?"

She faces him.

"How do you expect me to feel?" he asks.

"It wasn't planned. We've always been friends — I knew him before I knew you."

"What do you want from me?"

"Nothing — I don't care whether you go or stay."

He lets that sink in. Doesn't care.

"I thought we had a future together — I thought we — for fuck's sake, I went and had a vasectomy, June."

"That was your decision — besides, I thought when Karl... " She can't bring herself to say it — dies.

"What June? We'd live here in a loveless marriage and rear the kids and — "

"Something like that."

"We're a tough deal for — "

"Kids are strong — they're tough. They don't need you as much as you like to think."

"I'm staying here — for their sake — but I might also go because of them, for them."

"It's over between us — there's nothing... " she says.

"Did I do something specific or was it just general things?"

"You're just you — that's all — just you — I just. . ."

He raises a hand to signal he has heard enough. Staring into the fireplace he thinks how her love for him is colder than ash. You'd think that building a home, having two children would count for something, create a bond between two people, but the links have broken on the chain. Chain — isn't that it, how June sees it? Love sneaks up on you and chains you to someone and later on you find out there isn't such a thing as real love. Real lasting love for that person.

He doesn't feel anger or frustration – just an incredible sense of loss and sheer disappointment. Forced down a road he doesn't want to take. Forced now into asking that all important question, the one that'll sink the ship entirely and take the lifeboats with it.

"Do you love him?"

She utters without hesitation, "Yes, I think so."

"It's easy to love a dying man."

"It's easy when you realise that he's all you ever wanted in the first place – when the choice is there and in a few months won't be. Yeah, Harry, it is."

He nods. Rubs the stubble on his face, "I'm going to Al's for this book launch -

I'm telling you this so that you don't think I've gone and done away with myself, or that I've left the house for good."

"Harry... "

"What?"

"I am sorry – sorry, I'm just sorry."

"You'll get over it – I'm away for two days now and next week I'll be gone for eight. You'll get help I'm sure in getting over your being fucking sorry."

In the bathroom, under lock and key, his eyes bleed tears.

Al's aged a lot since the accident – his pronounced limp and the scar above his left eyebrow, its tail leaving a white niche in the brow itself, shows some of the physical toll.

"Ivan's poems are shite," he whispers to Harry in the Railway Hotel's crowded lounge. He goes on, "No publisher will touch them so he has to fork out the money himself – we've got shelves of his last two books in the flat. I ask you – he gives the fucking things away to customers as spot prizes."

"Still, I bet you tell them he's great."

"Of course – I'd die sooner than tell him the truth."

"I'll buy two."

"Good. He'll be delighted."

A ripple of applause erupts as Ivan takes to the podium. He's heavy-set with a goatee beard and wears a smile like he's used to smiling and not like some people who have to crank their faces to start a smile.

Later in the flat above the restaurant Ivan is still on the town with his literati friends.

Al makes cappuccinos and puts a box of After Eight mints on the glass-topped coffee table.

"What train are you taking back down tomorrow?"

"Ten."

"A flying visit, eh?"

"Yeah, yeah, it is, Al – can't be helped – I just can't fucking settle in myself."

He fills him in on his upcoming trip to Lebanon, steering clear of the last, even when Al presses him on it. Asking about the explosion – the one June said he had nightmares over.

"June – you were talking to her?"

"Aha. About, let me see, three weeks ago.""Did she say anything else?"

"No. Should she have?"

He winces, "I think we're fucked. Really fucked this time..." Al listens, taking all in as though his brother's words are rare jewels.

"Jesus – if Ivan cheated on me – I'd think I'd kill him."
"So – on the train down I made up my mind to get out."
"Leave her the house, the kids – first day out she'll have the locks changed."

Harry shakes his head, "I don't fucking care."

"Derek and Tony?"

"I'll keep seeing them, of course. They're my kids."

"I wouldn't fucking leave, no way – I'd stay put, move into the boxroom... "

"Only three bedrooms."

"The sitting-room then – turn it into a bedroom – you stay where you are, and you tell her you're staying and if she doesn't like –"

"I don't – "

"The kids. Don't fight in front of them. It takes two to fight... don't go, Harry."

He nods, sips at his beverage and turns the conversation to their parents. Al's not stupid but doesn't re-route the topic, yet. He says they should make peace with the old couple. The old man's on the way out. And just as Harry thinks he has gotten away, Al sticks him again, "What happened in the Leb?"

"That, you don't want to hear."

Harry holds up a hand and says, when Al looks like he's about to become persistent,"Some other time."

"You go and get help."

Those two words *Get Help* – how he fucking hates to hear them. Harry says nothing, just nods, pinches an After Eight between thumb and forefinger and says, "Now stop playing Mother Queer and get me a brandy – your good stuff, make sure."

"Only the best."

In Al's absence Harry closes his eyes – so fucking tired, so fucking soul-weary.

No matter what he decides to do he is aware that his actions will be those of a jaded man. And actions by jaded men usually result in things backfiring. Big time.

Chapter 15

Lines of thought going nowhere as he hops into a window seat. Al's final words of advice ringing in his ears — don't do anything rash; sit back and think. Think. Al doesn't know that he would like to stop thinking and have a blank mind, a clear screen, just for five minutes. Lines of thought in all the more of a rush as the train gathers speed and the window fills with Mayo landscape ... *fading to Irishbatt HQ near Tibnin and its crusader castle, Norbatt's HQ near Ebel el Saqi, FIJIBATT HQ in Qana, NEPBATT's HQ perched off the road near no village, and Ghanbatt's HQ in Kafr Dunin... other places... Madjil Silm, Al Sultaniyah, Haris, Haddatha, Saff al Havua — a flood of names — each branded on his mind with certain images.*

Srifa and the tattered olive uniforms of Israeli soldiers strung by a bomb blast onto the electricity pylons, blowing in the wind, ghostly rags that snap. There for years, the locals say, from the time a roadside bomb was detonated. Tibnin and the Lebanese guy who speaks with a Chicago drawl and says he will stop the locals from firing their weapons over the UN camps. And does. Amazing the power that one individual can wield. Ebel el Saqi, visiting the home of an eejit who collects dud shells (shells fired but which don't explode on impact) from the Norwegian firing range, and is injured as he tries to get at the explosive devices inside. Blinding himself and killing his son — his family looking for compensation — overlooking the fact that he had collected the duds from a hillside that runs at a steep angle from the Hasbani river, which even mountain goats have the sense to avoid. Qana and the camp that runs with the blood of 105 women and children who seek refuge in the UN camp, unaware that Israeli cannons are intent on searching them out. Troops and farmers find bits of bodies in trees and nearby fields for weeks afterwards. Harry had seen the photographs taken by the investigators but the ones snapped by soldiers were more graphic in that they were taken immediately after the shelling had stopped and the wounded evacuated — horrible photos — nightmares in albums. NEPBATT and Camp Trishul — skip and come back to it. Kafr Dunin and the Ghanaian major who died from a witchdoctor's curse (heart attack) — a young lance corporal with strange facial tribal markings who steps forward to claim responsibility and is promoted a month later to cast a witchdoctor's spell on the Irish team playing the Ghanaians in the UNIFIL Soccer Final — doesn't work — the Irish winning by a penalty goal.

Madjal Silm and the investigation of a UNIFIL SISU APC that collides with a cyclist, leaving the young boy in a critical condition — a key witness Harry discredits because he can't possibly have seen what he claims to have seen from his turret position in the APC. Other places... leave them, just fucking leave them. Think of Israel, a massage in the steam room in Canada House in Metulla, drinking Maccabi beer with Israeli soldiers he works with on the border, visiting the Biblical city of Dan and Tiberias where he meets an Israeli woman who asks if he is circumcised, and he looking at her, smiling, shaking his head. The smile diminishing when she says that's a pity — she only does it with circumcised men. She is beautiful, a little broad at the shoulders but she has terrific legs. And her voice, its Slavic cadences tingle the hairs on the back of his neck. Yeah, he could have been unfaithful if he had been circumcised. Typical of his fucking luck. Eating falafels, pitta bread sandwiches, on the street, wishing the hood would fall off his mickey. Thinking of something one woman had said at the Curragh races — a soldier's mickey is like a compass — always has to be pointing. The Israeli woman, Pam, says he looks like a lion, her favourite animal — he thinks courageous and then thinks of the cowardly lion in the Wizard of Oz. He feels like begging her to change her mind about having sex but doesn't. She's the sort who knows what she wants. A paddy mickey isn't for her. He blames his mother — she says she prays for her boys never to let down the Catholic faith — Jesus, Mary and Joseph, he can only laugh. Proves that in spite of their differences, his lengthy absence from her home, that Mum is praying away.

Always Kafra.

Welcome.

Stench of blood and the scent of roses don't go together, except in his dreams. A hand like the hand in The Adams Family inching towards him, black hairs like cat hairs on its back — a screaming hand fleeing from a faint miaow — his dreams go crazy now and then. Sees Basima dancing with Damar — the music stopping — he can never remember the music, something by Strauss he is sure, though that sort of stuff he only hears by accident and not design — and the pair falling to the ground when their legs disappear. Bloodless dreams, happy dreams all occurring in the same little square, and dreams so full of blood he wakes trying to wash it off.

His father would say he's losing his cards.

Drops of gloss-red blood on spina Christi, thorns of Christ, falling tip, tap on to bones bleached white by an arid heat.

Dad. A slight, bespectacled man with frowning features, as if life had given him too much to do and he feared he would not live long enough to complete his tasks. What is he at in Lebanon? Holding a black sack? Shooing at cats? Fucking eejit.

Fucked-up dreams. Fucked-up life.

A loud intercom voice breaks up his thoughts, "Portlaoise next stop... Portlaoise next stop."

He rubs his eyes and looks up and down the carriage as the train departs — not many people aboard — coming from Kildare the train had been packed, standing room only, and he had been squeezed against a middle-aged woman with BO as bad as he had ever smelt. He gets to his feet and makes for the service counter to grab a coffee.

Taking the polystyrene carton with its sliver of a spoon to his seat he studies the green fields, coming round to thinking that Al is right – don't act rashly, stay at home – sort out something, give things time, climb the hill then look down and decide.

June is quiet when she collects him. Wears Estée Lauder perfume – White Linen – that he got her last Christmas. Derek and Tony – their eyes are hungry on the plastic bag he holds.

"Wrestlers, boys – who likes wrestlers?"

"Me do," Tony.

"Me, too," Derek.

He hands The Undertaker to Derek and another to Tony. Figures they'll thump about in the miniature black ring Harry bought second-hand in the parish jumble sale.

"Thanks, Da." Derek.

"Ta, Daddy." Tony.

"Nothing for Mammy," Derek says.

"I have, of course... "

"What is it?"

"A surprise."

"Okay."

Harry takes June in. She knows his eyes are on her but ignores him, her eyes tightening on the windscreen, her lips coming together so that he can't see the normal view of her ivory teeth.

At home she drinks lots of water as if in an attempt to wash herself from the inside out. The chip-pan is on and so far, in the half-hour he's been home, she hasn't said a word to him.

He tells her his plans, and she nods, then says he's not to go near Karl. It's breathed like a demand and not a request.

"I think what I do, who I see has no longer got anything to do with you."

"He's dying."

"A week ago I might have cared, but hey, you know, since I heard about your shenanigans, I really don't give a fuck."

"You're – "

"And something else – "

"What?"

"When he's dead I'll still be here – and probably will be for a long time. Think on that the next time you're with him."

June stiffens and rakes her hair. For moments he thinks she's going to scream but she doesn't. Instead she points her forefinger, the one she can't straighten because of an accident with a slamming door on her thirteenth birthday, and says, "Back off, I'm warning you – go your way, do what you like, who you like, but don't torment me. If it wasn't for the kids I would be long gone – and it doesn't matter to me how long you live or how long you don't."

"I know that," he says, turning from her so as not to show her his hurt. Through the kitchen window he sees Barney rubbing his back against the ladder on the kids' slide.

Need to bring him to the vet – he gets ticks from rolling in the grass.

"Okay," he says, "I get the picture."

She doesn't respond.

He slips on his green waxed jacket and feels for the hood in the side-pocket – there's nothing so bad as being caught out in the rain when walking the Curragh Plains – the wind seeps through your clothes and into your bones, and the little heat in you leaks through your eyes. Barney knows the walk is on before Harry even takes his Wellingtons from the burner shed. He paws the garden door, tongue hanging out like a pink car flag, tail wagging, "Hold on. Take your time. Hold will you till I fit your lead." Once he had allowed Barney out without a lead and he ran straight for the road, earning himself a belt on the head from a passing car, leaving him dazed and wobbly on his paws, like a drunk.

On the plains he lets Barney run free. It's cold, an easterly bone-shaver blowing in from the rugged Wicklow mountains that are partially obscured by cloud. He keeps his back to the wind and presses west, towards a long rise that holds the all-weather gallops and a view of the plains sweeping to their hedgerowed borders. The clouds are racing.

His blue beret hangs from a nail next to his bedside locker. He has few possessions.

A Sony radio, some cheap perfume, a few packets of green plastic soldiers of the sort you buy at home, cheap, made in Hong Kong or Taiwan, someplace like that. Things he bought for his son. The officer motions a soldier to pack away the dead soldier's belongings into a new suitcase, one he had bought in bulk for all NEPBATT personnel just a week ago. Harry thinks how peculiar it will be to enter the Rubb Hall for a rotation baggage search and to find 350 pieces of like luggage all holding like packets of cheap cigarettes. He hasn't seen it happen before — but what he hears is that the uniformity is in complete contrast to other contingents' searches — wholly orderly, professional.

The tie-strings hang loosely from the back of the soldier's blue beret. Ends frayed like laces go when they lose their plastic binds. The cap badge is missing. A new cap he never wore. Soon to change, as it will lie on his UN flag-draped coffin a few days from now.

In Tyre, in the early hours, after the few beers and kava, Harry peels open the velcro-bound camouflage wallet. The colour photograph in the plastic inlay is of a smiling four-year-old boy, a stout woman with a pretty face and Damar with a bad haircut.

The plastic is broken and there are cracks in the photograph — you would know it is something Damar often took out to look at.

His blue UN ID Card is in the wallet's outer pocket — looks nothing like he looks in the family photo, looks unhappy in this, on his own — three crumpled dollar bills, money to last him until the final pay day before flying home. A pocket knife, a pack of LM cigarettes, slightly crushed, a lighter with a skim of fuel, a silver ring taken from his right hand by Sam before he deposited the severed limb in Musa's black bag.

Shiny dog-tags on a long chain that would have touched his flesh, felt the beat of his heart. Not much to leave behind, and yet so much.

Harry feeds them into the small cloth bag and swings it on to the nearest chair.

A week's leave — heading for Israel, leaving Lebanon and fucking Kafra behind.

Breaking across Roshaniqra Border at first light and eatingbreakfast in the Lite Bite Cafe above the cliffs and the cable cars, looking at the sea through the panoramic windows over coffee and croissants — a grey Israeli patrol vessel heading towards its port in Haifa, the long straggly beach that leads to Nahariya, a German- built town he thinks about spending his week in — maybe he'll hire a car, take in Jerusalem and Bethlehem. His mother had dropped him a few lines asking him to light a candle in Bethlehem for his dad.

On the road to Nahariya he flags a taxi — twenty-three shekels to town — Peters and Lee are playing on the radio — Peters was blind. Wasn't he? His mother played their songs all the time — theirs and Cliff Richard's.

He books into the Mount Ema hotel on Jabotinsky Street. It's run by Mickey who leaves fresh bread over to the MP detachment in exchange for tinned UN rations.

Cuts him a good deal for the week's stay. Shows him to his room on the ground floor. Comfortable if a little basic — TV and radio, double bed, wine-Coloured carpet, tan curtains with deep pleats. Orange trees out front.

He runs the bath, runs it deep, and slips into the hot water, sinking to the neck, feeling the tension-knots unwind a little. Closes his eyes and sighs. Doesn't know it but that balmy night is the night his nightmares begin.

The Curragh wind meets him full in the face as he emerges from a trail between the gorse. Ignores the wet arse he'll get and sits on the embankment of a rath and takes in the traffic heading towards Kildare. Smells the pine smell of the furze and hears Sammy's panting as he chases rabbits through the furze – it's the thrill of the chase he loves, nothing else – he'll get a start at the first sight of his shadow.

Lights up his Zippo and stares at the inch flame for moments before setting it to the thin cigar between his lips.

June – she's let him down badly – and yet she doesn't seem to realise that she has – what is it with her? She has to be mad at him in order to live with her guilt? Is that it? Or does she think she has to find so many faults with him, so many that, well, who could blame her for having an affair?

Karl, how long away from his deathbed? He's drowning, grasping at another man's wife for his last comforts. Childhood friends? She always wanted him but didn't know? Fuck that for a load of oul shite – he was away for six months; she got lonely and horny. Like he got lonely and horny, except his opportunity was blown out the window because the lady likes circumcised flutes. Like winning the Lotto only to discover that the winning numbers are on an outdated ticket.

Murder a drink. Murder for one. Has a tenner in his pocket. Enough. Breathes in cigar smoke – a soothing fog caressing the land of his troubled mind. Okay. Relax. June? Stay in your bomb-shelter and hang tight, forget about running away.

As for the nightmares – deal with it when you return from the Leb – go and confront the ghosts, see then, see – how many ghosts in an old haunt?

At the end of the cigar he flicks it to the ground beside a broken thistle and digs his heel into it as he stands. Calls Barney, claps his hands, and walks on a bit – Barney will come running after him, nothing surer. His mind is a little clearer, a little more organised – leave Barney home, head for a few scoops in The Rising Sun, pop a sleeping pill tonight and gain some respite from the dreams, keep the tide of them at bay for a night. Numb his pain. With luck.

Chapter 16

This time June doesn't drive him at dawn to the barracks. Instead, he waits in the kitchen, in his light green uniform and combat boots, for the doorbell to sound. His blue UN beret rests on the table; his military bag is in the hallway. Harry sips at his coffee and glances at his watch. His lift is five minutes late. June doesn't want a fuss with the kids so she brings them with her to Newbridge. She says nothing when she's leaving, not even when she returns moments later to collect her handbag – her eyes not answering the questions in his – just going, slamming the door in her wake, a fall of words from her lips, words he can't hear because of the window, but which are nevertheless distinguishable.

She's fucking him in and out of the ground. Her hatred for him is intense – what happened to her diffidence? Diffidence is better – you can live with diffidence.

Toot of horn. He gets to his feet, grips his bag, briefcase and cap and looks about the kitchen – taking a long look, like it's a face he loves but will not see again.

An early December misty rain shrouds the plains where a pair of red-blanketed horses make for the gallops, their riders' chins tucked into their chests, sure sign that they're feeling the cold, the wet chill in their very marrow being dried by a slight, almost imperceptible breeze. The horses' chestnut heads and neck columns are slicked greasy, ears lying flat to show they prefer the heat of hay in their stables than this battle with the elements. In the distance, in Camp, he sees a

Land-Rover turn a corner and ascend Lord Edward Hill. A plume of diesel smoke in its wake — not many Land- Rovers in service now, most replaced by the sleeker Nissan Patrols.

"All set?" Sarah says when he's in the car.

She looks beyond his chest to see who is waving him goodbye. Pulls a surprised face when she sees the closed door. Looks about and nods — his car is missing.

"That bad?"

"Yeah, worse than bad."

"Sorry."

She edges away from the kerb, doing a U-tum, heading for Kildare and the M50.

The Section's Astra is noisy, something rattling in its engine. Keeps going — the army is good at that, keeping things going, giving the taxpayer good value. Sarah asks about the boys and he tells her that Derek had the sense to know Daddy was heading away somewhere and to ask for something back, while Tony was content with biting on the blue beret and toying with its cap badge.

"It's over," he says, "between us — there's no way back — I see that now."

Funny, how it's sometimes easier to admit a truth to someone else before you admit it to yourself. Really admit it to yourself.

"Yeah, join the gang — Pete is gone back to his mother — just came in and said he was going."

"You've no kids, Sarah. So... "

"Yes, I suppose — still it hurts, you know — guess what he left me, Harry, as a going-away present?"

"I couldn't."

"Go on."

"Sarah... " He's not in the humour.

"Take a wild guess."

"A vibrator fitted with razor blades."

Her lips turn down, "You're disgusting, Harry — a pair of oven gloves."

"Yeah, and... "

"You know what he's driving at, don't you?"

"Keeping your nails covered. What else?"

"Actually, I thought he was telling me to practise my culinary skills."

"Oops."

"Actually, you're right – it's as you say – to keep my talons covered."

A lapse into silence then, as the cab warms and Sarah tunes in the radio to Gerry Ryan. He thinks of his parents – their surprise when he called around to see them yesterday, looking at him as though he was the Second Coming.

He had parked for a while outside the alders that hadn't been trimmed since he was a boy. Alders that ran the short width of a site Dad had given to his brother in the States, a site that his uncle will never see, unless the dead, their souls, can dream.

The house he grew up in has changed little – he could still be the little boy in the garden playing Star Wars – he acting Luke Skywalker and Al Darth Vader – Prince their shaggy Kerry blue a four-legged Chewbacca. Just switch back the clock twenty years and he could be in that garden, his father calling them a pair of eejits, his mother on the doorstep, an evening sun spreading red and amber above the Hill of Allen – a spell of time when everything seemed right with the world – not enough spells like them and those they had never lasting long enough.

What is it all about – this fucking life? he asked himself, walking the path.

A grey pebble-dashed bungalow with a crack along its chimney stack. Windows like oversized eyes in a small face. Gleaming. Mum kept her windows clean. The garden wore its winter's cloak of near despair – weeds pushing up between the ochre hexagonal flags, jaded hanging baskets in need of creosoting and repotting, some shrubs eaten to death by sheep which had taken advantage of a gate left open. Beads of sheep-shit and splotches of bird-shit were spots on the tongue of concrete leading to the front door. He knocked and when she answered she squinted against the light – her frailness, even though he expected it, surprised him – the corners of her lips held webs of wrinkles but her eyes, when she opened them fully, twinkled their old familiar blue. Recognising him, taking in his presence, her mouth formed an O and her lower lip gave the slightest of tremors.

He made his peace with them. They politely skirted the issues that had driven them apart – their ostracising of Al and Ivan, their lack of interest in their grandchildren, his father's dismissiveness of his army career and a host of other things – all inconsequential in light of, in Harry's case, what happened in Lebanon and is happening to him now, and his father's lung cancer.

They never mentioned June, or the boys – Mum did, but only after a long while, when she had run out of things to say, and he said, "Fine" and left it that.

A series of yawns preceded Mum's quietly spoken, "Goodnight". She shot Harry a glance to suggest that he stay a few minutes to speak with his Dad. Why not? He has come this far. An hour with the living is better than a sleep and time spent with the dead who refuse to remain dead. Silence. The small living-room smelt of wear and tear and of old food and fresh varnish.

"Never stops going – that woman," Dad said.

Harry took him in – he had always had a broken look about him, without being next or near broken. Now he was – a wreck of a man. Lungs full of phlegm, throat raspy, death chipping at his cheeks, giving him a hollow appearance.

"Will you have a drop?" he said.

"Yeah – I'll get it."

"You won't. Stay where you are."

He moved on painfully thin legs to a tall press and went a few fingers deep with Redbreast whiskey.

"Cheers," he said.

Their glasses met in a brief tinkle.

"Cheers," Harry said.

The old man started then, about the old days, when he was in his health, and how hard he had worked and how far he had walked on his rambling excursions. Paused and then continued. "I always feel the cold. It's in my insides – the chill of the grave. You know what I'm saying?"

"I do."

"Keep an eye on your mother."

"I will."

"Good."

There was no more for him to say and Harry had nothing to add, so they sat in silence in the darkened room and watched the coals dying in the fire.

They leave the roundabout and hit for the airport along the toll road. The skies are dark and full of the threat of rain. Gusts of wind buffet the car.

"He's very quiet in himself."

He is about to say "Who?" when he realises she's talking about Karl.

"Yeah."

"You haven't seen him?"

"No."

"But you will?"

He says, "I don't know... " Before she says anything he adds, "I might."

"Must be hard for you to work with him, knowing... "

"Knowing, yeah – listen, Sarah, you know –"

"Drop it. Right?"

"Yeah, but thanks for the interest."

Her "Okay" is quiet.

Harry senses that Sarah has a store of things that she wants to say – it makes him feel uncomfortable – the last thing she had to say blew June's secret – what other juicy bits might she have?

She drops him off at the passenger terminal, beeps him back when he forgets his beret, smiles and waves as she pulls away.

He smooths his hair. There's no way she is interested in him, other than as a friend.

And he feels the same about her – he is finishing with June only because she is finishing with him. He has no choice. Right now he needs a friend who doesn't want to be anything other than a friend. Besides, what's he got to offer? He's a guy with a drink problem (fighting hard to contain it), a vasectomy, kids, and an assortment of bad dreams – a whole range of problems he'll bring with him into any new relationship.

He meets up with the others in the departure lounge; a couple of high-ranking officers, four or five junior officers, a chaplain, a party of civilians from Finance and a couple of journalists. He knows one of the guys from the An Cosantóir, the army magazine, and has coffee with him, struggling to recall his name. Remembers it then as he chews on a cheese sandwich. The priest he knows too, a thin man with glasses that keep slipping down his short nose and freckles that cloud his high cheekbones. Rocks on his toes when he laughs – tilts his head when he's listening to someone. Like he has to exaggerate his interest in order to prevent the other from realising how utterly boring he finds him and his topic.

Battling the wind to the plane, Harry's breathing accelerates. Flecks of rain push against his face and dampen his hair. The wind is strong against him – the sighing of souls. His fingers clench the beret that he carries in his hand because of the elements and his rising fear. He is among the last to board the *Saint Brigid* airbus – he feels as though he is a little way out from shore and drowning – people on the beach not minding because they don't know. Can't know. Other passengers, destination Rome, begin to board, passing the military party. He feels warm and sticky.

Must look ill because a steward asks, "Are you afraid of flying?"

Shakes his head, No, just afraid of where we're going – I'm a coward – show me a soul who died a violent death and my mind will take him in and keep him alive – I'm a coward because I can't let him go and I can't deal with a situation that other soldiers deal with, which is, in terms of war and of people dying, a small episode. Two people died, not two dozen, and I didn't know them, had never met them. Why – for fuck's sake, why – they should mean nothing to me, and yet somewhere deep down, soul deep, they mean everything – is it because in what happened to them I see a true evil – a brush-stroke of the devil's work? Maybe my problem is that I think too much, too deeply about stuff I can't change?

He watches the ground dropping away, hears the underwheels tuck into the plane's belly, and closes his eyes not to sleep but to shut himself away from the chatter going on about him, He has two seats to himself. It is natural for other soldiers to incline towards avoiding the company of military police – the fact that he is on board means that someone is being investigated for something and it could well be a friend or a relation of theirs. When they speak to him it is as though they are choosing their words from a hand of playing cards. His MP brassard – white lettering on a black background – is like a chemical warning sign you see on the back and sides of trucks.

It is Father Pat McClure who touches his shoulder.

"Here... "

He can't remember Harry's name! Harry smiles. A Matrix medal with pale blue string passing through its eyelet.

"May it keep you safe."

"Thanks."

The priest nods, adjusts his glasses, and disentangles another medal from a fistful of them. "who else?" he murmurs, then cops that someone else.

Harry puts the medal in his black leather wallet. A wallet June bought him for a wedding anniversary when anniversaries mattered. They stopped mattering when?

He sighs — a rut, they fell into a rut — partly caused by money problems and partly caused by — well —, he isn't the best, is he, for being able to talk things out, while June is, or was — was. Definitely was. The wallet retains a slight leathery smell and has in it a photograph of June, Derek and Tony. Snapped last year in Dublin Zoo — you can see a lick of grey-blue like in the background, behind their smiling faces — a cold day in May. Shoulders hunched against the breeze. A lot can happen in a year.

He eats the in-flight meal of steak and watches a little of the movie *The Game* but grows tired of it and turns the dial under his armrest and listens to the ballad instead — lets back his seat and closes his eyes.

Last time in Beirut — landing there, walking a stretch of tarmac to the waiting lines of UN buses. Old Huey Helicopters riddled with bullet holes, the puncture wounds a stark grey against the choppers' green skins. One burned to its frame. Another with its cedar motif scorched and another with wounds to the Lebanese national flag.

All of them pockmarked to some degree. The sun high in the sky, the air shimmering on the runaway — heat haze, heat dance.

The troops bound for home remain penned in a giant hangar. Those that show their faces are tanned and relived-looking.

Cheer.

On the outskirts of Beirut he sees a sprawling refugee village on a hill slope — plastic-sheeted hovels with brown puddles here and there. And caves — people living in caves that are set like dark mouths in grey faces. Night-time draws in. The farther south they travel the emptier the roads. South of Sidon, just beyond the fish market and the crusader sea castle, there's a canvas of darkness — neither a streetlight nor a house light showing. Earlier on, this stretch of road was raked with gunfire from Israeli gunboats in a shoreline battle with Hizbollah guerillas. They meet the first UN CP — Checkpoint One dash Ten — shortly after passing Tyre roundabout and the Leb army barracks. The going is slow along the shell-marked roads. His window is open and he smells the sea, the orange groves, and when the engines are silenced he hears the mowing noise of a pilotless drone in the skies — snapping the landscape for Israeli intelligence.

At Checkpoint 1-25, a well-lit Fijian Post, there's a long wait as the Post Commander awaits clearance from UNIFIL Ops to clear passage through the Israeli-held Charlie Swing Gate — a border crossing that divides free Lebanon from occupied Lebanon. Here, he sees a file of tall spindly pine behind a wire fence — the trees in the middle are rust-coloured, scorched, caused, he overhears someone say, by a bomb blast that killed five Fijians some time back.

"Suicide bomber — fucker," says the voice from behind.

Scorched trees. Scorched earth. Scorched souls.

The voice.

"He got out of the car and argued with the guys on the checkpoint because they wouldn't let him pass to the Swing Gates. Then he gets back into his fucking Mercedes — they all drive fucking Mercedes — they get them from Germany mainly, turns the key and bang it goes — gone like that the lot of them. I was in the mess in Naqoura and dropped my fucking pint with the noise. And I wasn't the only one."

After getting the all-clear they inch towards the Israeli-backed South Lebanese Army — a militia known as the SLA — position. Ahead in the distance he sees the lights of Naqoura and UNIFIL HQ.

It's 120 kilometres from Beirut to Naqoura. And when you cross the border from Lebanon it's like stepping into two different worlds. Israel is cleaner and richer and organised. A space of inches reveals worlds that are poles apart. The same in Beirut itself — along the Corniche, the poor with you for halfway — on the beach, sewage-tainted sea; the very poor living in spaces that are merely dark holes, places they climb out from under at first light and steal back in when the stars are out. And the affluent stretch — awash with swimming pools and lounge areas fenced off from the poor man's eye — so he can't see them and they can't see him — so the guilt can't pinch. Hotels and cafes, and Kentucky Fried Chicken, and pubs and lounges — a stride, one fucking stride and you're in two different worlds — it amazes him — and yet the gulf is wider than just a step or two — wider than an ocean in real terms.

They've passed over Cyprus and are beginning to descend. Turbulence buffets the plane but not much, a gentle rocking. Lebanon comes into view — the sun isn't shining a welcome this time — Beirut is wet, grey and miserable. The pilot is on — wishing them a pleasant time in Lebanon and that he'll see them in eight days' time. Don't go wild.

Harry stares through the oval window, along the wing span, to the disturbed sea and two small twisters that lie offshore like a pair of devil's angels, dancing a crazy waltz. Feels the bounce of the wheels — here, less than two months after leaving the fucking place and he's back again.

Chapter 17

The burnt-out hangars he had seen on his last visit have been levelled and done away with. The few Huey choppers wear new motifs and olive-green skins – the Lebanese know all there is about starting over. Harry thinks a little ironically that they could teach him a thing or two.

The Liaison Officer from Irishbatt, Captain Boran, says that the original plan for the party to take a UN heliflight service to Tibnin has been cancelled because of inclement weather and a bus has been organised instead.

A wet, greasy and cold Beirut is something Harry hasn't seen or felt before. So cold that he zips up his parka as they head to the revving coaster. He shakes hands with the LO who stands by the door, checking people in, who says that Harry'll be staying with the MPs in Irishbatt and that those other individuals, Smart and Williams, will be reporting to him tomorrow for interview – he can then rejoin the visiting party and their itinerary or relax – but be in Camp Tara at 11:00 hrs sharp on Wednesday week for the return journey by heli to Beirut. "Okay? Understand?"

Harry nods. Breezes into the bus – understand? Does he think he's a fucking eejit?

Heading towards the back he finds a single seat by a misted window. Wipes a patch so he can see out. Beirut.

Lifoh books him on a heliflight and sees him off from the helipad at noon. Going on detachment to Beirut, replacing an

Italian MP who is travelling home on leave. Hates fucking helicopters — simply hates them — for no reason he can fathom. The whole machine vibrates as it passes low over the sea, hugging the coastline. Calm. Keep calm, natural-born coward. The sea is a variation of blues and greens and in places the deep coffee colour of shit. In a short distance from the coastline there's tobacco crops and orange groves and farther inland scrubby hills and wadis that are criss-crossed with trails.

The other day on speed-checks a flock of goats came off a hillside track and passed the jeep, except for one that stopped to give birth to a kid on the verge, near the front wheel. It happened quickly, with no great fuss. Born in the dust with the flock's bell ringing above the soft shush to shore of the waves, within sight of the Moorish keep, born for the market place, the oven and the plate — marked to die — the way humans are. Life before Kafra — a shell — then what? What is after Kafra for Basima and Damar? What is after Kafra for him?

Tyre looms to the right. He sees the ancient mosaic avenue and its flanks of Cipollino columns reaching to the sea. The area here is a sprawling metropolis of old civilisations — their skeletal remains awaiting more probing, more digs. Peacetime digs and not clandestine efforts carried out by thieves during the war, selling off a nation's heritage on the black market — Harry saw it with his own eyes, Roman artifacts offered for sale to a Norwegian MP — the bust of a Roman general wearing his helmet, exquisite craftsmanship — going for 5,000 dollars. A song. Septimus Severus must be turning in his grave.

The drug-dog Heppy is barking like crazy in its box. Od, the Norwegian dog-handler, is trying to quieten him. The co-pilot firing a look to show that his nerves are at him — shut the dog up. Please, fucking, please.

In UNIFIL House at Bir Hassan, Beirut, he wonders how the hell he is going to manage a Chevrolet Caprice through this cosmopolitan maze — roads up, leading nowhere, new roads, old roads, bombed roads — avoid this Hizbollah street, avoid here, don't go down there. All around — a chaos of beeping horns and drivers jockeying for position. Fucking crazy. Adam, the Polish guy, who'd flown with him, arriving in from the balcony through the patio doors, shrugging his shoulders, and raising his eyebrows, saying, "Jesus". The exact same word Harry used when he had come in from the balcony. It takes a week and a half to learn the basic routes. Then, one Sunday they get brave and head for the mountains, passing Chateau Bernini and the Bekaa valley, leaving the plains behind, and crawling into Baalbeck and its acres of Roman ruins.

The admission fee is 2000 Lebanese pounds for natives and 4000 for foreigners.

Harry wonders why that should be but doesn't query it — the ruins too alluring to quibble.

The Six Columns of Jupiter stand thick of girth and tall of stature and have a picture-postcard backdrop of snow-speckled Mount Lebanon — sun and snow, each living with the other.

When they're leaving, Adam draws Harry's attention to a child's shoe tied to a sand lorry's front bumper. These lorries carry colourful plumes on their high bonnets and most have the child's shoe. Adam asks why and Harry says it's a lucky charm, that the driver may never hit a child.

He sleeps a little, not wakening until outside the oil refinery at Sidon. They're approaching Monkey Junction where a guy keeps monkeys in a large cage — he wonders if they're being sold as pets or as a food delicacy. He fingers the sleep-crust from his eyes and massages his temples. Feels dirty, needs a shave. Dirt streaks the window he stares through. It's raining. The narrow road is wet and covered with a fine layer of red mud, the reason behind some of the accidents they come across.

The Lebanese drive too fast — indicators are ornaments — in his time in Beirut he came across one set of traffic lights and no one heeded the red light unless there was a cop present under his mushroom shelter.

He sits alone on a low parapet. His eyes turned to the sea. Close to him is a bush with pink flowers and a small shrub with red plumage. The evening sun is setting, a burning orange globe on the nib of the horizon. He had just been to the phone booth outside the Observer Lines, using the last units of his Israeli Bezek card to speak with Emma who said June had gone out — keep fit, she thought. He felt like asking if she were training for the Olympics but there wasn't any point in being sarcastic with Emma. Why is June out every time he rings — why isn't she writing?

He's called on the Motorola. When he reports to the Duty Room which is situated at the gates of the MP Camp he is introduced to the Ghanaian driver who, earlier that day, had knocked down a small boy in Mingi street, a one-sided street meandering snakelike, fracturing in three places: at its northern tail beyond the French Wadi-Gate, where the road slims to meet a tight bend before the Port; midway when the road shoots up a long and winding way to the hilltop village of Naqoura; at its southern outreaches where the bulk of the corrugated shops squat, leaving behind the disused whorehouse and a dump smoking its own filth. Mingi — a cheap present of dubious quality and a mingi man is a seller of such wares — Harry knows a few — Khalil Abbas the old man who sells electrical goods, Jesse the Commando who deals in liquor sales, Ata the hairstylist who wears short claret shorts and string vests, Sammy the Coffee Man and his roadside van cafe, Chicken George, one-armed Monsour the tailor, Pablo, Ali Strawballs, Tom Cruise — he knows them all, but had only struck up an affinity with two — Khalil and Pablo — both of whom know whatever there is to know on the street. Khalil had pointed him in the direction of the Thief from Beit Leif when UNIFIL stores were being raided at nights, a tip-off that led to his being apprehended along with three others in the Polish Transport yard. "Sit down," Harry says in the Traffic Office.

It's a balmy night with the mosquitos biting early.

Lifoh drops in, smiles and calls the other Ghanaian "my brother". The tall, thin Ghanaian gives his name as Patrick Dunne. Harry blinks, takes in the wiry ginger hair and the ID Card he produces.

"A real Irish name that, eh?"

"My father is a real Irishman."

"Oh."

Lifoh asks for his Driver's Permit and looks it over when it's produced.

Harry drops his pen and says, "Do you want to deal with this?"

"No dealing. The child is alive and this man, my brother, is lucky, so lucky."

The relaxed look on the Irish Ghanaian's face gets lost. Guilt swarms into his eyes.

Is the permit legit?

Lifoh, standing behind Dunne, rests his large hand on the man's shoulder, "You drove a truck?"

No reply.

"And your permit does not entitle you to drive a UN truck. Isn't that correct?"

"Yes, sah."

"Why were you driving the truck?"

"Captain Osufu told me, sah."

Lifoh nods and sighs. Harry knows the score. The officer wasn't aware that Dunne wasn't qualified to drive the truck and Dunne didn't tell him because he feared being charged with disobedience. The Nepalese have much the same discipline — driving and dropping a hand from the wheel to give a proper military salute — okay on the flat, maybe, but not while descending a steep wadi road.

Accidents Traffic — mostly routine work — administrative

duties — produce the Arabic card that tells the Lebanese driver to report to UNIFIL's insurance agent in Tyre on Saturday mornings, while the MPs deal with the UNIFIL driver and the investigation. You see accidents and extensive damage done to cars and you wonder how no one was killed in them; you see other cars with mere scratch marks and slight dents and you wonder how people had died in them. Yet it happens.

After Harry records the statement and sees Dunne off, who is relieved because he expected to be arrested, he finds Lifoh studying him.

"I heard about Kafra."

"Yes."

The room is too small to hide from Lifoh's searching brown eyes.

"Dobbs says you cry out at nights."

"Dobbs says a lot about lots, L -"

A wave of a stubby finger, like a magician's wand, "You can't live in the past, Harry. Always remember that. It isn't possible. Remember. "

Harry's fingers shake a little on his cigarette pack. He lights up, his free hand smoothing his hair. How can he stop himself from having dreams? They're not fucking movies he chooses to watch — he can't turn them off or walk away. "A long time ago, Harry, I picked up pieces of human body too."

Harry loosens a jet of smoke, waves it from his face, as though the smoke obscures his view of Lifoh.

"It takes a while for your mind to let go — sometimes it needs help."

Harry's lips run dry. Lifoh's fingers are joined in a steeple. He speaks easily of his experiences without actually being forthright about the cause of his dreams, his moods that turned and twisted. He is someone who has exorcised his ghosts by using time, his faith, counselling, and he says he now looks back on the incident with a steady eye.

Not so steady, Harry thinks, because he can't bring himself to speak outright of what he actually did. What was this fucking incident, he probes gently.

Lifoh nods, "Over a bottle of vodka maybe, but not like this."

Harry senses he could share many bottles with Lifoh and still the secret would not spill. He says this.

Lifoh grins, the white of his teeth are as bright as the humming fluorescent tube. He spreads his hands, "You don't play around with ghosts — I mean I am afraid if I think too deeply or talk that I will breathe life into them — I am just glad they are quiet. And they will leave you with that quietness too. I am sure."

"You try to forget it ever happened?"

"No, Harry, you move on — you put distance... "

Harry draws on his cigarette, "I hope I can do that — I fucking hope so."

The bus drives through Qana, taking a right turn outside FIJIBATT HQ. He finds himself wondering if Sam has rotated — probably has — the Fijians do a yearly stint overseas. Sam had said he hoped to spend his second six months in the Sinai — he needed time on an outpost there — time to be with his thoughts — nothing to do except radio in a passing camel, whenever.

They reach Irishbatt just after dark. Passing Al Yatun and flowing down the long gradient to the new Camp Shamrock. A long and narrow base with shelters dug into the embankments. He is last down the steps and last to remove his hand luggage from the undercarriage. Last to follow the others into the dining-hall where Boran says supper is laid on. Harry lingers a few moments — wanting to feel the cold because the cold makes him feel alive. There's no rain in the mountains, and there are only a few black powder puffs of clouds on the drift, sometimes veiling the moon's round face.

Some Lebanese stars shine brightly in the ink-dark sky — the full moon lends an eerie pale gold colour to the walls of the crusader castle on the hill in the village. He watches the bus edge uphill and swing into a parking space facing the RAP. Thinks about lighting a fag but decides to eat and enters the mess. Putting one craving ahead of the other and with a bit of luck he might get to sink a couple of beers in the canner before closing time.

He sits at a table on his own, bleakly aware that he is the only Non-Com in the mess — thinks about leaving and is wondering where the other NCOs had got to when Boran tells him they're next door, in the ante-room. He had come over specially to tell him, to remind him of his rank, his place — it's on the tip of his tongue to tell Boran the air isn't great in here anyway, too fucking stale, but he swallows his words. He's too tired to mix it with anyone and where he sits and with whom he sits to have his grub isn't all that important. Not in the big scheme of things — he could have been an officer, too — but having a brain-cell over-qualified him for the job. One of these days his thoughts are going to slide onto his tongue and spitfire from his mouth and he'll be on the mat for insubordination. He loves the army about ninety per cent — but ten per cent is sometimes a lot of shite to contend with — and sometimes he thinks he should go on his ticket and see what life is like in the real world — after all he had never held any other full-time job. Perhaps it might be better for him if he did just that — try a civvy job — see what orders he would have to take there. If there's the same pomp-and- ceremony shit, the rules about officers and men having to drink separately and eat separately. If you want to see a close-up mirror-image of how the classes are segregated then join the army. That's what his oul fella told him — the army typifies it. Most armies do. Not the Israelis though — they're one in the field and one in the mess then they've been fighting wars for the fifty years of their nation's rebirth, and they realise, because their enemies never let them forget, that the plot of earth is the same for all men of all classes.

Harry says he's lost his appetite and that he'll give the MPs a ring and turn in for the night. Boran wears a face that says he doesn't give a fuck where he goes once he goes.

He rings the MPs from the Ops office and gets speaking with a guy called Tony who says he'll collect him in half an hour. They're expecting him and have a room ready. Harry says he'll be in the canner. Then, abruptly, he says "No – I won't – I'll be at the fountain, the memorial fountain – okay?"

Won't drink. Fuck it. Go on. Have one. No! One? No! Throat is dry. Go on? No – no – no.

He sits at the fountain and takes in the names shining gold on the red granite memorial, illuminated by a shaded strip-light. It's bitterly cold, the air whipped up by a breeze that falls down the slopes of Mount Hermon. Goose pimples erupt on Harry's arms and though every few seconds he gets wild shivers he remains seated, the cheeks of his arse wet and numbed – pneumonia might take his mind off things?

Soldiers killed in accidents and from natural causes – KIA, which means *Killed in Action*, which in real terms means they were murdered. That is if you call a spade a spade – 'in action' to Harry means 'in battle, fighting' – some of these guys were simply shot at or blown up. Murdered. Skip the fucking platitudes – murdered – they were fighting no one, had not fired a shot in anger. Killed in Action. Yeah. Right.

Lambs to the Slaughter more like – being a peacekeeper means you can't fire your weapon until you or your comrades are fired upon – and even then you must only use as much force as necessary – *go on sir, Mister Hizbollah. Have the first shot. Go on, I insist. Please do.*

The sad fucking thing is that the Arab resistance fighters here, the terrorists, have international support and recognition for their cause – aren't they trying to drive an invader's force from their homeland – same as the French

Resistance did in World War II? Sure they are. There's something in writing, some UN rule or something – Harry is fucked if he can remember. So what the fuck are we doing here, really doing here? Peacekeeping?

"SLA One – NEPBATT Nil" he sees across the chest of a mingi mans T-shirt. Makes him take it off at gunpoint. When Harry takes his pistol away from his neck there's left the deep O of the muzzle, the watery fear in the other's almond eyes. No one to witness the incident because he and Harry were alone in the back of his van. Harry bums the twenty or so T-shirts in a skip outside the Rubb Hall in Naqoura, waiting for the call of complaint to come from whoever in the AO. But none comes.

Fuck them anyway – it isn't right to make a football score out of someone's death.

A soldier away from home, close to getting back, thoughts on seeing his family. Thoughts blown out of his skull and that bad haircut.

Harry sees the lights of the Cherokee at the automated barrier and gets to his feet.

Yeah, tired, need a good rest. Search for the sleep he is never sure of finding, wait for the dreams to come, lurking like starving wolves in a snowy forest, the hunted a hunter with his camp-fire dying and his rifle empty of bullets.

Chapter 18

The MP's small base is about five minutes' drive from Camp Shamrock. Set off the road, behind locked gates, down a short incline with tight parking space, it comprises two long corrugated buildings that once made up the RAP in the old, now-demolished Camp Shamrock. A shelter belt of spindly pine flanks the wadi side and beyond the trees there's a short range of bee-huts. Both RAP tin roofs leak in places and sometimes cats steal through holes in the floorboards and leave behind a feral smell.

The lads try to patch up things when work is slack and the materials available. The engineers who should be doing the repairs are rebuilding a post that took two direct tank rounds – luckily all the troops were in shelter or else they'd be filling bags with bodies instead of sand.

His room is situated at the back, away from the Duty Room and the Armoury, close to the generator shed. A single bed with iron-grey bed-ends and matching blankets.

Through the window, his view sieved by an external mesh grille, he sees the Irish-manned Hill 880 and in line with it on the hill range, a narrow valley between them, squats Charlie Compound, an SLA post that's often attacked by the Hizbollah.

Sitting on the edge of his bunk he gets ready for bed. Sneaks a look at his wallet photo as he sips from the bottleneck of an Al Maza beer – Derek's ruffled hair and gummy smile and Tony looking hungrily at the ice pop in his brother's hand as his own melts. His heart seems to load with something that's almost too heavy for it to carry. June? Try not to think of her. Try not to miss her. Try.

Tomorrow. See Williams first and then Smart – no big deal – suspects that there'll be no head for the GOC to roll to the media as proof that the army deals seriously with reported acts of sexual assault within its ranks. June? A weak try – what's June doing this very second? Lebanese time is two hours ahead of Irish – is she with *him*?

Will she be there when he arrives home? He should feel angry with her and murderous towards Karl, the bastard. And yet he isn't angry – just hurt, wounded, let down – the notion of them together – doing it – drives him nuts. But compared to the smell and sight of death, of Kafra, what he feels pales into, if not insignificance, then what – a lesser despair?

He doesn't dream of June. In fact, it's a long time since he's dreamt of June. Pleasant or otherwise. A question of degrees – at the moment Kafra is winning the race to do in his head.

Sleep stays in the shadows. His eyeballs ache from the lack of rest. Count sheep.

Fuck counting sheep. Think of... Israel. Yes. Last time in Israel – the last days on leave, when he thought his nightmares were beaten.

The battlemented seafront at Akko, near Napoleons' black cannons, sipping a head of cream from a capuccino, looking across the bay at Haifa and catching the faint smell from the sulpher mine, a smell slightly redolent of CS gas. Pans right and sees a soldier climbing from the back of a minivan. He wears olive green and on his shoulder the antlered deer flash of Israel's Northern Command. An M16 assault rifle keeps slipping from his shoulder and frowns of irritation ripple across his deeply tanned forehead. A black skullcap is clipped to a think thatch of brown hair. He draws a large kitbag from the van and taps on the roof for the driver to take off. Stands there, fidgeting for and surfacing a lone cigarette from his breast pocket. The match he zips to life dies before he lights up and he rolls his eyes to the skies questioningly, as though this minor mishap is the latest in a long day of them. He gathers his bag and rights his rifle and setting his lean face against the hill he advances in a depressed man's shuffle — is he going from war zone to war zone. Same as... ?

Then a blonde pushing thirty bothers him for the time and he loses sight of the soldier.

She has painted lips and a pointy chin and tells him she'll suck him off for ten dollars.

"No money, no mickey," he says.

"You Irish?"

"Yes."

"Always big mickey but no money. Irish no good. No fucky fucky good."

"That's right. No mickey."

She sees a tourist bus pulling in down the road and reaks for the steps. The noise is loud from her high heels. Brown handbag flapping against her hip like a wing.

He is in good form, heading off the back of two solid nights' sleep, coming on stream after he visited Bethlehem and sinking to his knees in the grotto where Jesus was born, fingering the silvery star under the altar indicating the holiest of spots. A tear for no reason falling, then another, and not giving a fuck because he would never again see the Japanese pilgrims who looked at him. Touching the earth where He was born — feeling that something he hadn't felt in Jerusalem or Nazareth — feeling that something strange and mysterious had happened here — or was it just because he felt tired from too many nights spent tossing and turning, too much feeding on Gold Star beer and not proper food, that he felt those feelings, that it was all so very very true? the Birth of a Saviour? Two nights' slep and he believed so.

Now, he is his little old cynical self again. He feels like an old house with glassless windows through which dead eyes stare.

With frustration seeping in he throws his feet to the lino and spends some time reading a year-old *Reader's Digest*. Reads till the sky gradually begins to brighten in the east and begins to show the contours of the Lebanese hills.

He takes a black coffee into the office, ushering Williams ahead of him. He's tall and good-looking, prematurely grey at the temples. Keeps twisting his wedding band like he's trying to stop it from choking his finger.

"You know why you're here?"

He nods. He has a cracked lip that looks sore. Nervous. Hands comforting each other.

Harry leans forward, "Enright's made two statements —you were friends, isn't that so. Intimate friends?"

Mutters, "No... yes, yes we were."

He tells a different tale to Enright's: she had been giving him a blow job when Smart staggered in with his mickey hanging out looking for the same — drunk as Smart was. Williams couldn't match him and he ended up being fucked out of the room by him.

"He's strong, Sarge, very strong — in the head as well as the body. He is."

"He threw you outside?"

Williams gives a semblance of a nod, "He got me in a headlock."

A slow smile plays on Harry's lips, "He had you in a headlock — I thought Enright had."

"It's not funny, Sergeant —not funny — I was hoping to get promoted — now, with this hanging over — "

"But you've another problem, haven't you?"

"I have, Sarge — if the missus gets wind of this I'm fucked — I've three small kids you know. She'll go apeshit... "

A pause.

"Go on."

"Smart doesn't give a fuck – he says he's going to tell the truth – she's a slag and he saw what he saw and he wanted some because he was pissed and didn't know what he was doing – the only loser in this is me."

"Don't whinge – you're not the only loser – your wife is, your kids are. And young Enright too – she has to contend with a prick like Smart mouthing off about her. And don't think your missus won't get to hear about it because she will and what'll you do then, eh? You know the army – the rumours – you can't keep anything a secret."

"I don't know – Lie, I suppose. Pass it off."

"Pass it off – you mean lie through your teeth?"

"Yes."

"That's right. Lie, and carry your lies to the grave – that's your fucking penance – I don't think you'll be able to do it. A good liar, are you?"

A strained silence. Harry intrudes upon by saying, "Think twice in future about parking your mickey in a strange mouth and if you do –"

"I won't. Jesus, I learnt my lesson."

"If you do –"

"I won't –"

"Stop interrupting and listen – if you do, make sure you've locked the fucking door."

When Harry dismisses Williams, he is hesitant about leaving. Stops twice on his way across the floor. Stuttering steps.

"What? Do you want to say anything, add to your statement?"

He turns, dropping his hand from the door's chrome handle.

"Off the record?" Voice weak – under strain.

Harry ponders, sighs, "Okay."

"He's doing drugs, buying hash from Gorky the Hairyman in Haris."

"What's this – you want us to get you some payback? Come on."

"It wouldn't make me feel bad – fucker deserves it."

"Yeah — I suppose he does — I'll pass on the info to the boys here. So tell me — where, when and how?"

Alone in the office Harry leans back in the chair with his hands behind his back.

A yawn escapes him then another. Wants a smoke, needs a drink. Williams is gone, and Smart is sitting outside the office — neither of the former friends exchanging a word, nor looking at each other during the time it takes Williams to walk on by.

Harry waits five then ten minutes before calling for Smart to enter.

He's short and well built. No hair, shaved to the bone, showing up his scalp in a hue of blue. He has green eyes like an itemising crook's. Loose lips that bounce a smile from one comer to the other. Harry susses him — that good at lying he would stay up late just to hear the ones he'd mouth off. Folds his arms and lounges in the chair.

"Sit up straight," Harry says. One sergeant to another — but Harry is in control.

Dirty glare, but complies.

"Have you anything in your mouth other than teeth and your tongue?"

"Chewing-gum," comes out low.

"Get rid of it."

Stares at Harry as he tips the gum on to his palm and puts it into his pocket.

"I wouldn't like your tongue to trip over anything, you understand."

"Don't worry. It won't."

"Won't what?"

"Won't trip, Sergeant."

"Good — you know why you're here, and that I have to caution you. You are not obliged —"

"I'll co-operate. No problem. Take this down."

Harry does.

Two statements — more or less saying the same —

Smart playing it cute – knows that he'll get away lightly. They can't very well screw him and not Williams and Enright – they've all broken military law. What Smart isn't smart enough to know is that if the army doesn't want you and can't get you out at first shove, it'll content itself to turning the screws in your coffin one by one. You're a number in the army, that's all. A red line drawn across your place in the record book, the LA 31, the day you leave. The army's been around for over seventy years – a lot of red lines drawn, and a lot of dead army numbers – the army can wait you out. That's what Smart is, a walking red line. No doubt. He's going to get his ticket over something. Someday. No doubt. He might want it to happen that way and he might not. It doesn't matter. He'll be gone and the army will go on. Business as usual. Every army has its red lines.

Every soldier gets one. Guaranteed like death. Some get it sooner than others – just like death – whether we want it or not.

That's it. Over the next day or two he intends to type up the statements, draft the Final Report and submit the lot on his return to the CO and be done with it. In the afternoon he's heading to Naqoura and will stay with the MPs there until Wednesday.

Things are more comfortable in HQ, more freedom – you can relax in your civvies after three o'clock, go out on Mingi Street and dine or cross the border into Israel and hit the Penguin in Nahariya for a meal and watch the girls go by. Get sloshed on the beach and sleep. In this weather? That's half your fucking problem – you're rooted in the fucking past. This is winter. Lots of rain and thunder and lightning that rips the skies asunder. The waves not lapping but slapping to shore. Beach sleep in winter – joke of a notion.

Drunk on the beach. So warm, lying on a beach towel, the weather beautiful. Night skies with bright stars pinned to them. The sea quiet, the discos silenced, empty buildings shuttered, the last of the dancing crowd moving off, the staff quickly following.

He and his bottle of Gold Star on the beach, hypnotised by the sea's constant drive of skinny dipped surf to shore. So warm. Perspiring heavily, his sweat falling in swollen drops on to the sand and towel. Looks at the cool water — inviting — on his toes, the sand squeezing up between them, the waves like a lover's arms, calling him forward, calling him in. The sea is his lover, naked, raising her knees and drawing them apart. For him. She has long jet-black hair that falls over full and ripe breasts, the vee of dark thatch showing through her fingers as she strokes herself in readiness for him. Low groans. He stops. The sands shifting underneath — he is falling, slipping under, the water smothering him, pouring into his throat, his belly, the air abandoning him in large bubbles — like bubbles he used to make in his Coke when he was a kid, blowing through a straw. They say death by drowning is an easy death — better than being cut up in a car smash, or being blown up by a bomb, better than being shot in the belly and looking at your entrails hanging out, hanging out the way he saw a sheep's hang after being burst by a speeding car. Sinking, floating — they'll find him, perhaps out to sea, his eyes missing, bloated, smiling. Seaweed like a scarf around his neck.

He is knee-high in the water and he sees this, how it would be if he were to walk any farther. He would not see Derek's or Tony's faces again, not know the unconditional love that children give without realising it — June, he would not see her again — it is something, the loss of him, he senses, that she would recover from quite quickly.

Women are strong when it comes to mourning the loss of husbands they don't particularly love. March from fresh graves with tears in their eyes and wearing black, but with a clinical resolve in their hearts to carry on. Tears, a few shed complimentary — he knows women who have done as much. He knows a man who did the same, except he was more ostentatious in his grief, had to be held back from jumping onto his wife's coffin as it sank into the ground — a week later he moved his new girlfriend into the bedspace left by his wife. Sincere souls. And Dobbs, too, cheating on his girlfriend, crying in their billet because he hadn't received a letter from her (she wrote daily, but sometimes the letters arrived three or four together) and then within the hour he was geared up to cross the border, smiling, to meet Agnes, the Filipino, with tits he says that are long enough to swing over her shoulders for him to suck on from behind.

He takes a few steps backwards and turns. Dries off and dresses. Sees a hypodermic needle near his feet, its tip bent by a considerate druggie. The sea is calling him.

He daren't look. Unsteady on his feet he starts for his hotel, and a short time later, in Mickey's. He isn't as much trying to sleep as he is trying to hide himself from the sea and its call.

Harry gets into the back of the MP Chevrolet. A damp, grey morning, with low clouds. Naqoura's about 36 kilometres from Tibnin, nestled by the sea. Harry feels a certain edginess this morning. Kafra lies along the route, a drive of a few hundred feet off the road to that fucking square. He says nothing. The pair up front he hardly knows, guys from Cork, going to MP Coy to deliver a report and collect another.

Passing through Al Yatun and Haris, Harry admires the fine palatial houses that somehow for some reason never get bombed. He hears that the owners pay the SLA not to shell them. Doesn't surprise him.

Kafra – almost there, at Checkpoint 5 dash 13.

"Lads – any chance of dropping into Kafra – if you've time?"

The guys look at each other, one taking it upon himself to say they've time when the other doesn't respond.

Harry swallows air when the road to Kafra is engaged. All the Nepalese soldiers snapping to attention, the NCO in charge shouting, "*Ram Ram,*" in greeting.

Kafra. A man on a donkey with creels of potatoes, the road bumpy – jutting stones and tyreprints in places where there isn't asphalt. The mast on the UN post is new, its flag lying flaccid. One of the MPs, Pat he thinks, asks why he wants to visit this arsehole of a place.

"I know the Mucktar."

Knows ghosts here, too, but of course, he doesn't breathe a word of that. Nor mentions that at night he spends his time running away from Kafra.

Chapter 19

The village is like something thrown as waste onto the hill, falling wantonly – thick walled houses leaning together for support, like a family clinging to each other over the grave of a parent, a misshapen spread of homes with a couple of shops serving the basics and a mosque with a tape recorder that calls the faithful to prayer – an old village bled of its youth, stinking from poverty, and dying. Caught in a firing line between resistance fighters and the SLA, its walls being battered and its people killed.

Harry rounds the bend and pulls up at the lip of the square, a short step up where road meets village. It is smaller than he remembers and more oblong than square. The olive tree has flesh wounds on its knotted bole, the concrete ground eaten away where shell fragments had torn into it, the gable end of a house all new, rebuilt, only in the last few days because the plaster has that wet look and reveals the outlines of the blocks.

A fall of dates by a rainwater puddle, a cola tin and sweet wrappers under the tree's rusted railing. The tree itself, gnarled and sorry-looking but yet tough, yet resilient – it has seen off a hundred years of people's lives and will count some more. A woman lost in a black chador emerges from a laneway, pushing a child in front of her, her deep-set hazel eyes flit to his blue and slip away like leaves flowing by on a river. The veil covers her beauty, he senses – for moments he visualises her form under the black robe. Thinks thoughts that would have him killed if he ever aired them. Lust here – in this place – the desire to make love! *Here.* The irreverence of it causes him to feel shame. Chance – Luck – Fortune – Fate – what led Damar and Basima to walk the square at the exact time they did? Seconds either way and they would have missed the shells and today he wouldn't be here and Damar would be at home with his wife and child, and Basima walking through the square, always in the back of her mind that shells had rained there and how lucky it was that no one was killed. She would hurry along. Always hurry along with a chill in her soul.

No cats.

He carries on, taking the narrow lane to Musa's café. The old man squints when he lifts his eyes from the backgammon board to look at who casts the shadow.

A smile exhibits uninhabited lower gums and an upper row of teeth poisoned yellow.

"Welcome, welcome," Musa says, excusing himself to an older man with a smile.

Clasping of hands.

Musa indicates the cafe. A smell of herbs and spices from a shelf arrayed with jars behind the glass counter. The room is long and narrow with grey-topped circular tables and black polypropylene chairs. Wooden condiment cellars too large for the tables add a touch of gaudiness. A dark and bleak place in which to take morning coffee – a meeting spot for frightened souls. A huddling venue for tortured minds.

Strong Turkish coffee in miniature glasses, highly sugared and black. Musa's thumb chases the beads on a string of them. Always smiling. His mouth emptied of good teeth knows no shame. He has little English and Harry little Arabic. Arab music is soft from a red Sony radio on the counter, keeping an awkward silence at bay.

Musa calls someone, his head turned sideways, facing a room with its door ajar, revealing a crack of dun-coloured wall and a sofa-arm with a worn patch. Moments later a heavy-set woman appears with a photo album. The old man takes it from her and with neither a word nor a look of acknowledgement at Harry's presence she departs.

Musa opens the album and slides it across the table, a blackened nail pointing at a photograph of a young woman.

"Basima," he says.

Harry stares. Now there is a face to the foot he holds in his dreams.

He had wanted to come here to face the source of his nightmares, that in doing so he might put an end to them. He is aware that his knowledge of psychiatric theory is akin to the level of a barrack-room lawyer who knows some things but not a lot – strengthening the credence lent to the old adage, *a little knowledge is a dangerous thing* – and can walk you into shite.

She is, and he thinks of her in the present tense, as he does with Damar, because they are not dead for him, beautiful. Long brown hair and large brown eyes, an oval face with high cheekbones and the tiniest of dimples. A way of looking at you that suggests she has a playful side – perfect teeth. Painted lips and touches of make-up on her cheeks the colour of amber cloud.

Musa sighs and spreads his hands as though to ask Allah, "Why?"

Harry closes the album slowly, as he would the lid of a coffin. A young man spills in from outside, smartly dressed and carrying books underarm. He has good English and allows Musa and Harry to conduct a short conversation through him – Musa calls for the woman again and this time she emerges with a wallet folder that contains an assortment of papers, loose photographs and a thick book with a loose cover. Harry is invited to rifle through them. All the time the student is telling him the history of the papers, a family's history, and all the time Harry is thinking, on a track parallel with other thoughts, that the hole he's in is getting deeper.

Sees the short story book Musa had shown him before and remembers the coffee- mark.

Taps the face on his Citizen watch when Musa goes to freshen his glass.

The old man sees him out. They shake hands and Harry leaves, making for the square, taking the same route Basima would have done in her last minutes. He is across the square in seconds and almost at the Cherokee when it begins to rain – rain as soft as tears. A low whistling wind seems to whip from the village, dancing with overhead wires – is the wind a communication from the dead? A song of the souls? A lament from those taken before their time, taken by acts of murderous violence, a cry of the innocent?

"Was he there?" One of the MPs says. Not the guy whose name he thinks is Pat.

"Yeah – he was."

"The state of this kip – dirty Arabs is right. Manky fuckers."

Harry says nothing. Wants to respond and say something in defence of Musa's village. But can't. He already has enough battles on his plate and besides his riposte would be weakened by the fact that he is listening to the wind, listening until they reach the road and a burst of Motorola static floods the cab and the rain becomes substantial, thrumming on the roof.

Beirut – Damar's coffin is fashioned from simple boxwood. In cold bright sunshine it is fed into the belly of a 737 plane. In the skies his comrades will eat, drink, and think of their families while Damar sleeps his sleep of the ages in the hold – as part of the cargo. Harry had driven from Bir Hassan early that morning for heliflight duty, keeping traffic back from the path of arriving and departing choppers and to check the hand luggage of the outgoing Nepalese chalk. The one Damar expected to take his seat on. He waited on the runway. Insects cheeped and clacked in the bush behind him. His mind a rubbish-heap of thoughts.

The heli angled in from the sea and Harry stopped traffic his end. Five minutes later there was the mounting roar of rotor blades as the heli prepared to take off for Naqoura. Shaking the dust from a stand of cypresses close to a Leb Army sandbagged position.

He's in the car staring through the windscreen as the plane climbs for the clouds, banking to the right. He flicks the wiper-wash to clear the screen of dirt streaks but it's futile, this doing of little things to distract his mind — the images climb over them.

He is freighted with a deep sorrow to know that a boy in Kathmandu will see his father's coffin in a few hours' time. And surely he will see the other soldiers and question why his father isn't among them — and surely he will ask to say thanks to his father for the gifts he brought him home. The remains are viewable up to a point, so perhaps he might be allowed to see his father's face — his mother will probably keep the wallet for him some place safe — in time, he will come to know that although his father was far away he always carried him about, and was with him the day he died.

Chapter 20

They turn the comers at Quasimodo's Curve and gather speed as they roll off the last, passing tobacco plantations, heading for the village of Al Hinniyeh and beyond to a final stretch of downhill road that for some distance is canopied by trees.

The Chevrolet pulls in, making room for a tractor and trailer to pass. Harry, his window down, catches the fleeting smell of diesel fumes and then breathes another of rain-freshened cypresses. The driver stays put as a stream of traffic appears – speeding – like a mad posse of wedding cars in chase of a runaway groom. A wedding party of Hizbollah going to or from an operation – he knows the faces neither by name nor sight but from experience – lean, hard faces with cold purposeful eyes.

Beirut — travelling from the airport with a high-ranking officer and his wife as passengers. A balmy night in a street corridor with electrical wires like a circus safety net above their heads. Frenzied march of a chanting crowd wearing sweatbands and carrying yellow flags with motifs of green hands holding Kalashnikov rifles — approaching them — a battering-ram of souls.

Harry edges into his right as much as possible, silences the engine and cuts the lights.

Coffins, many of them, floating on a sea of shoulders, sail by. Coffins with raised roofs as though to allow the dead some air to breathe.

"Where's my camera? I can't find my camera, Theo," the woman says in the back.

"I have it." Theo's voice is stem. Rippling with impatience, frustration and the apprehension Harry feels.

"I want to take some photographs."

Harry checks his rear-view mirror — how can anyone so beautiful be so fucking dense?

"Are you fucking mad, Bella? A flash of camera and they'll torch the car," Theo says.

"No need to use bad language. Give me my camera, please."

"It's in one of the suitcases — I forget which."

"What's going on?" Theo asks Harry, ignoring his wife's mutterings.

"Exchange of war dead — the Israelis returned twenty-two bodies for three of theirs — sort of telling the Hizbollah something."

"Not that they'll listen."

"Not that they'll listen is right."

After a few minutes Harry inches past the tail of the crowd and picks up a little speed.

In Naqoura he's being billeted in a room by a solemn-faced Fijian quartermaster. He turns the key and walks in ahead of Harry – flicks off a whining ceiling fan, opens a bedside locker from which spill three baby mice, pink and wriggling and blind, a chewed nest of newspaper in the bottom half of the locker. *The Sunday World.*

"I'm sorry," the QM says. "I've only taken over the job – the last quartermaster did nothing except sleep and drink kava."

Harry looks about. A shitty room – the slats on the Venetian blinds thick with black dust, the blue lino holding patches of congealed food and pellets of mouse droppings.

"I'll pass on this," Harry says.

"It is all we have."

"I'll find someplace else."

"Give me an hour. Say you come back then – I will make sure it is cleaned. Everything."

Harry nods. It isn't as though he has much choice in the matter. And he's right about the last QM – wasn't Harry here in MP Coy with him, guzzling the man's kava, looking at his photo shots of the massacre at Qana? It seems that all the poor man did was look at photographs – feeding his eyes with stuff for which his mind had no appetite.

"Yeah, okay."

Harry makes for the MP Club and in there puts his bag by an armchair, helps himself to a spoon of coffee and steaming water from a Burco boiler. The club is empty. Cold.

Mid-floor a pair of red kerosene heaters stand idle, their fuel gauges reading full. The wooden bar shutters resemble thick prison bars – the margin of the counter holds beer- spumed glasses, ashtrays, and beer cans. A smell of piss rends the air. Some things never change, especially it appears, a urinal that constantly clogs.

Stares through the window as he stirs his coffee. At the disturbed sea and the patrol boat bobbing up and down, and closer in at the grey rocks – winter throws a dirty rag on things. Tyre is obscured by a thick sea mist. On clear days you would think Tyre's tower blocks just simply grew from the sea.

Last days of the Grapes of Wrath, standing where he now stands, a Katyusha rocket landing fifty feet away in the sea, creating a loud burst. His coffee spilling. Waiting in the silence. Usually the Kaytushas – Little Kates – come in threes. Naqoura is located smack in the middle of the Hizbollah's intended target, the Israeli border crossing at Roshaniqra. No more rockets land. Even so it takes a while for his hands to stop trembling. And the silence, that penetrative silence – it's as though the very air holds its breath at how lucky he is. The sea is the camp's sandbag, swallowing the rocket's impact, drowning the shrapnel, leaving no slivers of steel to sear his flesh.

Drinks coffee black because the milk in the fridge is sour. Scalds his tongue.

The upper half of the walls are timber-slatted and festooned with plaques and pennants and framed photographs of units that have served in MP Coy down through the years. It's a familiar scene in the mess at home.

He recognises some of the names on the plaques – a beautifully crafted hand-carved piece from Ghana – Lifoh, Opare, Osufu, Aygiman, Wallace. A photograph of a Fijian section – Konasau, Waqa, Seru, Vaklurulu, Donumaibulu. A Finnish pennant – Sadimaki, Hietala and Borge.

The same names crop up a few times – regular visitors to MP Coy, to Lebanon, mostly Fijians and Irish with a sprinkling of Norwegians. His own name etched on the most recently displayed Irish present to the club, an ornamental plate holding a map of Ireland in its base.

Sam's name is fashioned on a piece of glassware – he doesn't notice his surname until he runs his eye over the list again, checking the rotation date – he left two weeks ago for home. Didn't get his six-month tour of Sinai. In fact he didn't see out his year-long tour of duty – Harry guesses at the reasons. Shrewd guesses.

He asks the QM when he comes in to tell him that his billet is ready. Ripples break out along his broad forehead.

"He got drunk and got out of hand – you know it is forbidden for us to drink beer."

"Yeah, I know... the kava and beer don't mix."

"Rocket fuel – Sam – his mind went to the stars. But he's okay. Now," a throw of his head as though Fiji were only feet away, "he's at home and he is fine."

Sam's phone is No 40 on Suva Island – Harry thinks he might give him a call. Why not? Two minutes to tell a pal to hang in there won't cost a whole ton – he can do it tonight after he calls home. He wants to call home, needs to speak with Derek and Tony. He feels a deep emptiness – fuck it, he might even ring the old man and Mam. Why not?

Surprise them. There's a pinch of pain in his belly, caused by a tension' knot – what's going to happen when he gets home? For fuck's sake, Kyle, get a brain. Your wife is being humped by a fucker who's dying on his two feet, and all you can do is dream about dead hands inching towards you and a young woman calling your name. Images so real that you see the sweat and dried blood on the back of a severed hand – fuck, you can even hear it panting – and the woman smells of a rich perfume, and after she calls your name she asks you in a flat Cork accent, "Have you seen my foot? It's got a blue legging."

Yeah – he can smile at them during the day, play them down when it's bright, but in the depths of slumber the images aren't funny.

In his room – he has forgotten to ask the quartermaster what he did with the baby mice and when he thinks about it some more is glad he has – he makes up his bed, tugs on a cord to shutter the clean blinds, and peels off his uniform. Wearing a towel and flip-flops he makes for the shower-room along a footpath that runs through the maze of accommodation prefabs – from the Fijian lines comes the beat of kava roots being pounded to powder.

He heads out to Mingi Street wearing a navy Adidas tracksuit he bought in Finbatt PX and which he brought with him this trip. It's cold, a dampish cold, caused by an earlier shower of rain and a slight breeze that the sea blows inland.

A recently tarred road slicks black and winding in front of Mingi Street. Half the shops have closed since the Swedes left and the French cut its force. Silent, dark corrugated ghosts with weeds growing about the door ends and perspex windows pushed in by storm or the hands of kids at play.

He climbs the steps leading into a shop that has two phone kiosks and which advertises international calls at a rate of a dollar and a half for a minute. He had intended to make his calls within UNIFIL HQ but the queue was too long – there'd been an influx of troops from the AO and only one of the three available kiosks was functioning.

The woman with dyed red hair motions him to a kiosk that has a phone ringing, signalling that she has got through.

The kiosk is warm and reeks of stale cigarette smell.

"Hello?" Derek's voice.

"Dad here, son – how are you?"

"Fine."

Harry does most of the talking and Derek answers, chipping in with what he wants to discuss – the drawings he did, the fact that *Hercules* was great tonight, that Arsenal won by four goals against – he couldn't pronounce the team's name. It sounded like Wimbledon to Harry. Says he hurt his knee out the back – he was playing soccer and Barney tripped him up. A dirty dog of a player.

"Tony?"

"In bed."

"Who's minding you?"

"Mum."

"Good."

"Yeah, Emma's sick so she can't baby-sit us. She has the flu, I think."

"What are you – "

"Do you want to talk with Mum?"

"I... "

Derek's voice drifts from the receiver, "Mum – it's my father – he wants to speak with you."

My father – kids.

June's "Yes?" is laced with impatience. Like she has a million things to do, wants to do, and speaking with him isn't one of them.

"I didn't actually look to speak with you – I think Derek just got bored and wanted to get away."

"So?"

"So?"

A sigh, "When are you coming home?"

"Thursday."

A pause, "I won't be here."

"Going on holiday, are we? Slut Tours."

Silence. No need for it, Harry old boy. Mother of your children and all that.

"The kids, are you – "

"You hardly think I'll leave them behind, do you?"

"To that bastard's place – isn't it – that's where you're going – Jesus Christ!"

"What? You'll mind them? With your moods and your nightmares – your fucking marbles – I can almost hear them rolling about."

"You're bringing our kids to live with your lover boy – how the fuck do you explain me away and him in to the kids?"

"They'll adapt."

"He's dying, you know that. What the fuck are you playing at? Moving the kids – upsetting them – will you start thinking through to the end result of what you're at, for fuck's – "

"We're finished – that's all you should concern yourself with."

He wants to ask if there is hope – any at all – of them working things out. But he doesn't ask. He had always thought that a person in a relationship who had an affair would feel guilty and be inclined to ask for forgiveness. So fucking naive. He never thought June was the type to brazen it out – never thought she was the sort to have an affair. He wants to tell her that she doesn't have to justify her affair by being hard on him, exaggerating his faults and trying to convince herself that she loves Karl. She doesn't have to soothe her conscience. He wants to ask her to stay for the kids' sakes.

She can carry on seeing Karl – why not? It's not as though he's going to be around for too long more – he doesn't have to ask her to give him up, because she's going to have to anyway. He says none of these things because he is holding on to a vestige of self-pride – the pain, it sucks, the pain of loving someone who has stopped loving you, just fucking sucks.

She doesn't love him. And if she didn't love Karl she wouldn't be going to him.

That's the truth about June. She knows who she wants and is going to make the most of whatever time they have left together. Karl's impending death has galvanised her into action.

"I'll leave a key under the mat out back," she says.

"No – it's okay. Don't do that. I have one."

"Then – "

"June?"

"What?"

The words won't come. They snag on the lump in his throat. Tears well. Temples feel as though someone is chiselling at them.

"You can see the lads any time – you know that – have them for a weekend or whatever."

"How fucking gracious of you."

A quick intake of breath from June – like the heat of his anger has touched her.

A break.

"Are you there?" June says.

"Yeah, yeah, I'm here."

"I'm sorry, Harry – the way it turned out."

Sorry? He supposes she is – "So am I."

She hangs up. For moments he feels as though he is living in a vacuum. He slaps at the perspex with his hand and emerges from the kiosk, growing aware that his action has alarmed the receptionist. He counts out single bills to pay for the call and apologises – bad news from home, he explains. A sympathy smile fires up and dies in an instant on her weary face – a look that appears to say, *who hasn't got problems?*

He strolls to Pablo's Bar at the top end of the street, the only pub in Mingi Street that sells beer on draught. Amstel.

The bar is set above an antique shop managed by Pablo during daylight hours; flintlock pistols with ivory chips embedded in the wooden handles, a musket, some coins from Tyre, a curved sword, a series of daggers, some paintings, one of the Moorish keep by the sea, the one UNIFIL HQ is built around, empty of Muslim headstones and the UN buildings, in its former glory, a man on a white horse by its thick honey-coloured walls looking out to sea at the setting sun. Harry knows the scene, knows that judging by the sun's position the painting was done mid-winter or close to it.

It reminds him of Kassam, the CO of the Leb Army in Tyre, with whom he had spoken many times, who used to ride a white horse along the white sandy beach between Tyre and Rashidiyeh, the Palestinian refugee camp, three kilometres away. A tall, educated man with distinguished features, who was gunned down on his way to barracks a week before he was due to leave for a job in the States. Harry heard that his funeral in Sidon was well attended — no one got to see the remains because they weren't viewable. Harry never found out why he was shot, or got to attend the funeral because Sidon was off limits for the UN — Kafra was two days away — a nightmare on the horizon.

Thinks too of Od, the Norwegian dog-handler, saying Heppy the labrador drug dog had gone wild in the graveyard at the Moorish keep. Harry polishing off his coffee and accompanying them to the keep — low headstones, a strong scent of burnt mint leaves that Harry explains isn't a drug smoke but something that is done as a custom by mourners in a Muslim cemetery. This one anyway. Heppy's snout is fucked from smelling too many narcotics — the most she ever detected during Harry's time was a mouldy salami sandwich. He walks through the keep — the ground floor holds a stable area and a winding stone stairs leads to two floors, all dust-covered. The view of the sea is magnificent — and others think so too, judging by the cigarette ends stubbed in the broken wall that serves as a low parapet. Some of the ends are hash ends but Heppy's nose is blind to them. Harry says nothing that might lead Heppy to an early grave in Norbatt's pet cemetery. Takes a breath — keep out of the grave, Harry boy, you too, for as long as you're able.

A drink. Need a fucking drink. He pulls himself from Pablo's treasures and takes to the stairs and the bar. A creak of lightning flashes in the skies – sunders the black of the night.

"A storm on its way," Pablo says, sliding a beer in front of Harry.

"Looks like it, yeah."

"So – you're back, for how long – there must be something wrong?"

"A week – and nothing's wrong – checking on guys – this and that."

Pablo is thin with grey hair and black moustache. His alert green eyes are always on the move and a cigarette never leaves his lips lonely for too long. He keeps a sawn-off shotgun under his counter, single-barrel -"Like a woman," he says, "good to have."

Harry says nothing. His mind is on June – sense of anger, sense of loss, sense of panic – the future is going to be new for him. Forced changes.

What the fuck is he going to do in a house full of memories? Alone? Life is just one big long kick in the bollocks. A short kick if you die young, or relatively young, like Damar and Basima.

"Another pint, Pablo, when you're ready. Put a decent head on it."

Chapter 21

Pablo helps Harry down the steps, puts him into his car and drops him at the French Gate, the one nearest UNIFIL's administration block. Harry isn't so drunk that he doesn't know what's happening and he thinks it's a shame that he isn't. It would be a pleasure not to know who he is for a few hours. A real pleasure.

Standing in the pouring rain, wavering on his feet, shaking Pablo's hand, telling him he's a star over and over, not letting it drop until a roar of thunder is such that it startles him. At the blue steel door, showing his UN ID card to a French conscript with more pimples than years, passing through into the grounds, the rain falling so hard that he is soaked before he reaches the kiosk, the one he couldn't get to use earlier that night.

Vacant.

There is no one else out in this weather, except the guards who remain ensconced in their jeeps, under their soft canopies. He espies them growling by on the lower road, the one that runs outside MP Coy — its surface beginning to muddy with the rusty red soil that the earth always bleeds when it pours.

Time? Two here. Midnight at home. Ring her. Go on, fucking ring her and tell her what a bitch she is. Tell her. Scream into the phone and let her fucking know what a cow you think she is.

No.

Do.

No.

Go on.

No.

Fuck – go on. Do it.

No! No!

Coward.

No! No...

His hand rests on the phone, his Bezek card in, reading 20 units. No, don't call her.

You never know what you might interrupt – some intellectual conversation perhaps – or maybe you'll arrest the fall of her knickers. A bit late for arresting those now, eh? You're a fucking eejit for trusting a woman, for trusting anyone. For putting your heart on a plate for someone to carve. Drunk – you're drunk – go to bed!

Would you ring her and tell her these things if you weren't drunk? No. Will it change anything? Not an iota. Like pouring your bitterness over her won't exactly show her your love for her. Will it? No. So, don't ring. Take the marriage bust-up on the chin.

He rings – disobedient fingers. Ought to be shot.

"Hello... " June's voice, sleepy.

He hangs up without saying a word. Annoyed with himself for ringing and for the fact that he hasn't spoken with her. He steps outside into the rain and starts for the billet, the path so narrow in places that the shrubs dry themselves on him. By the time he makes MP Coy he feels as though the rain is seeping into his bones.

Ascending steps, gripping hard on a handrail, into the toilet area where he pisses into a urinal. Takes in the wisps of pubic hairs that make the soak-hole look like it's growing whiskers. A touch of vomit in his throat settles back down, aided by a determined gulp and another – even so, he still gets the rancid taste of sick in his mouth. Leaking into the urinal while the rest of him drips beads of rain onto the floor.

The janitor, the guy who has to press a voice-box in his throat in order to speak, will be thoroughly pissed off in the morning. Harry laughs – pissed off – jacks-cleaners are always pissed off. Or they might get a pain in the hole – such a shitty job, see?

Hah. Down the steps. Easy, watch the shiny steps – one, two, three. Jagged streaks of lightning out to sea. Thunder rolls not as loud, somewhere to the east – Kafra, Tibnin. The rain teems. Always the rain. Steady on the steps – will you?

Finds his key in the last pocket he searches and lets himself in. Retreats in a hurry and vomits by the shrubs, retching so hard it hurts. Wiping his lips and staggering into his room he peels off his tracksuit and dries himself with a yellow bath towel. Falls awkwardly into a T-shirt and shorts. His head is swimming with thoughts. A crazy carousel of notions.

In bed, the- light out, he lies on his back, his heat trapped by sheets and blanket, feeling a little better in himself. Feels purged after vomiting, clean inside. A vomit a day helps keep the doctor away.

He falls asleep watching the pale blue flashes and listening to the distant rumbling of thunder.

Wakes late with a headache. The headache reaches from the back of his neck, across his poll and down the middle of his forehead where it branches out, a belter of a fucking headstorm – a class A blinder – a fucking headquake.

The camp is awake, well awake. He feels as though he is intruding by listening in – cars slushing past, a heli's mounting roar that in a few moments will pass overhead, its downward air current shaking the prefabs, two French MPs discussing something in their native tongue, the scraping of a yard-brush along concrete.

Harry sits on the edge of his bed. His lips dry and his throat raw. Almost midday by his watch on the bedside locker. He had slept – the ghosts leaving him alone last night. He probably got them too drunk to go haunting.

Pops a Disprin and chases it down with a swig of water from a bottle in the fridge.

Thinks of the mice as he opens the locker to remove a light pair of jeans, a clean T-shirt, fresh socks and underwear and a dark red fleece top. Catches a bad underarm whiff – he smells like he needs two showers. Headache begins to recede as he pulls the door behind him and the cool damp air catches his stubbled features. Lets the jets of hot water steam his neck in the shower – hates it when the draught pushes the plastic shower curtain against his skin – it feels like a hand's cold touch.

Later, he avoids encroaching upon the working life of MP Coy by going to Mingi Street where he sits hunched in Pablo's over a coffee. Pablo isn't around this morning, just a young woman who is busy pottering about behind the bar.

Orders a second coffee just to stop her tinkling glasses together and lights a cigarette.

In the light of day, as he threaded his way to Pablo's avoiding puddles and car splashes, he had reached some very important landmark decisions, and it is these he reflects upon.

His decisions give him hope for the future – a decision to quit drinking before it becomes too much of a habit and fastens too strong a grip on him. That's the starting point.

He draws hard on his coffee and then his cigarette. There is no decision to make about June as she has made it for him. He just has to let time heal the wound. The boys – he will take more of an interest in them – keep smiling for their sake so that when they grow up they might look back and remember, remember that you've got to take life's knocks on the chin, and carry on as best as you can for as long as you can. Either that or draw up a coward's charter and quit on yourself and everyone else by losing yourself in a bottle. Perhaps that's the road for him, but he'll go down it fighting all the way.

He is caught short with a case of Naqoura belly and has to rush to the loo — a harsh dose of the runs that makes a freeway of your arse — he sits there, the stench rising around him. Days after Kafra — so perhaps it isn't food that has acted adversely on his system — his pistol lying on the ground is encased in its green holster.

He removes it — polished black steel — a Browning 9mm, a magazine box fitted which he unclips. He stares at the brass rounds. He can, if he wants, end it all now, this very moment, this fucking instant, return the magazine, cock the weapon and press the muzzle against his temple and squeeze the trigger. Over!

It happens. People do it all the time. Call time up before time does it for them. Are they mad, strong, depressed, despairing or wise? He sees instances of how it is easy to do such a thing, to quit on life. If you have a cancer for instance, or you are living in such pain that death is a better prospect. But is it an option when so much can change in a week? Should it be an option when other people are fighting to save their lives — but should that anomaly of life bother you? It's your life — still, what does someone who is fighting for life think of someone who throws his away? What would Derek and Tony think of him? Maybe he thinks too much about what others might think. Unlike June for instance, on their Rhodes holiday, on an evening he was half cut, who told him, shouted in front of others, to mind his fucking business when he said she should excavate her bikini pants from her arse — he shouldn't be watching her arse. He was just a fucking animal. A dog. He apologised and said she was right he was only a dog — interested only in his bone and getting his hole. She hit him with her sandal. On the nose. It stung. He deserved it. Spent the rest of the holiday trying to make it up to her.

Life — mystery — one of God's private jokes if you ask me. Then, I'm only Harry — who gives a fuck about what I think?

When you have kids — well, you like to think life will be kind to them. So if you can — you hope. You live. You do your best to try and make life kind to them.

Damar and Basima are dead and they didn't want to die. Is it right he should be sitting in a toilet thinking about, if not planning suicide, then seriously considering its pros and cons with a pistol, a loaded pistol in his hand?

Think — bits of your brain spattered against the wall — your blood — slivers of skull and the cats, always the fucking cats, having a meal — Harrykebabs.

He keeps looking at the black piece — its serial number, ribbed hand slide, the grey showing on the trigger, the sights, and then with a series of long shuddering sighs he slips in the magazine and holsters the weapon, closing its flap and buckle.

He has two small seeds of hope, but it had been a dangerously close call — what if their faces hadn't winged into his mind?

He asks the young woman for another coffee. When she serves him he loads it with sugar and lights another cigarette.

He's hungry and fancies having a pizza in Ali's farther up the street. Glances at his watch. Yeah, grab something to eat and ring the boys, and the old man, maybe Sam, this time.

June asks if it was he who rang last night.

"Yeah, it was."

A pause. He thinks he should say something, "The lads?"

"They're fine — Derek is in his friend's house and Tony's out the back, trying to persuade Barney to be his gee-gee."

Another pause. The kids — though they are a lot to talk about, they are all they can talk about.

"So — anything else?" she says, finally.

"Weather's poxy."

It goes like that for a few more seconds, each searching for things to say, each keeping a calm air between them, a strained calm — it's a bit like trying to have a conversation with a person who stands on the other side of the hill. You know she sees things differently and because of the hill you can't show her what it is you see.

Is Karl the hill? Part of it – if it wasn't him it would have been someone else. He decides to wrap up the call. Says they'll have a chat next week, when she's gone wherever it is she's going, to sort out the kids and money and all the other shit.

She says, "That's fine – good – no whingeing, Harry – no begging me to stay for the kids' sakes... "

"No. I've accepted that it's over between us."

"Good."

"It's not good at all, but I'm getting on with it."

"I'll be seeing you," she says.

At least they had been civil to each other if not cordial. That's good – see – if you'd called her names last night you'd have gotten nowhere with her today.

On a whim he calls up Al but gets no reply, then tries home, his old home.

"Hello?"

The oul fella.

"Dad – Harry here."

"Howya – she's not here, gone shopping into Newbridge, on that new Rapid bus."

Funny – he always assumes that when either of his sons ring it's his mother he wants. "Yeah, so, how are things with you?"

"No cure, in spite of all her novenas." Chuckles the way he does when he hasn't his teeth in.

When Harry goes to speak he keeps talking, "Burns a stack of candles each week – I'll die in a house fire if she keeps going on with it. Ah, but the faith is great for her. Gives her strength – I wish I had her faith – it might make things easier for me to deal with. Huh, what do you think?"

"A pagan talking to an atheist, that's what I think. Don't ask me about religion and faith – I haven't prayed since I failed my – "

"Yeah, son – but what is it, what is it I hear about you and June? Is it true – only your Mum was telling me she's been hearing things back — you know from the sort who like running back to people with things."

Harry tells him everything. A moment's silence. Harry reads five digits on the monitor and says his units are almost used up.

"It happens, son — you're young enough to start all over — what are you — twenty-seven, eight — Jesus, you could start all over at fifty if you wanted to — so you've loads of time. Just —"

"Dad, I'm almost out — we'll chat when I get home, okay?"

"All right, son — oh, one thing... "

"Yeah?"

"Al was up. And... "

Beep, beep... card used up.

He'll never get around to speaking with Sam. Outside the kiosk he takes in a breath of air and then heads for the MP Club to have a chat with some of the Irish lads, if they're about. Most might be training in the Rubb Hall or gone to the AO. There's only a few anyway, unlike years ago when the Irish committed as many as twelve MPs to serve in the company.

Times change. Circumstances, too. If you don't change with the change you get left behind. Lost. Kafra has left a scorch-mark on his soul — until he saw Kafra he had experienced only little evils in short doses — petty things — jealousies, spiteful words, tempers, avarice, and greed, fuck, even adultery. But Kafra had shown him real evil — and though some would say it happened on a small scale it would never be a small-scale affair for him. A theft of a life is the greatest evil — he knows, he has seen, touched, lives with it, knows. Dreams.

Only the barman in the mess and he's watching TV in the ante-room. A scattering of old newspapers on a coffee table, steam raising the lid on the Burco, a spill of crumbs on a blue check oilcloth. Harry takes a coffee he doesn't really want outside, into an arbour constructed of bamboo sticks, and sits facing the sea.

Sips at his coffee, winces at the taste of lime – fucking Burco needs descaling. It's cold. Not as cold as it is at home for this time of year, but cold all the same. Glances at his watch – five – ticking towards darkness.

This time next week he'll be home. It can't come to pass quickly enough. Here, without a friend, without a purpose, living on top of the land of his nightmares – at least the Curragh provides his eyes with a change of scenery – shows him that he isn't anywhere near his dreams. A small respite. But nevertheless a respite.

Chapter 22

Four days without a beer in his hands – his soul, body and mind are screaming at him to have one. Just one. One won't fucking kill you. A glass of wine, even. For fuck's sake. A drink, please – one. No!

It's still raining in Lebanon. Driving rain, too. Everywhere there are loud smells of dampness and kerosene. You miss the open fire, the heat from the range, the oil that warms the veins of the house before you set toes to the floor. *You can drink a cup of tea without a shell landing fifty feet away from you – making you stain yourself.*

He's in the Lite Byte café in Israel, just beyond the blue gates of the border crossing.

As he eats a croissant and drinks mint tea an occasional squall carries the salt of the sea to his nostrils. He has walked the ten kilometres from HQ and will start on the return journey in a little while. It's a long stretch of coastal road, possessing one bend, a long and steep hill, and is flanked inland by scrub-covered hills, a sand quarry and UNIFIL's rifleranges and on the other side by the sea, the chalk cliffs, and the rusted bones of railway tracks that once carried the Orient Express – all watched over by a French base with a high watchtower, its nest perspexed, which must freeze the sentry's balls during winter and roast them during summer.

Tomorrow he'll be out of here, heading in convoy to Beirut. Home. He wonders what lies ahead, thinks of the cold greeting that awaits him. A house devoid of his wife and his children. Barney won't even be about. Seeing the emptiness is going to be shit.

A house as hollow as he sometimes feels. She's really gone on this fucker to put the kids through this upheaval, taking them from their home, their bedrooms – Tony's done up in *Teletubbies* and *Postman Pat* characters on the walls and Derek's with posters of Arsenal's players – chipping away at the kids' sense of security, giving them a new daddy – *because mummy and the old daddy were always fighting* – for adults it's too simply put for something so complex as a break-up, but for kiddie-speak it's spot on.

He walks, walks hard, shows his ID card to the guard and slips by the guardroom on to a pathway with more cracks than the haggard features of a man not necessarily old but broken.

He's almost at the gates leading into the camp – MP Coy is another kilometre beyond the entrance – a bit of a pain in the hole that last bit, the longest part he feels.

He experiences a sensation of achievement when he reaches the Duty Room and sees the unit's crest on the wall – crossed flintlocks on a red background with MP Coy in emboldened black underneath – it's a place where he feels he belongs – of course, he doesn't belong – he did six months ago when he was on the unit's strength – now he's just a guest.

Passing through. Tolerated with the same friendliness you'll find in a B&B – but kept at arm's length – he isn't really part of anyone's long-term plans, is he? Story of his life. Whine, you're whining, Harry – feeling sorry for yourself – don't whine.

Look at it this way, things are looking up – you woke up this morning with an erection. First rise in a while. Not a piss-horn either – a good standing erection. You had no nightmares. A good sleep and a horn. Something to be grateful for – if June had been there she'd have said something like, "Take a photograph before it goes away," or "Jesus – Lazarus mickey." That's if she looked – she thinks mickies are disgusting so she seldom looks at his. During foreplay it used to remain locked up in his underwear like the family freak in the attic in old movies – an instrument to be produced when the passion was at its most intense – only then did June forget about the ugliness of his 'Bill Clinton dip'.

She eats with her eyes he tells her.

He didn't really mind her insistence on his langer being kept under wraps before she needed it – after all, everyone has likes and dislikes. Quirks. He used to ask her for blow jobs but quit after she refused a number of times. He gave up on her because it's not the same when you have to ask. June's the sort that when she wants to do something she'll do it very well and when she doesn't she'll make a hames of it – a hames of it in his case is leaving teeth-marks on his column. Risky ...

Well, if he can make light of a poor sex life he must be on the mend – having a *craic* with himself about getting no crack. Perhaps revisiting the scene did something after all – perhaps.

Showers. Eats in Pablo's, gratis, and calls Sam.

"Bula," Sam says in his thick, syrupy voice.

"It's me, Harry."

A pause. A long pause. Like a pause that says what the fuck are you ringing me for?

"Harry?"

"Harry from Tyre."

"Oh ... "

"Did I catch you at a bad – "

"No, where are you ringing from?"

"The Leb."

He goes on to tell him about the reason for his trip, and then, one eye on his disappearing call units and the other on the window sill on a cockroach as large as his thumb, he queries Sam about Kafra — straight out, on the button, nail on the head first fucking time.

"Do you have nightmares about Kafra — is that why you went wild, Sam?"

Silence.

"Come on, Sam?"

"No — no, Harry, I had problems at home — I don't think of Kafra — those people — they are nothing to me. Nothing."

"Nothing?"

"Of course — they are in God's hands now, not mine — I said a prayer and I can do no more — I can do nothing for them by thinking about what happened... "

"So, you've no nightmares, no... "

"No." Smart change of topic, "How is your family, Harry?"

"Fine, and yours?"

That's it. Sam has nothing to say about Kafra, or has but won't free the words. What does he expect Sam to say? What does he want to hear from him? It isn't so much that he wants to hear what Sam has to say, it is more a case of wanting Sam to listen to him — Sam would know exactly what he was on about. Know exactly. Should have opened up to him after Kafra, when they returned to Tyre, instead of smothering things with kava and booze.

Fuck him.

It's time. His turn to get into the heli for the shuttle flight to Beirut. Applies belt and and closes his eyes as the heli dips its nose on take-off. He had a friend who died in a chopper crash and another involved in a forced landing on the beach at Sidon. Thirty minutes to Beirut — the longest half-hour. He spends a lot of time in the air for someone who hates flying. In a couple of hours he'll be sky-bound again, this time in a jet, taking in Beirut until cloud covers cloud and he can no longer see the city.

Aboard the plane he slots in by a window. The runway

is wet and greasy, the skies grey, the mountains above Beirut showing snow when the clouds drop a stitching. Up, up and away, over the inshore waters, reaching for the clouds, buffeted by the wind, tickled by the rain — pale yellow neon displaying no smoking which he thinks is a load of bollocks — it's during take-off and landing that smokers really need to smoke.

The two most critical times of every flight — every fucking pilot will tell you that. Then he realises that this is worse — a no-smoking-at-all plane — shit. Once a hostess, nervous as a soul's first day in Hell, sat beside him on a flight to Rhoose Airport two years ago, blessing herself as the plane turned for the runway, telling him in a panicky voice that she hates take-offs. That at least if you crash during landing you're on the way down, there's a shorter drop. She put the wind up him and the other passengers within listening distance — he suggested that she try another line of work. He watches hostesses' faces for any sign of concern during flights, and here is one in bits in front of him! Thank God the flight was short.

Shuts his eyes. Opens them. Craves a cigarette — fuck non-smokers. There's the usual reminder about alarms in the toilets. The in-flight movie stars a guy with lips sewn to a cigarette — balancing it in the comer of his mouth when he's talking and not flicking the ash off until it's well over an inch long — then judging by his wince, the absence mere milliseconds, he suffers deep withdrawal pangs. Can't watch. Closes his eyes and tries to sleep. Sees June and the boys and the house standing idle. Sees the flowering furze on the Curragh, feels the soft caress of a mild autumal breeze on his cheek, the velvety feel between his fingertips of wild mushrooms, and hears the brittle snap of their stems under his gentle squeeze — hears too the thunder of hooves on the gallops, the burst of machine-gun fire on the rifle ranges, and sees a trickle of mass-goers walking the footpath behind the trees, the arc and swoop of a linnet, a dead badger at the mouth of a pillbox beginning to reek, scald crows in attendance, diving in with their beaks. Squawking like crazy at a feast provided by death. To the east the mountains are inky blue and shorn of their purple heather... Opens his eyes. The army chaplain is talking away, some of the others in the party are trying, like him, to lose some of the journey in sleep, but it is the sleep of the easily disturbed, a just-below-surface sleep, the brain on green alert in readiness for red. He closes his eyes again.

Goats by the roadside, tinkling bells, dust clouds kicked up by Mercedes tyres. Contrails from jets fading in the clear blue skies — walking the marathon walk from Camp Shamrock in Tibnin to UNIFIL HQ to raise funds for the orphanage in Tibnin. A march of 42 kilometres in flak jacket and shouldering a Steyr rifle. Setting off in pairs at staggered intervals when the first cracks of light appear above the crusader castle. A castle Harry visited yesterday evening, driving into the village, passing the waterhole, green slime on its surface lending a face to its dank smell. He pulled over and walked the castle way, a narrow dirt track that reached the honey-coloured walls and veered abruptly to the right and met an arched entrance with a lion's faded head and a coat of arms. It is an austere fortification with four comer towers and grounds that are home to scrapped cars, a couple of derelict shacks and a pack of ribby dogs. Red flowers grow in cracks between the walls and lean towards the evening sun. Riveting views from a tower of a Mount Hermon dressed in white, the great wadis below where many roads meet at one, what would have been a main trading route in the Levant — Tyre and the glare of the sea visible through a vee in the hills.

Harry loses his partner shortly after Haris, wanting to be alone with his thoughts, to take in the air, to chase a respectable time. A month before Kafra, a village he passed on the walk, not knowing its name, more interested in the compound on the hill, the way its Sherman tank was rolled out from within the enclosure of high embankments, its barrel a dark threatening stick in the skyline. Like God's toothpick.

Blistered feet and perspiration-soaked clothes, the ache from his knee joints as he crosses the line in Naqoura — feeling miserable, tired, carrying seven pounds less body weight, glad to be free of his rifle and flak jacket, his shoulder red and raw from the chafing of the rifle sling. Nursing a beer in his billet, taking in his sopping uniform, the boots that are stained white on the uppers and rims, dried froth caused by socks darkened with sweat, all lying on the green lino — you would think a body drowned in them.

The Irish Sea, familiar housing estates, a bleak day but with no rain, a half-moon lying on its back wearing a broad smile, like it had just had a good ride.

Sarah's waiting for him in the lounge, catches his elbow, "God, you're blind, Harry – and deaf – I've been calling you." She's taller than he is but not by much. Talks with her hands a lot. Drives with her mouth open as though it's a third eye. Pretty though, she's very pretty. Hair smells of apple shampoo and her features are finely honed, as though Himself had taken time out to practise his sculpturing. Asks himself why he hasn't noticed how attractive she is until now. Nails, she's clipped her nails short – they have almost a bitten look to them.

"I've some news," she says, glancing sidelong.

"Good?"

"He hasn't shown in for a week."

"Who hasn't shown – Pete or Karl?"

"Karl."

"Sick?"

"In hospital for two days – out since then. He looks bad. Really lousy."

"Yeah."

Sarah lifts her brows and that action frees a silent question.

"You aren't going to see him, are you?"

Breathes, "I will." Adds, "When I'm ready."

"Don't be hard... "

"You mean don't kick the crap out of him for screwing June."

"So coarse."

"Watch the road. Do you want to get us killed?"

"Coarse."

"Coarse."

"Yeah."

Silence for a long way then, until Johnstown Garden Centre outside Naas.

"I got you a small something... a bottle of Baileys," Harry says.

"Lovely Harry – thanks – you shouldn't –"

"Isn't it almost Christmas?"

She laughs, "So it's a Christmas present?

"No and yes."

"No and yes?"

"No, but maybe we can share it over a meal at Christmas." Feels like a fucking fool for propositioning her – worse than a fool. A fool would have tried to pass the suggestion off as a joke, making it easy for her to shoot the notion out of the skies. The silence is uncomfortable. She shifts on the seat like her piles have suddenly popped out for the occasion of his invitation.

"Harry – Pete and me – we're back together."

"Oops."

"Sorry."

"I shouldn't have asked – I'm off the rebound on a lot of things."

Something shrinks in him – his heart? Probably. What sort of a fucking dope is he? His marriage is dead, not long dead, and he needs to get his mind sorted out long before he lets a woman back into his life, for her sake and his.

Sarah pulls up outside his house. The lights are on in the sitting-room.

"Thanks, Sarah... see you tomorrow – oh, shit, almost forgot – the report."

Can't meet her eyes – fears what he might read in them. He surfaces a green folder from his carrybag, "Give this report to the CO for me – no results, no head for him to roll. Just a messy affair, that's all."

"Aren't they all messy?"

He looks down at the rain puddle by his feet and sees the reflection of a streetlight on its wind-combed surface. "Yeah, messy," he agrees, embarrassed.

"You don't want to interview Enright again?"

"For what – to tell her she's a liar? She's a friend of yours – isn't she? You have a word in her ear."

Waves at her as she honks the horn. Picking his way up the path he looks into the sitting-room. The Christmas tree is up, lights blinking on and off. The crib on the Mexican pine coffee table is missing the infant Jesus – Derek keeps him under his pillow until the time is right. They're watching TV and Scooby Doo being chased by a ghost in an old house. So quiet, so clean-looking, in fresh pyjamas – his two sons. Harry takes to the gable end and hears Barney whimpering a welcome – swallows a breath then a couple more, rubbing Barney's ear as he turns the handle on the back door.

What the fuck is going on? Probably decided to put the move on hold until after Christmas. Makes sense not to unsettle the kids.

Chapter 23

She's lost weight – that's the first thing he notices – perhaps she had lost it before he went away and he hadn't noticed. But if a week is a long time in politics then ten days can be a long time in a marriage and a crash diet. She's had her hair cut and coloured – cut too short and bleached blonde. What sort of a fucking statement is she trying to make? It bugs him that she won't even turn around and greet him. Her normal thing – ignoring his existence – it wouldn't hurt her tongue to say hello. She is wearing black ski-pants that are so tight he sees the rims of her knickers and a blue sweater he likes on her.

The devil in him suggests he should walk up behind her and slip his hands under her arms and grab her breasts. The angel in him suggests that it would not be such a good idea. It could be an act that would lead to open war – a feel of her breasts could burn his hands.

"Honey, I'm home," he says, to annoy her.

She whisks about – twin peaks – no Wonderbra. Eyes so bright you'd think she'd had them washed with juice squeezed from the stars. Legs crossed – a toe showing through a slipper. Painted.

"I'm jumping up and down," she says.

"I thought you were to be out of here."

"Change of plan."

"Decided to stay and beg forgiveness – is that it?"

"No – I'm not upsetting the kids so close to Christmas."

He feels burned out, tired after the flight and the worry — he could sleep for a year. The blood is tired in him.

Christmas is two weeks away — upset them? No. *Dún do bhéal*, least said, you know yourself. Okay, you want to scream at her — scream and ask what the fuck she's playing at. And what of the others in the unit? They must know, too. Everyone fucking knows. Of all the mickies in the world she has to pick one that loses him a bit of face, leaving him nowhere to run, to hide, to put on a brave fucking smile and say to himself, 'What the hell — who'll miss a slice off a cut loaf?'

"I'm going to change... " he says wearily.

"It's too late for that."

"I'm talking about my clothes."

Snorts. "Your clothes are in the boxroom — I've moved the lads into the — "

"Everything planned out, haven't you?"

"Until we can make a better plan, yes."

Halfway up the stairs he hurts his small toe on a toy soldier — shakes his head — picking it up he sees that it's a Japanese World War II figure, on the charge with his rifle and bayonet, half a bayonet because its top has been chewed. A little Nepalese in its miniature features, which might explain how he ended up under his foot, in the wrong place at the wrong time. He peels off his uniform and heads for the shower, not disturbing the boys from their cartoon until he has freshened up a little, putting a little fuel into his patience-tank. Sometimes he feels as though he has got old very quickly.

Dressed casually he knocks on the sitting-room door and puts his head round it.

Smells the smell of pine — last year he forked out a lot of money for an artificial tree at June's behest and this year she wants to go *au naturel*. There's no pleasing her.

Derek swivels on his behind, eyes widening — washed in star-juice like his mum's.

The boys run to him – to him and the packages in his hands – spoil them a little, why not? Harry sits on the chair by the fire. Tony edges onto his lap, smiles his toothless smile, chats his baby words, nods and says "Ta, ta, Daddy," when he peels off the paper and sees his Action Man. Runs to June to show him off. Derek shrugs, the blue wrapping shredded at his feet. Like his sky has fallen in.

"What's up, son?"

"Have him. He's uselesses and this is uselesses too."

"So you've got two the same?"

Nods.

"Oh, sorry, son."

"You're a fucking eejit of a daddy – do you know that, do you?"

"Yes."

"I'm going to ring my friend and tell him all about the stupid father I have."

"Where did you get the other one, Derek? This is a Parachute Action Man – I don't remember – "

"Uncle Karl got me him – not this time – the other time when you were in Lebanon."

"Uncle Karl... "

"Yeah."

It's like a lone skater cutting through the thin ice covering his nerves. Something comes on TV that Derek likes and he says, "Mister Bean, Dad – I love him. Be quiet, won't you?"

The innocence – be quiet? He hadn't said a word – he's too fucking shocked to speak. Sitting there, his son glued to TV, the lights on the tree colourful, he thinks of how things are sliding from his grasp in degrees – June, and now the boys, soon it will be the house and the car, and probably his job, his willpower, the nights he sleeps, his ability to focus on a problem and deal with it – Jesus. Going back to having nothing. Go to bed. You are tired. Sleep. Too fucking agitated to sleep. What if the dreams come back? Come back. Do they ever go away?

During the ads, after Bean catches his teddy's head in a bedside locker, Derek says, "Guess what I'm getting for Christmas – I have my letter wrote out – it's gone up the chimney – guess, go on, squeeze up your brain and think – like this."

Derek knits his eyebrows together and squints.

"A football, an Arsenal shirt, football boots... "

"What else? Daddy, think."

"Games?"

"Yeah, what else?"

"Wrestlers, an artist's set, soldiers, a rifle... "

"A Scooter Robot."

"Ah sure, I suppose you were a good boy, weren't you... "

Nods, "And a cat."

Something bums in Harry's stomach – feels like lino after a hot coal lands on it. Veins in his temple begin to pound.

"No, son, no cats in this house."

"I want a cat – Timmy my friend has kittens and he's going to give me one, so he is. He looks like a baby tiger and I love him." June is in. "Mum – Dad said I can't have a kitten."

"Of course you can have a pet – I said you can – now come on in for your supper." Harry calls her as she makes to follow Derek.

"You know... you know what I think of cats... "

"Cop yourself on – anyway, he'll forget about it if you don't go on and on."

A fob – it doesn't matter what he thinks.

His insides feel like jelly, all cold and shivery, but on the outside he feels warm, especially at the temples. Sits there, takes his goodnight kisses from Tony and Derek who says he's getting the "kitty".

"Amn't I?"

He asks although it doesn't matter what his dad thinks. Mum has spoken. Derek fears a row breaking out over it.

There's a tension in his eyes, his raised shoulders and in a faint worry line along his forehead. Harry can see life furrowing that drill deeper and longer and wider.

"Yes."

A hug, "You're the best father I ever had."

Harry smiles. Nothing official, but an agreement was reached – there'll be no rows between Mum and Dad over his kitten. He sighs, wonders if there's anything in the drinks press. No! But he looks anyway. Nothing, not even the ghostly smell of drinks long consumed.

In the kitchen he butters a few slices of soda bread and cuts some slivers of cheddar cheese from a block. June has the portable TV on, watching the news. Legs crossed – a new habit of hers – as though she were keeping something locked from him. Shutting him out. Done so determinedly in her heart that it shows in her physical actions – legs crossed and arms folded.

"We need to talk about getting in things for Christmas," she says, without looking at him.

"I thought we had all the boys' stuff?"

"They need new clothes and shoes – and –"

"So, go and get them – there's money in our account, extra this week because of duty money and we didn't spend every penny of that Lebanon money."

Silence. The weather forecaster says there'll be high winds and heavy rain tomorrow evening. It'll be very cold. "Why are you telling me this?" he asks.

"So you don't start whingeing about the account being down money."

"Why the fuck are you out to needle me every fucking chance you get?"

"Don't use that language towards me!"

"Well then, fuck off and leave me alone – you have an affair, tell me you're leaving and now you bring a cat in here... "

"Jesus, you're going to start about a cat now, are you? A

cat – you make it sound as though it's worse than having an affair," she pauses. "You make it sound as though there was a tiger coming into the house."

A smile plays between them, fleeting. Tiger...

Harry feels the clouds gathering within. Tries to blow them away by using Tony and Derek's names as sky winds – to keep the peace for their sakes.

"You don't understand."

"That's right, Harry, I don't – why don't you have an affair and get even – it might take the chip off your shoulder."

He sighs, "I won't say I haven't thought about it – but – "

"Of course – you don't have the what... means to satisfy a woman."

She's taunting him. Trying to draw a reaction from him – make him lash out. What kind of a woman wants a fracas in the house? One in which there can be no winner. Doesn't she fucking realise that they have two kids in bed? Is she starting to lose the run of herself? Is she trying to goad him into hitting her – why? Is there a smidgin of guilt breathing within her, enough to make her feel she should be punished in some way? Or has her hatred for him become so real for her that it is as tangible as concrete? She has taken the seeds of hatred, planted them, and now they blossom.

"You can't rise my ding-dum and I won't let you rise my temper."

"You're a disgusting bollocks. A fucking creep, Harry."

He breaks into song, "Tis the season to be jolly... tra-la-la-la-la... "

Takes his tea and sandwiches to bed. A little dig at her because she doesn't like to see food upstairs. Knows she won't say anything because she too is trying to rein in her tongue.

Spite is like shite in that it has to come out – Old Confucius saying.

He drinks his tea but leaves the sandwiches alone, his appetite dying somewhere between the first and last stairs. New arrangement for Christmas – the boxroom is his. In bed, a single bed, the blind raised so he can see the sky and its stars, he tries to unwind. A few beers would help to loosen the knot in his neck and stroke his nerves to a quiet and pleasing, most welcome, numbness.

Facing the night without a drink is like a knight measuring up to a dragon without his armour.

Freeze-frame images. Picking up Basima's foot and looking at bone and blood and thinking this couldn't be really happening, he couldn't be standing here with a woman's foot in his hand, with the smell of death all around him, the smell of blood burst from a body of flesh like his. The legging is dirty. Her toenails polished pink – there is almost no space between her small and inner toe – almost Siamese toes. Peculiar. He wonders if she fretted over such a minor imperfection? He drops the limb into Musa's black plastic bag where it lands with a soft plop on other flesh. A thread from her blue legging snags under his thumb nail. Waving at him. Specks of her blood on his palm. A stigmata of sorts. Never wash his hands enough.

A cat, white with a grey and black tail, nibbles at flesh near the olive tree, its whiskers twitching as though with satisfaction at a rare delicacy it has chanced upon. Reaching for his pistol to shoot it when Musa shoos the creature away.

Later, in the Duty Room, listening to the cheeping of insects, his hands on the desk, he turns them over. A long lifeline holds a spot of blood, so minute, but it's there, always there no matter how often he washes his hands. There that night, after he had scrubbed from the elbows down with Dettol, soap and water almost too hot for him to bear. The thread under his thumb he frees and watches as it spirals under a flowing faucet into the sink's soak-hole. Sometimes he feels as though there is something caught under his thumb nail and cleans under it without ever looking to see what might be there.

Can't sleep. These images he runs as he looks at the

night sky. Seconds, mere seconds, like an excerpt from a movie — playing the same scene over and over.

He waits until he hears June emerge from the bathroom, check on the boys and close her door before he goes downstairs to have a smoke. The night might be old for her, but it is young for him. It isn't a good sign when he sees his dream before he falls asleep. Sleep would bring the main event, the big show, twist his images into grotesque sights — bring the dead back to life — a cat singing *Food, Glorious Food.* A Harry Kyle horror show — held over by popular demand. Keeps the kitchen dark — lets Barney in when he paws at the door — so fucking tired.

It's as cold as what was forecast, windier too. He leaves for work when June puts her nose in the kitchen and takes over making the boys' breakfast — egg on waffles.

He asks if she needs the car and she pretends not to hear. "Do you?" he says.

"What?"

"Need the car."

"You're hardly going to leave it stuck outside the barracks all day, are you?"

"If you don't need it, I do — that's all I'm saying."

"I need it."

"Fine."

The wind blows the rain into his face. Hard and icy cold, coming from the east. He keeps to the footpath, off the plains because they hold large puddles and are cut up with horse hoofs. He would lose time by having to circumvent them and the wet and mud would ride up over his ankles.

He has a few things he's going to say to Karl, clear-the-air talks, let him know exactly what he thinks. Why wait until he's gone to the grave, why wait until then to dance? Let him fucking have it. But keep the hands by your side, because if they start they won't stop — and haven't you enough blood, no matter how atom in size, on your hand?

You have.

Chapter 24

Harry reports into the Duty Room and runs his eyes over the previous ten days' entries in the Unit Journal. Nothing unusual – juveniles breaking windows in the Gymnasium, an attempted break into a store, a woman complaining about a dog's barking keeping her awake nights, a naked woman walking along the camp's top road, after leaving one of the messes, taking an epileptic fit in the Nissan Patrol car en route to the hospital.

Christmas – a bit of a fucking funny season. March is on duty – smells of stale booze and fresh cigarette smoke. He coughs, sniffles, then says, "The CO wants to see you first thing – he's in his office already. Early for him – his missus must have thrown him out. Again."

Dobbs is leaning by the window, looking across the road at a woman in the phone kiosk, "He must have heard about your nightmares keeping Naqoura awake half the night." "Why don't you fuck off with yourself?"

"Touchy."

What is it about people like Dobbs who like to stir shit just for the sake of stirring? He's a little older than Harry, with a cruel mouth set in Nordic features. March's drinking buddy – a pair of sarcastic fuckers. Like those old Muppet men in the balcony.

Harry sees Sarah and Pete pulling into the car park – thinks how they've got it made with two army pay packets coming into the house, but how they've got a major problem in that they're not right for each other. He can tell. Just can, more than a hunch. Sometimes you see things and you don't know how you see them but you do. You know something is going to happen before it does – you get a feeling. Like the feeling you get when you visit some place you've never been and you sense otherwise, that the place is familiar.

He enters the admin block and knocks on the CO's door, which lies ajar.

"Come in!"

"Sir, you want me?" No salute because Harry wears civilian clothes to work, for which he receives a small daily allowance. He lets it build up and claims a month before Christmas – it usually dresses the kids for the big day.

"Yeah, Harry – take a seat."

Duggan has a ring of grey hair and a shiny poll that is red as though from embarrassment at its baldness. Fleshy features with large intelligent eyes that are hooded and critical.

"This sexual assault case – I'm not happy about it."

Harry waits. The CO riffles papers through his fingers, shaking his head.

"It tells me nothing."

"Amongst other things it tells you that Smart entered the room and wanted Enright to suck him off."

"Don't act the eejit – I'm not in the humour – there's no charge sheet for Smart. And none for Enright or the other gobshite involved."

The CO pauses, goes to continue but Harry says, "Look, sir – okay, she shouldn't have had Williams in her room – and Williams knows he shouldn't have been in there. That sort of thing is against regulations – but do I charge them? So Smart comes in and he's drunk and he wants a bit of the action. He's by nature a bit of a bollocks, a bully – but he's cute as a hawk – he's quite willing with the truth. He knows that everyone in this, if it goes to a court-martial, comes out smelling shitty. How does Williams explain it away to his wife? Enright's character gets more mud thrown on it while Smart just apologises and says sorry for a drunken escapade and that it wouldn't have happened if she had kept her mouth shut in the first instance."

"He walks so — walks away from assaulting Enright and Williams, and fuck it, Harry, they all walk away. Women in the army — I always fucking said it. Trouble."

"What else can be done?"

"Enright's mother is bothering my ear — she wants the army to do something about it."

"She should have taken an interest when her daughter withdrew the complaint she made to the guards."

The CO sighs, picks up a Biro, prises off its blue cap and uses its pocket-clip to clean between his lower teeth.

"So — otherwise your report is quite good, but I want one change, at Para Nine."

"Change?"

"I want you to recommend that Private Enright should be transferred to a unit of her choice — I think a clean break is needed."

"A reward for lying to me — for her lack of co-operation?"

"Just see it as a tactical manoeuvre, eh?"

"It's a buy-off, sir. She'll be happy. Mama will be happy."

"Aye, and Mama won't make media waves and the whole thing can die a happy death." Pauses, "A happy death, right?" Harry nods. Thinks that perhaps this is what Enright wanted all the time. A transfer from a unit that's hard to leave, an operational unit constantly busy. Fuck it, it's over. Not much left to do except give Enright a bottling for lying to him. Might not even bother doing that — why bother? Why give a fuck? His bottling won't stop her lying.

"I'll amend that para, sir."

"Good." Smacks his lips.

Back in his own office Harry stares through the window. Pete has left in the saloon for Wexford to check on why there's army tentage in a farmer's field. Sarah's gone for milk for tea. No sign of Karl. His bad days are coming in strings now and not in singles and pairs. A robin lands on the sill, beak full of bread, flutters to a branch and perches there. Harry looks at his palm, folds it quickly when he sees the speck of blood, unfurls his fingers to look again. A glance. Not there. It only comes when he looks hard.

Al and Ivan have gone to the Canaries for three weeks. Al left a message on his answering machine to that effect, with Cliff Richard's *Summer Holiday* playing in the background. Christmas abroad, well for them – he wonders if Al left a contact number with Mum in case Dad – no, Al would prefer to ring home once a day and find out that way – ring and expect to be told bad news instead of it coming to look for him. Harry'll drop around this evening to see the oul fella. It'll take him out of the house for a while. Maybe he'll bring Derek around. Though June doesn't like the child to visit. She says you just don't know what diseases are being coughed up. Besides, and she takes much pleasure in kicking him in the balls with this, they don't give two shites about their grandkids, just giving a cosmetic wash to their relationship – a card here and money there – never their time. Mum says your own kids grow quickly and leave, and that grandkids would grow twice as quickly and the odds were you wouldn't get to see them maturing into adults. Kids, their developing years signpost the road to your grave. Harry thinks they have a bad way of looking at things, but he can't change them and they are his parents. It's the only anchor that had kept him from severing his connections with them – like you can do with a friend who turns out not to be one – you can drop him easily enough.

Slips on his jacket and makes for the mess for morning coffee. Sarah hasn't returned with the milk which means she has met someone and is having a chat, or doing something on army time she shouldn't be doing, like getting her hair done, or a good manicure. Whatever.

The mess is a mess – beer bottles holed up on bar tables, cigarette ends flooding ashtrays. Beer spume in glasses and in spills on the tables, soggy beer-mats. March says the barman has reported on Sick Parade. Dobbs is peeling off his greatcoat by the coat stand beside the jacks. There are grains of snow fastened to his shoulders. Some of the other lads are hovering at a circular table that's loaded with crockery and chrome tea and coffee urns. Like vultures crowding around a carcass, each looking to break the circle to get his fill. Dobbs rubs his hands as he approaches them.

"God, you wouldn't take it out in weather like this."

Harry ignores him, quaffs his coffee, draws on his cigarette and holds the smoke in his mouth for moments. Then, leaving his cup down he massages his right temple with two fingers – imagines that the vein throbbing there is clearly visible, like the beating pulse of a river reaching flood level or a red neon light flashing where one shouldn't.

"How's things?" Dobbs says.

"Okay," Harry says.

March shows the yellow of his few teeth as he sits beside Dobbs. His tobacco-stained fingers ring a handle-less mug that no one else ever uses because they know of March's recurring mouth ulcers and bleeding gums.

"Did ya sort out that sex case?" he asks.

Dobbs wags his cigarette, "Of course he did – it's his personal sex case that he can't solve."

The silence, it falls. It trickles from soul to soul, from wall to wall, so that all idle chatter and minor guffawing dries up. Dobbs realises that he's gone a step too far, a foot into a minefield and the lump in his throat moves up a floor. The only noise in the mess is the sound of Sky News breaking on the hour.

"What exactly can't I solve?" Harry says through clenched teeth.

"Only messing, I was only messing."

"You worry about your own sex case, Dobbs."

"Mine's done with – I got rid of her."

The chatter starts to rise, to smother the voice of Sky's reporter. Nothing's going to happen – no wild swing of a fist.

March says, "Jaesus, Harry – it has to be tough on you – working in the same office with the guy who's, you know yourself, rattling your missus."

Harry snaps, "Back off!"

"Ah, but shure he's never in work, is he?" March says, his tongue running along his cracked lower lip. His tongue enjoying the hunt.

"According to what I hear he's always in," Dobbs leers.

Harry connects with his first punch. It catches Dobbs flush on the jawbone and sends him crashing against March and on to the floor. Stabs at air with his second.

Dobbs gets to his feet, makes a charge for Harry but the others hold him back.

"I'll get you for that, you bastard – your missus is a fucking whore, a tramp of the highest order – and I thought mine was bad."

Harry rubs his knuckles, his head hanging a little. Shame. March is looking at his fly, saying his balls had been scalded with tea and after a moment's hesitation adds that Harry should be arrested. No one makes a move on his words. Harry sits down. The hands on Dobbs' shoulders usher him towards the door. Digging in his heels he says he wants his greatcoat and beret and in possession of them he storms from the mess, holding his jaw.

"If either of you bother me again I'll do you. I don't give a fuck as to the consequences – do you hear me, March?"

March looks east and west, towards the long windows on the walls. His eyes refuse to meet Harry's.

"Do you hear me?"

A nod. Short and brief – says as much as a picture. Gets to his feet, fingers like a spill of brown twigs reach down for his coat. Tea break's over. The mess empties.

Harry stays behind. Regretting that he had lashed out, that he had lost his composure, but fuck it, you only allow someone so many pokes at a raw nerve.

Door slams. Sarah. Speaking as she walks, "Harry, I heard- you're in shit – he's gone sick – jaw's coming up like a balloon. Fucker's getting March to photograph the injury." Sits opposite. "Harry?"

"Yeah, I... "

"Jesus – Harry."

"Sarah, what? I hit him for a reason, the same way you tore Pete's face."

She looks away, at the spill of butts on the carpet.

"Sorry – Sarah – Jesus... "

She sighs. Concern for him spreads across her pretty face. Her hand guides her hair from her eyes.

"You better tell the CO, Harry, before the others do. You know what he's like – he'll go spare."

"Yeah, I'll tell him."

"Then, maybe you should take some leave – get some help."

"Help?"

"Come on, Harry – you're going through a rough patch – what with June and that incident in Lebanon playing on your mind... "

"Help?"

"Counselling – don't play the thick with me, Harry."

"Did I tell you about the Leb?"

"You mentioned some of it – when he came back Dobbs went on about your famous nightmares."

Harry nods and says he'll follow her over to the office in a few minutes. Sarah goes to say something but joins her lips, her words changing direction, "Right, I'll see you there – in a few minutes."

When she's gone, he pours his face into his hands and breathes hard. The wheels are rightly coming off his wagon – even the fucking spare – you can hear the screws tap dancing on the road, the spokes whirring on their sides, the slide of the wagon towards the cliff, smell the dust clouds in its wake.

He makes for the toilets and a cubicle. The seat's up and a shit-stain rides up from beneath the waterline. Looks away. Far away. The tears, they come hot and scalding, uncontrollable. He shudders. It's as though an earthquake affects his heart — he feels a pain there and a complete and utter heaviness. Dries his tears with the back of his hand and pieces of toilet paper he hesitates to use because of someone else's finger indentations. As quickly as he dries them more tears arrive and all he can do is lean his back to the wall and let them come.

In the office Sarah hands him coffee. He washed his face in the mess but he couldn't wash the red from around his eyes.

He's pale and shaky in himself — his thoughts all over the place. Fingers nervously clinging to a cigarette, the way the driver of his wagon clings to the cliff, looking down at the wagon plunging into the darkness.

"Maybe you should go home?" Sarah says.

"No — I'll be fine."

"You're not fine — don't see the CO in this condition — he'll use it to block you for promotion — you know how they keep the bad bits about you in their memory — go on, Harry. Go home."

The phone rings and their eyes meet. Sarah lifts it and tells the CO that Harry has left for the office.

"I have to go down and give him a report," she says. "It's better if you see him after he hears some mitigating evidence, eh?"

Harry gives the slightest of nods, slips on his jacket and pulls a pair of Wellingtons from a locker, "I'm going for a walk, to clear my head. I can't face June in this condition, either — can you spare some fags? I'll fix — "

"There's a packet on my desk — take those."

Harry smiles, "Easy known I'm in bits – can you imagine a smoker coming home from Lebanon without his duty free – a bad mistake, eh?"

"Not if you're trying to quit."

"Now isn't a very good time for me to quit."

"I don't think so either. No."

He walks by the admin block and its corrugated fence, into the trees, making his way to the last timber-framed shop in camp and beyond that to the plains. It's freezing. The grassland's coldness pushing up through the soles of his boots. Pockets of frozen snow here and there, ice covering the puddles, sheep hurrying from him. A fox in the distance making its way to its lair, hunched as though its bones were being compressed by the bitter cold. Sprigs of furze and a Mars-bar wrapper trapped under the ice. The mountains obscured by fog – on a patch of the plains there's a fall of sunlight that withers too quickly. He's at his favourite spot, the ring fort mostly covered in dense furze. He and Barney sometimes rest here on a visible portion of ridge during summer evening walks and watch the red sun sink beneath the Hill of Allen, caping the woods, skyline and fields with red and amber. Too cold to sit around now and he misses having to call Barney back from chasing rabbits. Home – he feels as hunched in himself as the fox, but not so much from the cold as from apprehension. Things are sliding. He feels things are sliding. In blunt-speak, he tells himself: okay – in your face – you're losing your fucking grip.

Chapter 25

Harry reaches home just before dark. He had walked from the rath to the tunnel under the rail tracks, along the Race of the Black Pig trail, past the fox covert, the golf club, and lonely spots in the furze where two women from Kildare Town were murdered, and another place, a clearing in the furze he had stumbled upon as a lad with his friends when playing hide- and-go-seek – a woman with her legs wrapped around the small of a man's back. Her head to the side, eyes closed, wisps of dark hair lying across her profile, the man's fat hairy arse pumping, his lopsided balls hanging like a bull's, slapping her. He grunting like a mad thing. She saying, "Hurry, Mikey, you're hurting me." Then she lapsed into a soft moaning. Harry saw that she was enjoying it – her hands slipped on to the big arse, pulling him into her. Both coming at the same time in a fit of orgasmic twitching. Harry took in the red knickers lying on the grass and the black bra that cupped a thistle. He backed into the furze, dropping to his hunkers as his friends' voices cut the air. Coming this way.

She slipped from underneath the man and getting to her feet arranged her long skirt and oversized sweater. The man tucked away his mickey and zipped up, smiling to himself as she ran her knickers up the twin masts of her skinny legs. The lads on top of them, saying, "Howya, Mrs Shields – howya, Mister Kennedy?" Saying it like it was normal to come across a pair of adults in the furze.

Off-the-cuff reponse from Kennedy, "Great, lads, and yourselves?" Nothing from Shields. Through the haphazard bramble pattern of the furze, Harry saw that she was worried. She knew that tongues would wag, rumours would blaze and she'd have to think of some classy lies to tell her husband. Harry never told a soul what he had seen — he kept it trapped in his mind and the images played there for a long time, fading as the months passed. But the images returned fresh and vivid when he saw Mrs Shields and her swollen belly in town one market day, her husband walking by her side, linking her arm. Red knickers and black see-through bra, her satisfied smile, her hands rocking the hairy arse, his balls thumping against her. Her stifled pleasure groans. Close to them the sun was shiny on beads of sheep shite.

"They were riding in the furze," a friend said at the time.

"She's the greatest ride going," from another.

"Takes mickies off a conveyor belt," a lad he didn't know.

"Bag o' Mickies," someone said, "that's her name — she charges a tenner a jaunt."

Harry feels near to despair as he sits in a chair by the fire sipping at a mug of tea. He was fourteen then and the images are still ripe — and sometimes his feelings swing from one of excitement to another of disgust. So it still affects his thoughts, how he feels — a simple ride in the furze. What hope has he of ever shifting Kafra from his mind? Of looking at the images in his head with an indifferent if not cold eye?

The house is empty.

She hasn't left him because he checked the wardrobes and her clothes stared back. Probably rounding up the last of the Christmas shopping — June's the sort who buys for Christmas the whole year long. He doesn't like such forward planning. Never did. Less so since a fella in work lost his wife and he thought how harsh an ordeal it must have been for him to open the Christmas presents she had bought during the year. She took it for granted that she'd be around to hand them out. Fate's a fucker like that – lets you start something it knows you aren't going to finish. Fate gives you ghosts to play with – memories of dead friends – who sometimes, without warning, flit into his mind and present him with a scene from the past, a time they shared, and always he's left to wonder about them, where they are now, really are now.

Harry doesn't believe that the grave is where it all ends. He doesn't believe in much, but he believes that. He can't even offer himself an explanation as to why he believes. Now and then, because of his upbringing as a Roman Catholic, it is necessary for him to believe in something. Fuck, even an atheist believes in something – a world without God, maybe, but it's still believing in something. Cracking. Mind racing, thoughts whirring about as though they are at Mondello Park in Formula 4 racing cars.

Thinking of many things at once. Chequered flag waving like crazy.

Draws on his cigarette and stubs it in the ashtray when he hears the side gate opening. Derek rushes in, cheeks reddened from the evening cold, saying he had a McDonald's in Naas and that Tony wouldn't eat anything – he was so bold. Claps his hands. In an awful hurry to shed his coat as though it is a second skin he hates.

"I got him," he says.

"Who?" Takes a few seconds to register. Realises then just as Derek breathes, "My kitten – I'm calling him Bobby – Mum is bringing him in – we got a basket for him and all."

Barney's tail is out of joint. He stands with his head at an angle, probably feeling like an old toy. Sulking and worrying about his status. Aware that he is no longer the choice plaything. A fucking cat. A scrawny white thing, miaowing weakly. Harry feels the revulsion he feels every time he sees a cat. It starts with a tingling sensation in his toes and ends with a prickly feeling in his scalp.

The boys surround the basket. Derek puts an old sweater of Harry's under the kitten in its basket and spreads some paper on the lino.

"Do your wee-wee on the paper, right – good girl."

Harry meets June's eyes. Doesn't notice till her eyes tell him that his fingers are going everywhichwhere at once – like Riverdance dancers gone crazy on stage.

The cat in Kafra is large and wild. Domesticated gone wild, which is probably the worst kind of wild. Knows enough about humans not to trust them, to eat them when the opportunity arises.

He never saw its eyes but imagines them to be green and shiny as opals. Darting from the lane, stopping behind the olive tree, razoring flesh with its teeth and claws – jumps onto the roof when Musa shoos it. In fading daylight Harry sees a morsel of human flesh silhouetted in the cat's mouth, its whiskers like miniature wires, strumming, he imagines, as it chews and then swallows. Licks its paws. Looks down at the square, like a shopper on the watchout for a bargain, something free or ten per cent off, with extra bonus points. Harry regrets he didn't shoot it – but Musa and Sam – they have things to show him. Licks its paws, and settles down on the roof, waiting for another opportunity to feed on a bombshell's leftovers – human slivers.

Derek says, "Do you want to hold him, Dad?"

"No!" Then softly, "No – later, son, later."

Tony rubs the kitten's ear and Derek pushes his hand away. Barney's looking over from his corner and his folded blanket – a worried-looking hound – one who never owned a basket.

Harry starts for the sitting-room. He feels a little ill. June follows him into the hall,

"Harry?"

"What?"

"After Christmas – I want you out after Christmas. This atmosphere isn't good for the kids. Can't be for us either."

"A fucking cat – I told you, I told you... "

June looks over her shoulder and closes the kitchen door behind her. He knows she's going to raise her tone because she always glances about to see if the lads are within earshot before she goes into her harsh mode – it's like her mouth is a weapon and she needs to carry out a safety check before loosening her words.

"It's a cat, Harry. You must have seen a load of them since you came home."

"I try to ignore them, shut them out – you've brought one into the house – for fuck's sake – you're torturing me. Why?"

"Derek – wanted – a – cat."

"And you want me out of here – how very fucking convenient for you – I can just imagine you saying to yourself, 'I know just the pussy to shift him'. You're a bitch."

"Listen here, you – "

"No, you fucking listen – you cheat on me and you want me to leave. You've a fucking nerve."

"I don't put the fear of God into my kids – I don't snap and shout at them – I don't push them away, keep them at arm's length. I don't put them on tenterhooks – you do, Harry. They're afraid of you."

"Fuck off, will you? You would say that, wouldn't you – you're making ammunition out of what I'm going through and throwing it at me."

"No, I'm not. As far as I can see, Harry, you're shooting yourself in the foot – go and get help – we're finished – old you or a new you, it's over – but the boys think the world of you, and I can't be shut of you as permanently as I'd like to be – they want you, and need you to be a better father than you are – right now you're just a shell, an empty husk of a man. Impatient, abrupt, wearing a scowl. . ."

"I thought you were moving out – what happened?"

Derek shows his face.

"Go in, love, we're having a chat about what food to leave out for Santa," June says.

"Where did I go wrong with you?" Harry asks.

Shrugs, "I don't know — I find you too boring, too depressing to be around, and when you went to Lebanon it was like a load had been lifted from my shoulders — I came to realise I didn't want to grow old with you — sounds clichéd — but it's how I felt."

Harry takes a step back. If it's over then her tongue should be treating him under the Geneva Convention. Boring? He thought he was being dependable, reliable.

Love withers. It blooms, has its time, and then dies. She is so certain she doesn't want him. So positive. About the only time he has ever seen her so positive about anything. Jesus Christ, when is it all going to end? Are You as deaf as some soldiers?

Listen to her. Heed her. It's over. Definitely, fucking definitely.

Do you love her? When's the last time you told her? A year ago, two, longer? When's the last time you bought her flowers? Wasn't it when Tony was born and wouldn't she expect that of you? No — you got her flowers after her father died, remember, a month or two afterwards. She put them"on his grave. You didn't get them to end up in a cemetery. Perhaps it was a symbolic gesture — she was burying her feelings for you? Only she wasn't aware of it at the time. Yeah, he loves her. But he's fucked up everything. Whatever chance he had of saving the marriage died in Kafra — June doesn't want a shambles of a man — bad enough to love someone who is dying — but it's a waste of space loving a fellow with a bockety mind, who could be around for ages — she doesn't want to be his mind's Zimmer frame. Soldier, my arse — Macho Man, me hole — Professional soldier. Christ. Two war casualties and he wilts like a scorched pansy.

"Yeah, okay, I'll move out after Christmas," he says, voice cracking with the strain.

She says nothing.

He smacks his lips and shrugs his shoulders. The mood

he's in – it isn't fair to spoil the boys' Christmas. Mopey-hole. So wise-up – don't ruin it for them.

Derek again, "I have to go to the toilet."

June goes into the kitchen, Derek takes to the stairs, while Harry takes in the small optic Christmas tree in the hall, its changing colours, the drawings of the Middle East he brought home – their tinselled frames – copies of David Roberts' sketchings from the late 19th century – of Tyre and Sidon in Lebanon and of Akko and Haifa in Israel – of places Harry knows well – changed, of course, the people in them long dead. Only the places live on, albeit wearing a different face, but there, as always. Like Kafra.

Fuck this. He reaches for his jacket, slips it on and feels for money in the pockets. Passes through the kitchen like a breeze, saying he's going out. Stating the fucking obvious. Like June does every so often, airing the truth of her feelings, as if he doesn't know – airs them because a notion isn't born until it's said – repeats the truth every so often to make it fasten in his brain, until he accepts that it is over. He accepts. *I do, I do, I do, I do, I do – an Abba tune* in his head. Mentaller, he is.

Outside the back door he listens to the noises of the night – the distant beep of a car, the gentle clickety clack of a train, fading footsteps, an electric drill – upstairs the toilet flushes and then the taps run as Derek washes his hands, lathering them with liquid soap to kill all the soldier germs. Harry's hands – he can never get them spotless. Can't kill his soldier germs.

Tony asks where has daddy gone and June says to the shop for a newspaper.

Tony wonders if the paper is for the kitten to poo on. A low miaow. Harry pulls his collar up against the stiff breeze – almost five, most of the lads in barracks will have gone home by now – almost dark. Streetlights guide his way to the shop.

Takes a cab to see his parents. Either that or get drunk in the Rising Sun and he hasn't enough money to get drunk –

there's no slate for him in a civvy pub – unlike the messes.

The old man smiles when he sees him. Harry thinks how a smile is the one thing that age doesn't change in a person. He wears a blue turtleneck sweater and a sleeveless cardigan with brown buttons that remind Harry of chocolate sweets. Maltesers with a criss-cross pattern. A Carmelite scapular around his neck, only its strings visible. There's a screen fitted around him to ward off draughts only he can feel. Mum is watching Coronation Street in the sitting-room. She had answered his rap on the door and let him in, saying she would be out in a moment, to head into the kitchen and see his father.

Harry says, "How are you today?"

"Tired."

"In pain?"

Doesn't answer. Slight downward plunge of his bushy eyebrows indicates that he shouldn't have to ask. His lips are rimmed with scum and some whiskers Mum had missed with the razor.

"I'll see a month or two of next year – the heart is strong, you see," he says, like someone who has lost pride and found regret in something once esteemed.

Harry plugs in the kettle. Turns on the radio. How does the old man stick the silence in the kitchen? There's a portable TV on a shelf across a corner, but it's only there for the racing and Gaelic football matches.

"Al rang – he rings every day – rang twice on Sunday," Dad says.

"Yeah – that's good – I'm glad you've mended things." "Ah, not mended, Harry – it's just an agreement to put aside our differences – so that I can die in peace and afterwards he can live in peace. Guilt's a curse of a legacy to leave someone."

Harry makes tea with the loose tea leaves that Mum insists on using. She says putting hoods over tea is like using a condom when there's no need. You have to laugh at her sometimes, the way she goes on, the things she comes out with.

"If it wasn't for Ivan... "

"Jesus, don't mention his name in this house. "

"For fuck's sake, Dad... "

Makes a face, "Sorry, Harry — don't want to hear. Its near broken your mother's heart... there's nothing gay about having a gay son."

Harry says nothing. Though he wants to say a lot in defence of his brother. Hands the old man his tea, winces at the wasted forearms, the burst blood-vessels like purple clouds. Brings his mother in a cup. Back in the kitchen, seated in at the table, Dad says, without turning his head, "June?"

"It's over."

"You can move back in here, son — me and your mum have discussed it — the house is yours when we're gone."

He looks about. It's more appealing than a billet. Easily. He could fix up the garden and carry out some repairs — guttering is sagging a little, shed door is hanging by a single hinge. Small jobs he always promises Mum he'll get around to fix but never does. He's forever searching for enough time.

Maybe he should quit the army. Mightn't have a choice in the matter. Dobbs will probably take a civvy action against him. Perhaps not — a judge might think he deserved what he got. Dobbs might think so, too. But certainly the CO will take a dim view of a sergeant clocking a corporal. It's a court-martial offence. Fuck it, anyway.

"It's okay, son, really — you can move in any time."

"Thanks, thanks, Dad. I probably will. Soon."

In the taxi on the way home he decides he has one other call to make. If he can't sleep in peace then why should that other prick? Karl. He's in the mood for dealing with him now. Unloading some of his grief. But keep the hands by the side, eh? Say what you have to say and go, just go. Leave him with heat in his ears — a bum on his soul. It's the least he deserves. Bastard — for taking his marriage to the grave with him.

Chapter 26

Lebanon. The old man in the mingi shop coughs into the back of his hand. Snuffles. He sits behind a walnut desk, worn and unsteady, with small glasses for the pot of black tea close to his elbow. He rises from the chair carrying a pained expression, as though the effort causes suffering, and extends his hand, saying, "Welcome, my friend, welcome." He wears black slacks with the ends tucked into ankle boots and a brown leather jacket with enough wrinkles to match those on his round face. When he sits he rests his hands and chin atop a cane. He sells watches and pens and little knick-knacks, like plastic kettles that come to boil quickly and alarm clocks that waken you at cock-crow with a cock's crowing.

Harry is in Naqoura, his first night back in HQ after his detachment in Tyre. It's late. The skies are rich with stars and a moon's thin smile. A chill sea breeze cools the air. Winter is early this year, the old man says.

His name is Khalil and he has helped Harry with MP matters, passing snippets of information in exchange for Harry's assistance in tracking down UNIFIL soldiers who owe him money and who, as it edges near rotation time, don't look like paying. He comes from Beirut. Had to leave there in a hurry — shrugs — the life was better there before the war. War is no good.

Harry buys a Swiss Army watch to replace the one June bought him for his last birthday. Its glass cracked in Kafra. He doesn't know how. In Tyre he had left it on the duty-room floor beside the bunk and stood on it the next morning, finishing the job.

A watch meant to die an early death. He took it as an omen and it bothered him the whole day.

"Sit. Have tea," Khalil says.

Harry slips the watch on his wrist and lifts his change from the table, a pair of crumpled dollars that Khalil had difficulty in retrieving from a stiff drawer. "Money doesn't like leaving me," he smiles.

Harry sips at his black, sugary tea. Khalil scoops a tiny spoonful of sugar and tips it into his glass. Stirs. The stirring is done frantically — the only noise in the shop.

When he rests the wet spoon in the bowl it stains the sugar.

They talk for a long while. An old man and a young man from different backgrounds and cultures who each see a sorrow in the other's eyes. Khalil draws the blinds and turns a sign on the door to read Closed.

Khalil mentions a nephew who was conscripted into the SLA and who shot himself days later. He speaks in the low voice of someone who is depressed.

"I remember the day he was born, his first steps, the way he smiled, and I think of how he died and I feel it in my heart that somehow I am to blame. It is the children I feel sorry for, and the men who were children during the war for they know nothing else. Nothing. He was my sister's only son, and when she came to me for money so she could send him to the States to live with her husband's brother, I shook my head, and said, 'No'. I say it again and again after each time she begs and then I say it no more I say she is to pay me what she already owes and it is then she leaves. Somehow to blame? I am all to blame "

Harry says nothing. Thinks of the stiff drawer. He would have spoken of Kafra then, that evening, with that old man, freed some of the poison, had his wife not come in from an adjoining room. She carries a small rectangular brazier with smouldering coals and sets it at the floor, sitting next to Harry.

She smiles. Khalil nods, looks at Harry and sighs. She carries his pills on her palm and nods for him to take them. The lines on her palm resemble those on a well-creased map.

"I'm not a well man," he says. "The heart it is bad."

When Harry returns on his eight-day trip he finds that the shop is closed and Pablo tells him that Khalil is in Marajoun hospital — "It is not good for him."

It doesn't matter what your name is, what you are in life, how rich or poor you are, the end result is the same. Money sometimes delays the inevitable — yes, it does. If you're dangerously ill, you can wag a chequebook in front of a doctor's face and if he can he'll operate, put in the effort to prolong your life. Money can do. Talks. Negotiates.

A hospital in Beirut that wouldn't treat an injured child unless it got ten thousand dollars up front. The child fortunate that his bike collided with a UN vehicle and not a Lebanese car — the UN could afford to foot the bill and save his limbs. Money is a god. Better than prayer? Don't tell the poor.

The taxi driver wants to talk. It's nearly Christmas and he wants to talk about prices, about people puking in the back seat and how one late night/early morning he copped in the rear view a young one wanking an oul lad. He talks even though he knows Harry isn't paying him much heed. Harry stares through the fly window at the passing darkness. He finds the driver's constant chat irritating and asks him to pull over. He fixes him up with the full fare.

"You're three streets away, you know?"

"Like I said I need the air and the walk."

"Suit yourself."

"Thanks."

Crosses the street, making for the footpath that'll lead past the housing estates to Karl's house. The path is narrow and up in several places where new dormer bungalows are being built on small sites. He pauses on the bridge over the M50 and looks at the slick of tar sweeping towards Dublin —

listens to the language of the road – the noise of traffic, the trees rustling on the steep banks, a creaking road sign near to parting from its pole, the rush of cars under the bridge. The other day he had to drive to Naas to have the car serviced. It spilled. The rain thrummed on the roof, but passing under the bridge, for milliseconds, the rain stopped and the silence gave him a start. And then the thrumming noise resumed. A familiar annoyance – something that Harry was glad to hear, because he had been thinking about Kafra and was trying to leave there by focusing in on the noise of the rain. Thinking of someone walking through a field, how wet she must be, thinking of her smelling turf smoke as she reached the house. Basima.

The light is on in Karl's sitting-room. A large, stylish Tudoresque house with front gardens full of shrubs and trees and a gravel drive. A security light comes on when he is a few strides from the front door. Pushes in the doorbell. Waits. The woman who opens the door is pretty. Really pretty.

Model slim. A brunette. Harry's nostrils ride the scent of her perfume. Christian Dior? Estée whatsitcalled?

"May I help you?"

A voice booms from behind, "Who is it, Dav – at this hour?"

Harry doesn't recognise the man's voice. He says he's here to speak with Karl.

"He's up, okay – in the lounge. You say you work with him?" Dav's voice is silky.

Nods. "He knows why I'm here."

"Really? You'd better come in."

Harry keeps his features glued together when she introduces herself as Karl's ex. The brute, she laughs, on the sofa, is Karl's brother, Damian. He has film-star looks, and a wrestler's physique. A larger version of Karl – the sort of guy you'd only take on in a fight if he had his back turned and you'd a baseball bat ready to pounce.

Dav excuses herself for a moment and disappears into an adjoining room. Harry admires the floorspace, the tiles and rugs, the gas fire with its artificial coals – this is what June wants. This and Karl. He sees now why she hasn't moved in – because the vultures are already circling. Have got in before her. Eyeing up the flesh.

Damian says nothing. Yawns. Picks at the knees of his jeans. Harry says it's a cold night. He says it to stop him from ignoring him – to make him recognise his presence. All he gets is a look. A cynical look. Hard eyes. Clinical.

"Yes, Mr Kyle, he'll see you."

Harry walks through into the room. A lounge converted into a bedroom. Karl's dressed in clothes that think badly of staying on him – so loose. Aye, he's fucked.

When Karl nods for him to sit, Harry says he prefers to stand.

"You know?" Karl says. His words low.

"Yes. Of course, I fucking know. June told me and the eyes of every fucker in the unit told me – but only one had the balls to tell me up straight."

"Ah, that had to be Sarah."

Karl sits on the edge of the sofa. The TV is on, a video stilled.

"June doesn't want you – if it hadn't been me... "

"It was you – all the years we've worked together and all this time you've – "

"I've always wanted June... we grew up together, you know?"

"I... "

"I'm dying, Harry – there's no future for me with June. She wanted to come live with me – but look," his eyes tour to the door. "You can see the problems she would have encountered after my demise, eh?"

"My kids are all that's important to me. I'm losing them –"

"You're losing yourself, Harry, for fuck's sake. It's as clear to me as my shakes are to you. You need help – I heard about Dobbs. Not like you, Harry, is it? To lash out. What's next, who's next – me?"

"I came to see you – to let you know how I feel – I feel so fucking hurt, and if you were a well man I probably would go for you. Crush you."

"I know how you feel."

"No... "

"I do. Christ, I do – look outside and open your eyes – why do you think I waited so long for June? I wouldn't make a move because I knew exactly what it felt like, that certain pain only treachery causes – but because I'm dying – I didn't want to die not knowing her, not having her – and she wasn't happy with you – I – "

"Shut the fuck up, Karl. Just shut up."

"I had all the reasons – "

"I love her. She's my wife."

Silence.

"I'm sorry. Harry – but you've lost her, and you can't live in that part of your life – "

"Who the fuck are you to tell me where I can live?"

Karl sighs. The TV screen goes snowy. Tears well in Harry's eyes – brought there by anger and frustration and truth and a deep sorrow. He has nothing to offer – he can change nothing. There is Kafra and there will always be small Kafras – there are marital break-ups and there will always be marital break-ups. There are voids in his life and always will be.

"I came to tell you that I think you're a bollocks. Karl. I want you to know that."

Karl's lips go thin.

"I came to tell you other things – rant and rave, but I'll leave you thinking about what I think."

"I don't want forgiveness, Harry – never that."

"Aren't you lucky? You'd go hungry."

Harry turns at the door. "Have a happy death, Karl."

"You're sick, Harry, get help. Do it for your kids – now, fuck off and leave me alone."

Dav eases the door behind him. He lights up a cigarette in the porch, pulls his collar against the night's damp air and makes for the road with each step broadening his regret at his parting words to Karl.

An hour and a half's walking ahead – much of it along the edge of the Curragh where it'll be pitch black when the town's streetlights peter out. Alone with the night, his thoughts, his pains – a starless sky no fit companion for a mood as black as his.

They – Karl and June – say they've known each other for a long time. But he and June have a history, too – they met at a disco in Newbridge. A simple meeting of eyes, a simple request to share a dance – the song? *Feelings*, golden oldie – *nothing more than feelings*. A late-night walk along the river bank, the lights from the dormitories in the Dominican college shining pale and oblong on the quiet and brooding Liffey waters.

Dropping her home, seeing her to the door, sharing a last laugh together before she turned a key in the door and disappeared inside. What on earth did they laugh at?

Where did the source of that laughter go – the easy abandonment of life's shackles? They had taken a rich pleasure from being in each other's company. Spring days growing into summer and a rash of hot days – days when they trekked mountain trails in the Glen of Imaal, returning from the hill walks with an evening dew on them, drying off and drinking beer and eating roughly fashioned ham sandwiches, the sort an old bachelor uncle of his used to make, fat left hanging over crusty lips. Like shirt-tails that need tucking in.

Innocent days. First row at her twenty-first birthday party when she relayed a reefer to him and he passed it on without stoking it with his lips. He didn't do hash, he said. She was pissed and unreasonable, and when she turned her shoulder to him and teased him by laughing and joking with the guy next to her, some poor man's version of Bob Marley, he got up and walked out. She didn't call him for three days. Said a little hash now and then didn't do anyone any harm – that he shouldn't be too square about things. Square? It's square to force someone to smoke something they don't want. She said it was nothing to fall out over. He agreed and they picked up the reins of their relationship. An easy road to travel – the road to marriage, when you're in love.

A pair of "I do's" uttered to each other in front of a priest who later defrocked himself and married a sheep-woman from the Curragh. Harry sees him sometimes – he looks as though he would prefer his collar to have a stranglehold on him – love, if it exists, distorts the brain's workings. Deludes people into believing in some sort of fantasy world of Happy Ever After. Is it all just nature's con job – a meeting of male and female who are attracted to each other – nature's business deal? Isn't running a marriage like running a business – credits and debits in love and money, children and time?

Harry – walk. You're thinking too much about too much. Rest the brain. Don't be cynical. You think cynical when you think too deeply. Harry, walk. Just walk. Don't think. Think, then, because if you don't the eejit in the car coming your way will drive you off the road. Harry steps onto the plains, the grass soggy beneath his feet.

The car passes at speed. Harry doubts the driver saw him till the last instant, till it would have been too late to avoid hitting him. Bollocks. Only that he moved off the road he could have been lying in bits, broken up, a fragmented human – knowing his luck the cats were waiting in the wings. Bastards. *Let's eat Harry. Yum, fucking yum.*

Walks on, increasing the tempo, down to his last fag. Love. Yeah. Loves Derek and Tony. If anything happened to them he wouldn't want to live a second longer. Don't think of that. Amazing how that nightmare doesn't surface – holding Derek in the foetal position while a nurse performed a lumbar puncture – restraining him as the long needles went deep. On a drip, unable to straighten up, contrary – in pain – he and June by his side in that small cubicle with the double doors open to let in sunlight – waiting on test results. The relief pouring through their veins when they're told that Derek didn't have the deadly strain of meningitis. In the corridor snapping up coffees from the vending machine and seeing a weeping couple clinging to each other for support – the fact is, that summer's day, one child went home to start a holiday and another went home to be buried.

Fact is that near scare didn't bond a faltering relationship, didn't make him or June take stock of the important things in life – didn't he leave for Lebanon and didn't June start her affair? Risking his life in Lebanon for money, taking six months out from his kids, and that time is a long time in a child's mind. And June, too – maybe they got such a scare with Derek they just ran away. Ran away. Not cowards, though, not that. Just the initial impact of realising how close they came to losing Derek – if you're lucky you get to run from nightmares. A headful of nightmares – honest to Christ.

She's up. June. In the kitchen sipping at coffee. The kitten's pissing on the floor, on a newspaper photograph of Charlie Haughey, former Taoiseach – seems appropriate as everyone else is having a slash at him.

Harry wants to kick the kitten in the ribs. Wants to hear its bones break, watch it die, and its mouth lie still. Realising what he wants makes him feel ill. If it were a passing thought it wouldn't matter – something mad you think about doing but you know in your heart and soul you'd never do, not in a million years, because you just know, know you've a safety net locked inside you – the most harm you'll do is bitch and scream, but Harry knows it isn't just an idea of his, a floating idea. It is something real, which he believes can happen so very easily – and his stomach is upset because he has already, to all intents and purposes, killed the kitten. There remains just the physical realisation of his mind's actions.

It is then, when he thinks of Derek and Tony seeing their dead pet, the tufts of white hair on their father's shoes, that he realises he is never going to get better by himself.

"You were in Karl's," June says.

"So?"

"I don't know why you bothered – will you go and visit all the future men in my life?"

"Sounds like something a whore would say to her pimp."

"I'm no whore."

"I didn't say – can we just drop it I don't want the kids listening to any more of the shite that goes on between us."

"Fine by me."

"What are you doing up so late, anyway?"

She fixes him with a level stare. "I can't sleep. I've a rock in my stomach."

He pours himself a coffee and because the kitten's in the kitchen he moves into the sitting-room. Sits in the darkness. The Christmas tree a dark shadow by the window – like a nightmare waiting in the wings.

Chapter 27

The truth is like a glare of sun on a wet road that bounces through the windscreen. It dazzles. You can fit shades, pull down the visor or perhaps take a direction away from the sun and have the truth always at your back. Nagging the heart out of you because you know it's there, and will, nothing surer, glare you full in the face — sometime.

He needs a beer. Finds a six-pack of San Miguel, Spanish beer, in the Christmas hamper June had been paying off every week. Six bottles — three pints.

In the kitchen he opens a drawer and surfaces a brass bottle-opener. It's in the shape of a naked woman with her legs crossed and he bought it in Beirut's Armenian Quarter because he thought the crossed legs held some special significance for him — June's reluctance to make love to him during the weeks leading up to his departure was an indication of something serious, a shift in sands — he had felt this without being able to specify, until months later, what had caused this reluctance, this drawing away from his touch.

She reminds him that it was his choice to leave for Lebanon, his choice to have a vasectomy — his choices.

A load of oul bollocks, he tells her. She just hasn't made up her mind about the marriage — that came later, when his mood swings showed no sign of settling.

"What do you want the opener for?" June says, through the cloud of smoke she exhales.

"It's hardly as company – though she's probably the warmest woman in the house."

"You didn't open the hamper?"

"I did – I opened the fucking hamper – I'm parched."

"It's the last beer you'll drink at my expense."

"Yeah. Seems my going is the big event in your life."

"It's something to look forward to."

The kitten's in front of the fire. She's so small she would burn easily – all that would exist in the grate come morning would be a scatter of brittle bones. Have to choke her first. She wouldn't take much choking. Need help – how long before thinking becomes doing? How long before he fucks himself up in his sons' eyes – has them looking at him through June, with a mixture of pity, contempt, love and hatred? How long before he lessens himself as a human being in their eyes? Gives them something to have nightmares over?

"You and that bollocks – you had it all planned – you were seeing him before I left for Lebanon the first time, weren't you?"

Nods. Takes in the ted eye of her cigarette.

"If I'd been killed out there it – would have made your year."

"Don't be stupid."

"David did that, you know – King David. He sent Uriah to war in the hope that he would be killed – he wanted to marry his widow, you see? I think that's the gist of it."

"So, what are you driving at?"

"Nothing, I'm driving at nothing – I'm just saying it."

"You know, Harry, I felt guilty over what I did – it was wrong – but you came back from Lebanon a man who was easy to hate – a drunkard, an abrupt ill-mannered little thug, tossing and turning in your sleep, shouting, whingeing about what you saw and what you did out there – sure, it's awful – but you live your life in the fucking past as far as I can see. What happened out there is over, finished – as we are. Stop living there. Stop living here. Cop on and get a life."

So easy to say – cop yourself on. Lift up the head.

He says, "Get a life? I thought I had one with you and the kids."

"Yes, well – "

"I know, it's over. It's fucking drilled into me."

"Don't be hoping for a miraculous change of heart on my part."

"You'd have to have a heart to change first, wouldn't you?"

"Let's not – "

Nods, "Yes, let's not start."

The sitting-room window reveals a strange sky, a purplish hue ranging the width of several mountains. There isn't a whisper of a breeze – unusual for the Curragh. He sits by the window, music on low on an all-night radio channel, and sips at his beer. June's fall of foot on the stairs is tired and laboured. The kitten is next door. Safe. And he safe from her.

Closes his eyes after his fourth, beer. Thinks of old pals he hasn't seen for years, thinks of his schooldays, teachers and thinks of pets he has owned. Never owned a cat. Always dogs. Had a tortoise once but he fucked off behind the fridge and wasn't seen again for a couple of years, not until Mam was getting in a fitted pine kitchen and the fridge had to be moved.

Buried a dog belonging to a friend once. Pat came and asked him to help bury Shep. He was in the field behind the ESB shop. A fucking alsatian. Harry dug the grave and had to grab Shep's legs and drag him to it because Pat was bawling his fucking squinted eyes out. Then when he stopped bawling he asked Harry if it was okay to say an *Our Father* and Harry said, "Why the fuck not – maybe there's a heaven for animals."

"What do you mean, maybe?" Pat snuffled.

"Say the prayer, will you? It's getting dark and It's going to piss."

"You say it, Harry. I can't, just can't... "

"Jesus... "

So he said the prayer and then he had to push Shep into his grave and cover him with a hessian sack. When it was over Pat said he was the best friend he ever had. Harry said not to mention it – Pat said he was talking about Shep. Smiled back then – smiles now. Whatever became of Pat?

Another beer – so much for trying to quit.

Quit!

Calls the old man. It's late but he seldom gets to sleep at night because of the pain.

"You're drunk, son."

"I'm not."

"It's late."

"Are you going somewhere?"

"No, no chuckles – like where he would be going?

"Good."

"Okay, so talk to me. What's on your mind?"

Talk? What's he going to say? Thoughts are swimming. He tells him about being in Lebanon and booking a flight home from Israel because he didn't want to take a chance on the road to Beirut Airport being closed – and what happens? His flight is cancelled in Tel Aviv because birds feeding on a nearby municipal dump had caused a plane crash after they'd been sucked into a jet's engines.

"You know what I mean, Dad? you can't run away from fate – I just wasn't meant to fly that fucking day."

Pauses – the lead-in is done. He tells the old man about the kitten. And the old man doesn't come back and tell him to go and get help. Doesn't betray any disgust – no 'What the fuck have I reared?' Like he once said about Al. He sighs, his teeth skidding off each other, telling him, "Son, you know, you know yourself what needs to be done."

It is sometime near dawn when he consolidates his future – and he has done this with the regret of a man left with no choice. Like the slow dawning of an alcoholic's awareness, he knows he needs help, needs to go somewhere for it – before it is too late. Driving him there is the fact that he wants to be around to see Derek and Tony grow up, to have an integral part to play in their lives, so that in time he might be the lifebuoy for them that they are at this moment for him.

She asked him to stay until Christmas was over, and he had agreed. He didn't tell her that he would stay for ever if she asked – it was hard not to. The way it's going, the way Karl is, the way she keeps finding excuses for him to stay, he had begun to hope that he might not be going anywhere – kidding himself – he's good at that. Christmas dinner and practised smiles in the kitchen, boys playing with their toys, Barney and the Kitten (Derek calls it Tiger) in the garden – the weather is mild. It occurs to him that this is his last Christmas with them – from next week on he'll be on the outside looking in – a visitor on Christmas morning – a weekend father – an interruption in his sons' routines. He hopes that things turn out better than he envisages.

It isn't easy waiting to see the man behind the doors in the General Military Hospital. Everyone knows the name of the shrink and when Harry breathes his name to the orderly clerk the crowded waiting-room fills with nods and winks. Small coughs and short silences. The bulk of them await their turn to filter in and out of the clinics housing the conventional doctors with their conventional answers to conventional problems.

What does he say? How does he begin? Like in a confessional? *Bless me, Father, for I have sinned*? I can't handle the shit my brain keeps fucking my way. The pictures in my mind weigh a ton on my heart. I want to kill my kids' pet for fuck's sake. Oh, yeah, through the morass of bomb smoke and blood and a cat burping on a full stomach – my marriage sort of broke up along the way. So, I'm back living with my parents – the oul fella's dying in the back room upstairs – he can hear the horses whinnying in the stables from there and see the tops of trees. There's a guy called Dobbs who's taking me to court for tampering with his jaw and my CO wants to demote me — so, I mean, we've lots to go on. What I want to know is, straight up, can I be fixed right as new man or am I a patch-up job? If you want me to talk this to death with you, I will, you know. I'll take you through all the reels my mind plays, frame by fucking frame, I'll tell you everything because I don't want this, I don't want any of it — I want to let it go. If talking doesn't do it, what will? You tell me.

There are two others waiting to see Doctor Baines — the Baines of my life — Jesus. This other pair, they're wrecks. You don't have to look twice to know they need a shrink. Perhaps they think the same of him?

His turn. The door opens. There isn't a black leather couch — room's so tiny it wouldn't hold a flea circus. Drab, grey walls hold nothing for the eye to seize other than a scab of bubble-glass window and a clock.

The doctor's got a craggy face — it looks like a harbour for the secrets he hears.

"So, you're Harry Kyle, Sergeant Kyle?"

Galway accent?

"Yes."

"Sit. Sit down, please."

Harry sits almost opposite. He's nervous. Hopes it doesn't show. Baring your soul isn't easy. But. . .

He takes in the clock, the steady upward crawl of the second hand. Everything he says will be committed to paper, everything he says will be taken apart and scrutinised — but there is no other way, no helping hand except for this one here, in this hospital, belonging to this civilian psychiatrist who works for the army.

"Who are you, Harry? Tell me all about yourself — your family, friends — let's get a start on this."

Harry takes a breath. Begins.

451
Editions